Warrior Betrayed

"A great series . . . Montana and Quinn are a great pair and the sensuality is contagious. Ms. Fox is definitely an author to watch."

—The Romance Readers Connection

"An absolutely breathtaking journey from start to finish . . . Sexy, action-packed, and just plain impossible to put down. If you enjoy paranormal romance with the lure of mythology, this is definitely a winner. . . . A highly enjoyable read—perfect for the beach, on the couch, or in bed snuggling under the blankets."

—Romance Junkies

Warrior Avenged

"Alpha heroes, strong heroines, paranormal plots, gods and goddesses, and terrific storytelling await you. Don't delay. Try these books today!"

—The Good, the Bad, and the Unread

"Addison Fox has given her readers one more Warrior to fall in love with . . . a fantastic series."

—The Romance Dish

"Powerful and sexy . . . with a twist of Greek mythology that is exciting and fun."   —Fresh Fiction

continued . . .

Also by Addison Fox

THE SONS OF THE ZODIAC SERIES

Warrior Ascended
Warrior Avenged
Warrior Betrayed

ALASKAN NIGHTS NOVELS

Baby It's Cold Outside

WARRIOR
ENCHANTED

THE SONS OF THE ZODIAC

ADDISON FOX

A SIGNET ECLIPSE BOOK

SIGNET ECLIPSE
Published by New American Library, a division of
Penguin Group (USA) Inc., 375 Hudson Street,
New York, New York 10014, USA
Penguin Group (Canada), 90 Eglinton Avenue East, Suite 700, Toronto,
Ontario M4P 2Y3, Canada (a division of Pearson Penguin Canada Inc.)
Penguin Books Ltd., 80 Strand, London WC2R 0RL, England
Penguin Ireland, 25 St. Stephen's Green, Dublin 2,
Ireland (a division of Penguin Books Ltd.)
Penguin Group (Australia), 250 Camberwell Road, Camberwell, Victoria 3124,
Australia (a division of Pearson Australia Group Pty. Ltd.)
Penguin Books India Pvt. Ltd., 11 Community Centre, Panchsheel Park,
New Delhi - 110 017, India
Penguin Group (NZ), 67 Apollo Drive, Rosedale, Auckland 0632,
New Zealand (a division of Pearson New Zealand Ltd.)
Penguin Books (South Africa) (Pty.) Ltd., 24 Sturdee Avenue,
Rosebank, Johannesburg 2196, South Africa

Penguin Books Ltd., Registered Offices:
80 Strand, London WC2R 0RL, England

First published by Signet Eclipse, an imprint of New American Library,
a division of Penguin Group (USA) Inc.

First Printing, May 2012
10 9 8 7 6 5 4 3 2 1

PUBLISHER'S NOTE
This is a work of fiction. Names, characters, places, and incidents either are the
product of the author's imagination or are used fictitiously, and any resem-
blance to actual persons, living or dead, business establishments, events, or
locales is entirely coincidental.
   The publisher does not have any control over and does not assume any responsibility for author or third-party Web sites or their content.

ALWAYS LEARNING   **PEARSON**

In loving memory of Rose Milardo

Mom to Chris, Ellen, Greg, Andrew, Margaret, Heather and Mark.

Rose Marie to a true hero.

Grammy to two beautiful grandchildren, who carry many of your gifts, most especially your smile.

Rosey to two brothers who've bookended you in age, height and mischief (not to mention lively Friday evenings at the A&P). And to your family, who never spent more than a minute in your company before being enfolded in a tight hug.

Rose to an exceptional number of friends, whom you've always treated as though they were family.

Mrs. Milardo to decades of students who now love science just a little bit more because of your love for the world around us.

Regardless of the name by which you were called, you've touched each and every one of our lives with your love. I can think of no more fitting way to describe your beautiful light than to quote the immortal words of the Wizard of Oz:

"A heart is not judged by how much you love, but by how much you are loved by others."

ACKNOWLEDGMENTS

My deepest thanks to:

Holly Root and Kerry Donovan—your belief in my work is matched only by your ability to help me make it better.

The marketing team at NAL—you bring to life the ideas in my head, and your amazing work leaves me in humbled awe. One of my most favorite moments is when I open my e-mail to find a new cover. You outdo yourselves each and every time! And Kayleigh Clark, thank you for working so hard on my behalf to bring my work to readers.

The Writer Foxes—Alice, Lorraine, Jo, Tracy, Kay, Suzanne, Julie, Sandy and Jane. There's no one I'd rather be on this journey with than you guys.

And to Tracy Garrett—your love, friendship and support mean so very much. And your understanding that wine can only make the day better ensures you are one of the most enjoyable people to share a bottle with. Here's to the Ledson!

Pisces Warrior

Compassionate and sensitive, mysterious and always charming, the Pisces Warrior will often surprise others with the depths of his emotions. Thoughtful and devoted, deep inside his quiet reserve beats the heart of a leader.

Ruled by mystery yet capable of decisive action, he will vanquish his enemies with swift, determined justice.

My Pisces rules with his heart, trusting in his feelings as he trusts the tide to come in and out each day. He is adaptable to the ever-shifting currents that swirl around him, all the while seeking the best in others and himself.

The woman who will capture him is the woman who understands him. Who accepts him. Who allows him to be exactly what he is—a dreamer with a Warrior's soul. For the woman who can love him just as he is will find a love that returns to her a thousandfold . . .

—The Diaries of Themis, Goddess of Justice

Prologue

May 334 BC
Where the Dardanelles and the Aegean Sea meet . . .

Dracas, the fiercest Warrior of Alexander the Great, lay on the banks of the Aegean Sea, the water lapping at his worn boots.

How long he'd lain there, he had no idea, but the soft lash of waves comforted him as he slowly cataloged the pain ravaging his body.

"The dragon," his fellow Warriors called him. If they could only see him now, he thought bitterly as he rolled to his back.

Fire consumed the right side of his body, and he reached for the wound that throbbed from the center of his hip down to his thigh. Unwilling to give in to the pain, he pressed harder at the injury, not surprised to realize it had become infected in his mindless walk toward the sea.

The sounds of battle still rang in his ears along with

Alexander's sole command—no mercy—as he tried to piece together the last several days. Rubbing his hands over his cheeks, he estimated five to six days based on his growth of beard, the coarse sand on his fingers abrading his skin.

For years, he'd followed his leader with blind faith and devotion, losing count of the number of men he felled in the long hours of battle.

No mercy.

Until recently, this blind devotion had defined him.

And until this last battle, he'd thought himself infallible.

The Persian warrior had lain in wait for him. Had waited until the precise moment he had a clean shot and leaped with his sword. Pain seared Dracas's flesh anew as he remembered the downward slash of the sword, the dark glee in the soldier's eyes.

No mercy.

Without warning, a soft murmuring of his name on the breeze captured his attention, dragging his mind from the ravages of battle. Was it possible? Could it be the woman his fellow soldiers had spoken of in hushed whispers?

Themis. The woman who made immortals.

Since hearing of her great gifts, he'd longed to see her face. Longed to pledge his service to her, even as it meant a betrayal of Alexander.

A soft voice called to him once more, and Dracas struggled to his feet.

He took no more than a few steps—not even enough to escape the lapping of the sea's waves—when she materialized in front of him.

Long red hair framed her face and fell down her back in brilliant waves. Her slender form was clad in a white robe that covered her straight back and stiff shoulders.

"You are she," he exhaled on a wondrous sigh, "the one I have looked for." She was more beautiful than he could have ever imagined, yet to his surprise his body didn't respond with desire.

He felt only the desperate need to prove himself worthy.

"Aye, I am."

"Why are you here?"

"You seek me, do you not?"

"They say you do not allow men to seek you. That you seek them."

She nodded. "That is not entirely true. But if others believe it and it discourages them from looking for me, then so be it. They were not meant for the journey."

"They also say you take men as they are dying."

A nearly imperceptible lift of her shoulders. "I find men in many ways. Some as they near death. Some in their prime. And again, the select few who seek me."

"And which am I?"

"You are a seeker, Dracas."

He gingerly touched the wound at his side. "I am also near death."

"Hardly so. Your body fights the wound and you will heal. You will resume your life."

"Death does not await me this day?"

"Not this day, warrior of Alexander."

He'd searched for her for so many long years. Over campfires, he'd listened for any hints of who she was and on the brief absences from Alexander's campaigns he'd sought her.

Who knew she'd find him when he'd least expected it?

"I have searched for you and wish for your gifts more desperately than you will ever know."

A curious light filled the brilliant blue of her eyes. "Why?"

"I grow tired of Alexander's battles. War and destruction for the sake of nothing but greed. I am pledged to him, yet I loathe what he's become. What his army has become."

"My Warriors battle, too, Dracas. There is no escape for them from battle. No escape from the need to protect humanity, for there are many Alexanders in this world and the next. Many who wish to show their might and do much harm."

He studied her as she spoke and knew she sought to prepare him. Wanted to give him a full understanding of what service to her entailed.

What hand of fate had brought him to this place? What magic had befallen him that he be visited by a god on this day?

"And you believe I am worthy?"

"Aye, Dracas, I do. But you must know, the choice is yours alone. I do not endow my gifts by force."

Images of the battle he'd left behind assailed him and Dracas could still taste the ash on his tongue from the destruction Alexander delivered freely. Could still smell the blood and the suffering that suffused the air.

Would service to this woman really be any different?

Aye, he'd wanted her gifts, but were they simply a mirage created to distract him from the reality of service to her?

"Do you seek to battle like Alexander?"

Her smile was as gentle as her voice when she spoke. "I battle for humanity, and I ask that my Warriors do not back down from a fight."

"So you seek power of a different sort." Dracas couldn't explain why that bothered him so, but it did.

As if she read his thoughts, her gaze softened with compassion. "I seek the power to protect humanity and Warriors who will help me attain that goal. Nothing more than that."

He searched her youthful face, the porcelain skin nearly translucent in the bright sunshine.

Did he dare believe her? And could he really afford to deny her? Deny what she offered to go back to . . .

Dracas thought of the long, long years he'd spent in Alexander's service. He had no choices save one— obedience—for Alexander's words were law.

No mercy.

Stepping forward, he stood before Themis. His gaze was unwavering as he stared down at the goddess he'd sought for so long.

"I choose you."

"Do you choose freely, Dracas?" Themis answered, her gaze unwavering in return.

The response hovered briefly on his tongue, the magnitude of the moment not lost. "Aye."

"Then like the Pisces that fills the sky, your decision this day shall bind you to me and I to you. We will be tethered with rope like the two fish of the constellation. You are my Warrior and I will stand with you always."

A great, blinding light turned the daylight around him to a blazing white as Themis's sword lay against his right shoulder.

He'd made his choice.

Chapter One

Today
New York City

Drake Campbell lay on his bed and watched the woman walk toward him in the light of the moon. Her small, lithe frame belied an untold strength and the short spikes of her hair caught the moonlight.

In all his years, he'd never seen a woman more beautiful.

Had never wanted one more.

She moved alongside the bed, her thighs brushing the silk sheets, her high breasts beckoning for his touch. With the dark, desperate ache of desire, he reached for the peaks of her nipples, his fingers seeking to give her pleasure.

Only pleasure.

With quick, sure movements, she climbed on top of him, throwing her head back as he cupped the fullness of her breasts, the thumb and forefinger of each hand relentlessly caressing her nipples into hard points.

Wet heat painted his thigh as she rode him there and he shifted one hand from her breast to the dark triangle at her core. The tight bud of her pleasure pulsed under his touch and a soft cry fell from her lips as he pressed his thumb to the tight bundle of nerves.

Her head fell back on an aching moan and her small hands balanced behind her on his thighs as she allowed the pleasure to capture her.

To consume her.

Desperate for more—for everything she could give him—he embedded two long fingers inside of her and pushed his erection into the pressure of her thigh. On another erotic moan, she convulsed around him as he pushed her to peak again, the tight sheath of her body promising even more pleasure once he was inside of her.

Like quicksilver, the moment altered and re-formed; the object of his desire became the tormentor as she reached for the hard length of him. Shifting, she painted herself over him, teasing the tip of his cock with the wetness at her core.

"Emerson."

They were the first words he'd spoken since she'd entered the room. He'd hardly breathed since she'd arrived in the light of the moon, fearful she was only a dream.

A mirage leading him to certain madness.

She ceased torturing him with her tight warmth, instead shifting to press a line of kisses down his chest, over the hard lines of his stomach and down, until her lips hovered over his straining body.

"Do you want me?"

"Always." *And forever.*

"Then how can I refuse?" Her smile was beatific before those lush, sensual lips closed over his cock. The room spun around him as Drake battled fiercely to maintain control over his body. Fought to prolong the pleasure. Struggled against a desire that consumed him.

Desire for a woman he could no more control than the raging tides.

He craved her. He was utterly bewitched by her. And he knew he'd no more be able to hold her than he could hold water through his fingers.

Waves of pleasure assailed his body, the epicenter at the base of his spine.

He needed her.

Now.

"Emerson." With a ragged breath, he pulled at her slight frame, dragging her up his body until her core was again positioned over him. In one flash of movement, she impaled herself on him, the tight warmth of her body consuming him.

Wrapping her in his arms, he shifted, rolling her to her back as he held his weight above her. With rough hands, he dragged her legs up until she wrapped them around his hips and mindlessly drove into her, satisfaction whipping through him as her movements matched his.

Dark cries echoed around the room as they drove each other toward a shared goal. Sweat slicked their bodies as they surrendered to a passion that refused to be sated.

A passion she refused to bring into the light.

Drake felt her body tighten around his, felt the tell-tale tightness as the walls around his cock closed in. On a triumphant cry, he shouted her name again and buried himself to the hilt, desperate to drag a response from her.

As the pleasure crashed—over him, around him, within him—he heard it. Whisper soft and the antithesis of the vibrant, effervescent woman in his arms.

From the eye of the raging storm she whispered one word.

"Drake."

Drake wrapped his arms around her from behind, the curve of her ass pressed against his all-too-eager cock. They'd barely settled from the firestorm and again he was ready for her.

Who the hell was he fooling?

He was *always* ready for her.

He slammed a leg over both of hers, anxious to keep her there, even as he knew it was a futile exercise.

Emerson Carano danced to no one's tune, least of all his. As she'd proven all too often over the past year, she'd come and go as she pleased.

And the going always came far too soon for his tastes.

With a swift slap against his thigh, she struggled against his hold, scrambling toward the edge of the bed. "All right, Sweet Cheeks, enough cuddling."

He let her go, fisting his hands to keep from reaching for her. "We're back to Sweet Cheeks?"

She shifted and shot him a sideways glance out of

stormy gray eyes. "You preferred last week's nickname?"

"Hell no." He shuddered at the thought. Although he might like what it suggested, Lord Pantymelter was too twisted, even for her and her endless series of nicknames.

On a devilish grin, she leaned in. "You're right. Sweet Cheeks is so uninspired. I think I'll switch back to Wonder Stud."

"Emerson."

When she looked at him with a wide-eyed, mischievous gaze, he couldn't stop the words. "How about my name? Just my name."

"I use your name."

"No, you don't."

"I use it when I come."

Why the hell was this so important to him? He was getting no-strings-attached sex. So why did that simple fact chafe so badly? "That's the only time you use it."

"That's enough."

"No, it's not enough."

She thrust a leg into a pair of jeans, the storm clouds immediately evident in her gray gaze. "You know the rules, Ace. This has to be enough."

"Well, it's not, damn it."

"Too bad. My body, my rules. Take it or leave it."

She dragged a navy blue tank top over her head, the tight points of her nipples visible through the cotton, and damn it if his gaze didn't laser in on that fact. Anger balled in his stomach at his helpless reaction to her.

He had control.

A great deal of it, truth be told.

So what was it about this one pixie-sized woman that made him lose every last bit of it?

Dragging his gaze away from her chest, he focused on her face and the wry quirk of her lips. "I know it may come as a surprise to you, but I actually enjoy your company."

The slight smile fell as she gave him a nearly imperceptible shrug, the tight set of her slim shoulders a direct opposite to the casual gesture. "Every man enjoys getting laid."

"Fuck, Emerson. Don't insult me or yourself. I like you. The person you are. And I like spending time with you."

"Fine." She ran a hand through the short spikes that covered her head in a soft cap of black. The tribal tattoo on her inner arm flashed, the dark ink exotic against her pale white skin. "You want to talk to me. Fine. Talk to me. Tell me about your day."

"That's not what I'm talking about."

Moonlight reflected off of her form and he didn't miss the sly grin that lit up her face. "Then what are you talking about?"

"Shared conversation and interests. Time spent together. *Intimacy*."

"It takes an intimate relationship to have intimate conversation. We have sex, Ace. Don't tell me you haven't been paying attention."

Drake fought the urge to fist the sheet in his hands. He had been paying attention, damn it. With his dick most often, but more and more with his head.

And the sex wasn't enough.

The sat phone on his night table lit up and he reached

for it as the ringtone—"Under the Sea"—offered a dead giveaway as to who it was.

"Ah, saved by the bell." Emerson leaned in and pressed a loud, smacking kiss to his lips. "Or Walt Disney."

He didn't disavow her of the notion, even as he cursed Brody and his damn idiot sense of humor with the ringtone.

Although she knew what he and his brothers were, he refrained from discussing what he did for a living in too much depth.

Or his immortality.

She was prickly enough about a relationship; he didn't need to complicate it with information that would send the average woman running for the hills.

The ringtone continued to peal in the silence of the air between them and he fought the urge to turn it off.

Why hadn't he changed the damn song?

The sugary-sweet notes of the music couldn't diminish the power of the instructions that would be conveyed from the other end, but at least he wouldn't have the immediate reminder of what he was.

Of what he'd chosen.

While he lived with his choice and was grateful for it more often than not, the all-consuming nature of his service to Themis came with a price.

Drake picked up the phone and offered up a terse hello as he watched Emerson sashay out the door. Listening abstractly to his latest orders—something about overthrowing a warlord causing trouble off the coast somewhere in southeast Asia—Drake couldn't help but wonder how he'd gotten himself into this position.

Traipsing through third-world countries with nothing but a gun and a backpack for days on end, a slave to the constant demands of human depravity as he fought in service to Themis.

No-strings-attached sex with the only woman he'd ever wanted to tie himself to.

And then he remembered.

Oh yeah, he'd agreed to all of it.

Emerson snuck down the dark hallway, throwing a long shadow on the wall as she moved. The spikes of her hair waved back at her from her silhouette as she hot-footed it down the stairs, desperately hoping to avoid detection. Unfortunately, the small table lamp in the middle of the foyer threw a surprising amount of light.

Just enough to ensure she'd be easier to see . . .

"Emerson?"

She had nearly made it to the front door—and freedom—when Callie's voice stopped her.

"Oh. Hey."

"Visiting again?"

Emerson couldn't resist giving the raised-eyebrow treatment as she sized Callie up. The woman knew why she was there. She'd probably also known the moment Emerson had walked in the house, had entered Drake's room and had even had her first orgasm—the first of three, damn that asshole—that she'd had that evening.

"Just hanging out with Drake." *He showed me his tattoos. Every luscious inch of them.*

"Where is he?"

Since "I left him behind" sounded bad even for her,

she grasped at the straw offered by his late-night phone call. "I think he just got called on a mission."

"Which he'll no doubt come home from bloody, bruised and mean as a wild rhino. Ah well, there's nothing to be done for it." Callie let out a soft sigh. "Do you want a glass of wine?"

Emerson nearly said no. The reply was on the tip of her tongue, but something held her back.

Maybe it was embarrassment at the way she snuck in and out of this house like a thief. Or maybe it was a sudden desperate need for the sisterhood the other woman offered.

A sisterhood she missed desperately.

She kept other women at a distance, the nature of who and what she was difficult to share. Add in the shoddy relationship with her own sister and there wasn't really a female sounding board in her life save her grandmother.

And, Emerson acknowledged, one didn't exactly regale one's grandmother with tales of the hot next-door neighbor who banged your brains out on a regular basis.

A hot, *sexy* next-door neighbor who increasingly twisted her thoughts in unexpected directions.

Dragging herself from an endless loop of questions she never seemed to be able to answer, Emerson opted for one she could. "Sure. I'd like that."

Five minutes later, she was swirling a dark red Cabernet at the heavy butcher-block counter in Callie's kitchen. She hadn't spent that much time in here; she avoided the room most often reserved for family gatherings and dinners like the plague.

Even if Drake had extended an invite.

Repeatedly.

"You're up late."

Callie swirled her own glass. "I could say the same for you."

"I can't sleep."

"I know your grandmother is far more expert than I am, but I could make you some teas. Something to help take the edge off."

On a shrug, Emerson took another sip of her wine. "Nothing helps."

"Not even Drake?"

"No."

"He might be able to if you let him in."

She raised a practiced eyebrow. "I don't need the lecture, Callie."

"You'll get none of that from me. He's a grown man. He can figure out his own mind. That one only looks dreamy on the surface. A hell of a lot more goes on underneath."

Emerson rubbed a spot above her heart. Didn't she know it.

Which was the entire problem.

The all-fun, no-strings sex fest she'd looked forward to carrying on with her hot neighbor had turned too serious.

Way too serious.

She took a sip of her wine in an attempt to chase the suddenly raw taste of fear on her tongue. "Why does everyone want to make this more than it is?"

Callie's voice was quiet across the butcher-block counter. "Maybe because it is?"

"It can't be. I'm not wired that way."

"Is anyone?"

Emerson laughed at that one. "Hell yeah, lots of people. They're the ones that live those nice comfortable lives in the suburbs, with two-point-two kids and a minivan." People like her sister, who believed if she simply ignored the gift she'd been given—ignored the gift that lived and pulsed and *breathed* under her skin—it simply didn't exist.

"You don't really believe that, do you?"

On a quiet nod, Emerson stared at Callie, unable to lie to her friend. "No. I don't. Nor do I think anyone has a carefree life without pain or suffering or their own personal brand of misery."

"So why can't you have it, too? Love is what makes all the pain and suffering and personal misery worth it."

"I'm just not cut out for it, Cal."

"He loves you, you know."

The words struck as hard as a blow to the chest before being replaced with something else.

Delight.

Yet even as the hot bloom of satisfaction suffused her veins, Emerson fought to cut it off. "Then that's his problem."

"It's *your* gift, Emerson. Yours and Drake's."

"I can't give him what he needs." *But the goddess help me if I can give him up.*

Drake clawed his way through the afternoon heat of the jungle. Themis's intelligence had been spot-on, as always. The scumbag drug lord was exactly where

she'd said he'd be. Other than the land mines the asshole had embedded all along a two-mile radius from
his home base, the hunt had been quick, the kill justi-
fied.

Themis loved her humans far too much to take such
decisive action, and he'd been more than a little surprised at the order. The goddess of justice rarely, if ever,
ordered killing as a means to solve a problem.

After he'd seen the shallow graves full of the drug
lord's victims and the devastating pollution that filled
the nearby river—a result of runoff by the man's manu-
facturing operation—Drake understood Themis's decision.

All of her Warriors had a job to do—a contribution
that made the whole of their unit greater than the sum
of its parts—and he believed in his. His military training had set him up as the perfect person to handle ops
like this. He knew how to execute military strategy and
could be counted on to get in, do the job and get out.

He stayed cautious, keeping an eye out for the hastily set land mines stationed every few feet. He'd already tripped one and narrowly missed having to
regrow a few limbs thanks to a quick port back to
where he'd started. He did sport a nasty burn on his
foot that hurt like a bitch and his attitude—already
prickly from Emerson's standard exit strategy—had
gotten worse with each heat-filled, passing step.

Why did he let her affect him like this?

Kneeling down, he settled his backpack next to the
river and rubbed a hand over his chest. The once-clean
river showed the ravages of the drug lord's greed as
several dead fish bobbed along the fast-moving cur-

rent. It was moments like this—those quiet moments he spent all alone—when he wondered if he'd have been better off taking his chances, living the life he'd been given and dying like a normal man.

At least then he'd have had only one lifetime of seeing how humans fucked one another instead of a never-ending parade of lifetimes to experience it again and again.

Stripping off his clothes, he stepped into the river. The cold shock of water rushed over his burned foot and he winced before ignoring the pain to step deeper, the mud and silt of the riverbed soft under his toes. As he continued stepping farther and farther into the raging current, the water sluicing around him, he opened up his senses.

The pollution of the drugs assailed his skin in harsh rivets, like a thousand daggers along his nerve endings. Through it, he felt more than heard the screams and suffering the poison had wrought, from the thousands upon thousands of souls it had touched.

Addiction.

Violence.

Death.

And through it all, like a thread that grew stronger and stronger, was anguish. Soul-deep anguish borne by humanity for centuries.

The fish on his back, tethered together by an unbreakable string, came to life in his aura. He heard the splash as both dropped into the water to swim in circles around his body, driving against the current. The animals pushed Themis's power into the water to begin the process of eradicating the damage done by the drug lord.

Drake closed his eyes and allowed the gifts of his immortality to do their job.

Although he couldn't save all the life in the river, he could begin the process of healing it. Biting down on his back teeth, he fought the rising pain as it assaulted his senses—fought the drug-ravaged water as it branded his skin with poison—and held firm against the raging water.

He allowed minute to follow minute and hour to follow hour as he stood in the water, patiently waiting for his aura to repair the damaged river. His body weakened against the assault, yet he fought on. Fought with the stoic determination he'd spent his life with.

Only as the sun was setting in the sky did he finally give in to the pain. Crawling out of the river, he fell onto the banks facedown in the scrub that lined the soggy ground. He'd done all he could do.

Had taken all he could take.

He could only hope it was enough.

The sounds of the rushing river faded as sleep took him, and just before he fell fully under, Drake whispered one word.

The same word he'd whispered each and every night for the last year.

It was his prayer. His benediction. His comfort.

"Emerson."

Chapter Two

The cool, slightly dank smell of her family's brownstone basement surrounded her as Emerson ground herbs with a mortar and pestle. The satisfying crunch of stone on stone and the soft, airy scent of rosemary offered a soothing balm to the raging thoughts she couldn't get under control.

Drake loved her.

She'd known it, of course, but the evidence—the acknowledgment from another person—was a swift kick to the head.

And to the heart she'd tried so very hard to keep distant from him.

She'd allowed her hormones and her brain to think they knew better—to think they could keep him at arm's length—and she was paying for it.

Who was she kidding? She ground the pestle harder as the contents of the mortar grew to the consistency of the finest dust. She'd loved him since she was a young girl.

She could even name the very first night she'd seen him, during that full moon the August she was fourteen. Emerson remembered it like it was yesterday. The moon had been high in the sky, the oppressive heat of the city in late summer breaking slightly overnight.

She and her mother and grandmother had prayed to the goddess that night, chanting their prayers skyward. Emerson had asked for extra help that evening, trying to find a way to get through to her older sister, Veronica, who refused to celebrate the moon with them.

Her throat was still tight from the horrible fight they'd had that reduced them both to tears.

Sadly, she now knew, they'd have many more along the same lines.

After their ritual prayers, her mother and grandmother had eventually gone inside, but Emerson had wanted to enjoy the night sky a little longer. Wanted the time to stay wrapped in her thoughts as she tried to puzzle through her sister's unwillingness to accept who she was.

Who they were.

It had been that moment when she'd stood, angry again and ready to pace, that she'd seen the tall head bob past their fence. Curious, she ran to the large wooden play set that now sat empty since she and her siblings had grown too old for it and climbed up the wooden slats that ended in a fort.

The cotton robe she'd put on after the prayer ceremony wrapped around her legs, slowing her motion so she had to take the rungs at half her normal speed, but some sense of urgency pushed her on. She'd just cleared enough of the ladder to see into the backyard next door.

The man whose head she'd seen at the top of the fence was at the back entrance of the brownstone connected to theirs. He was bloody and bruised, looking exactly like she pictured the heroes of her books—Robin Hood, Ivanhoe and the Knights of the Round Table—after they returned from battle.

He rested his head against the door as she stared at him, his shoulders slumping. He looked utterly defeated, like it was an effort to even stand there. Like the doorframe was the only thing holding his body upright.

Emerson watched, fascinated that someone so large—a man so seemingly invincible—could look tired.

And so lonely.

Then he'd pushed off the door with some inner reserve of strength and stepped back. In quick movements, he shucked the filthy shirt he wore and her breath caught in her throat as moonlight coated his body. The heat of the summer night and the noise of the city faded away in that moment and she could do nothing but stare.

At the large form of his body—the broad shoulders and thickly muscled back that tapered down to a narrow waist. He was powerfully built, and the only thing Emerson could think was, *This is what a hero looks like*.

Her gaze drank him in and an odd awareness settled low in her stomach. She'd felt a slight tingling between her thighs. The sensation was foreign but exhilarating.

Feminine.

Powerful.

He'd stood there for only a moment before pushing through the back door, but it had been all she'd needed.

The man had captivated her.

Emerson waited at least a half hour, watching and hoping for another glimpse of the man, until she finally climbed off the play set and moved into the house to her room on the fourth—and highest—floor of the old brownstone. And it took until dawn peeked through her curtains for her to finally fall asleep.

After that night, Emerson stayed alert to any and all news of the occupants of the house next door. She'd always sensed the large brownstone held secrets, but now she had a face to put with those secrets. Stories had filled her head about the men next door—the made-up fantasies of a young girl. In addition to the man she'd seen, she knew of the others who lived there—large, imposing figures who looked like ancient warlords.

She imagined them on covert missions, saving princesses and keeping the world safe for humanity. And him . . . the large Warrior she'd seen in the moonlight. He'd fueled her fantasies for so long, always hovering in the back of her thoughts. Always causing her to take the men she dated and try to make them measure up.

But no one ever did.

"Emerson."

Dragged from her thoughts, it took her a moment to focus on the dark brown eyes of her grandmother.

"What?"

"Where were you? I've called your name about five times."

Emerson glanced down at her hands as her grandmother gently took the pestle from her. "I think you've done well enough there."

"Just wrapped in my thoughts."

"I can see that."

Gram took the stool next to her worktable, a light mischief bubbling in her smile. "I suspect I know just who's got you wrapped up, too."

Shades of the conversation she had the night before with Callie came back to her. "Grandmother."

A withered, gnarled hand stopped her from saying anything further. "I'm not prying and I don't need the sass. I'm just teasing you."

Emerson dropped onto her own stool, the wind effectively knocked from her sails. "Sorry."

"You're a grown woman entitled to your own business."

"Thank you."

"But I can't help notice you're not sleeping. Or eating all that much. Has Drake done something? Has he hurt you in some way?"

The fierce set of her grandmother's mouth had Emerson reaching for her hand. "No, no, no. Of course not. He's wonderful, Gram. Really."

"Wonderful?"

Emerson didn't often find herself backpedaling—she was far too comfortable speaking her mind—but the urge to do it in this instance was strong. "I meant he didn't do anything."

Gram's eyebrows rose at that. "Nothing? He doesn't look like a man who sits there and does nothing."

"Gram!"

"I've got eyes, Emerson. And that man is a vision."

And didn't she know it. On a quick sigh, Emerson resigned herself to how neatly her grandmother had boxed her in. "What I meant is that he's very good to me and you don't need to worry that he's not treating me right."

"That sets my mind at ease."

"Your nosy mind."

Emerson leaned over and pressed a kiss to her grandmother's cheek. Like a spring wind that lay gently against your face, the familiar earthy scent she'd always associated with her grandmother filled her senses and offered simple comfort.

Although her gram's skin was thin and papery, the hands that clasped hers were strong. Firm. Capable.

"I guess that leaves only one question."

"What's that?"

"Are you treating *him* right?"

"Of course I am." Emerson diverted her attention to the worktable and reached for the small sheet of parchment paper she'd set aside earlier. Emptying the heavy mortar over it, she worked the finely ground rosemary from the bottom of the thick bowl.

"That's an interesting choice."

"What is?"

"Unless my senses deceive me, that's rosemary."

"Yes. I'd like to have it on hand for the ritual tonight."

"It's a very intriguing choice."

Emerson stopped the process of extracting as much of the fine powder from the bottom of the mortar. "What is, Gram?"

"Rosemary. Dew of the sea. Makes one think you had the Pisces on your mind the whole time."

The heavy mortar wobbled in her hands as Emerson's attention snapped toward her grandmother. She juggled it momentarily, but managed to keep the heavy bowl in hand before settling it back on the table. On a deep breath, she gathered her thoughts, willing herself to remember why she'd selected the herb in the first place. "Rosemary is for remembrance. It's for Mom."

Gram nodded, and her shoulders seemed to contract from the weight of her own remembrance. "Of course. Well, then, I'll leave you to it." Their conversation at an end, her grandmother slipped off the stool, her grip firm on the worktable as she got to her feet.

Guilt nipped at her heels as Emerson reached for the mortar once again. "I'll come up in a little while and we'll have some lunch, okay?"

"Of course, dear."

It was a long while later, after she'd packaged the contents of the mortar in a small vile, that Emerson remembered rosemary's other use.

It was traditionally associated with weddings.

"You look like hell, Drake." Rogan slammed his cards down on top of the green baize card table and muttered a resounding "fuck" before continuing the inquisition. "What the hell happened?"

Drake shrugged off the question and reached for a beer in the full cooler next to Quinn. "Nothing."

The Taurus slapped him on the back as he reached for his own beer. "Well, it looks like a whole lot of nothing planted itself across your face. Where've you been?"

"Mucking through drug-infested waters in Southeast Asia."

"Why'd Themis send you there?" Brody threw his cards down with a sigh of disgust as Kane leaned forward and dragged the pot of chips toward him. "Couldn't Takahashi take that one?"

"She's got him in Tokyo right now and it couldn't wait." Drake took a long drag of his bottle, the ice-cold tang of the beer a balm on his throat. His body had almost fully shaken the effects of the drug-infested water, but he was still edgy. The way he saw it, a few beers and some cards should go a long way toward dulling those edges.

Insults were tossed over the next several hands and Drake was already well into his second beer when "the wives" bustled into the room. He enjoyed the company of Ava and Ilsa and he'd already warmed to their newest addition, Quinn's wife, Montana.

"I know it's poker night, but none of us could resist showing off our new shoes," Ava sang out as they descended on the table en masse.

"It's our lucky night, boys," Rogan ground out around his teeth, which were currently clamped around a cigar.

"Oh, shut up and go back to smoking that smelly piece of shit in your mouth," Ilsa shot back at him as she dropped herself into Kane's lap. "I'm sure my husband doesn't want your opinion of my FMPs anyway."

The question was on the tip of Drake's tongue before Rogan beat him to the punch. "FMPs?"

Drake saw Kane shake his head before Ilsa merrily chortled out, "Fuck-me pumps."

"What the hell, Ilsa!" Rogan gently stuck his cigar in the ashtray next to him before shoving his hands over his ears. "You've scarred me for life."

"Oh, come now. You're a big boy, Rogan. I've no doubt you've seen more than your share of FMPs," Ava crooned as she reached over her husband's shoulder to sneak a peek at Brody's cards before grabbing a handful of chips.

"Yeah. On women who should be wearing said articles of footwear. I have no interest in envisioning them on my sisters."

"And it damn well better stay that way," Brody muttered under his breath.

Drake took another swig of his beer as Kane tossed a handful of chips around the slender woman in his arms. Damn, but this felt good. A few hands of cards with his Warrior brothers and a bunch of good-natured ribbing and trash talk. Even the women had added a dimension to all their lives none of them had expected.

Family.

They'd always had a bond, but the women had turned their house into a home. And had formalized their relationship into something large and familial.

So yeah, he and his brothers had to hear about FMPs in addition to terrifying conditions like bloating, bad manicures and that horror of horrors, split ends. But these women had their back—not to mention some serious powers in their own right—and each and every one of them knew it.

Drake figured it was a more than fair trade-off.

"Speaking of FMPs," Ilsa ground out before her gaze made a bull's-eye on him. "There's been some sexing in our Pisces's room of late. In fact, I'm quite sure I heard someone sneaking out just last night, which, I believe, made for the third night in a row."

"Ilsa!" Ava hissed.

Drake's good mood fled on swift wings as Ilsa's words hung over the room. And before he knew it, the double-edged sword of family skewered him clean through. "Drop it, Ilsa."

Montana added a low-level "shhh" to Ava's unspoken admonishment to shut up, without success.

"Come on, Drake. We're all dying to know." Ilsa shot a pointed glance at the other two women even as a bright pink color spread up her neck and into her cheeks. "All of us."

He refused the bait. "I'm sure your immortality can withstand the torture."

Heavy, awkward silence replaced the jovial air and Drake bent to review his cards and pull together the chips for his bet. Within a few hands the women got bored and disappeared to have their own bonding time and then he waited a few more hands to make his leaving as inconspicuous as possible.

"I'm heading up."

"Drake? You sure you don't want to try and win that grand back from me? It'd be a shame to let me keep it without a fight." Brody's voice boomed even as his smile was forced.

Drake snagged one last beer from the cooler. "Nah, consider it a favor. Especially since it looks like your wife just spent it on shoes."

Five minutes later, he found himself wandering up to the top floor of the house, where they maintained an observatory. Long and narrow, it ran the roof of the brownstone and offered a clear view of the sky.

Through an elaborate set of physics having something to do with astral planes he had no earthly clue how to understand, the observatory wasn't actually visible to anyone who might be staring at the roof. The brownstone's simultaneous cohabitation on both the island of Manhattan and Mount Olympus ensured it was not only far larger than it looked, but that much of what made it a fortress for him and his brothers made it invisible to the average human.

Drake's gaze was drawn unerringly to the Pisces constellation, where it bound the twinned fish together in the sky. No matter how disillusioned he grew with the depraved actions of humanity, he always found comfort in the proof of what he was.

The balance in the heavens Themis used so many millennia ago in her Great Agreement with Zeus. That same balance that allowed a disparate group of men— all with different strengths, skills and abilities—to work together on her behalf.

To save the humans worth saving.

He didn't know why he was drawn there this evening, but couldn't argue with the impulse once he sat breathing in the night air, watching the stars.

Long ago, before technology had made their lives both easier and harder, he and his brothers could communicate with each other through the stars simply by using the ink that marked their bodies. Now their sat phones did the communicating and the night sky was just something nice to look at.

"I thought I saw you head up here."

Drake ignored the voice in favor of a deep drag on his longneck.

"I'm sorry for what I said."

He kept his gaze on the stars, but his voice was easy when he finally spoke. "Don't worry about it, Ilsa."

"It's no excuse, but I still haven't mastered that fine art of knowing when to shut the hell up."

Drake turned to look at her and saw the tense lines that bracketed her mouth. No matter how heavy the urge to brood, he couldn't stay mad at that winsome face with the sky-blue eyes. He knew what it had taken for her to begin to feel a part of their lives after her betrayal by Zeus, followed by endless millennia of soul hunting for Hades.

"Don't worry about it."

She hesitated for a moment, clearly weighing her thoughts before they tumbled out in a rush as if she couldn't help herself. "We're only curious because she makes you happy."

"Happy?" What a joke that was. And even if it were true, he sure as hell couldn't find a way to return the favor.

If he made her happy, he'd have an armful of witch on his lap right now as he played poker, all the while imagining her clad in her own pair of fuck-me pumps later in the evening.

"You can't possibly see what I see," he muttered on a harsh laugh.

"What's that?"

"A woman who wants nothing to do with me."

Ilsa moved forward until she stood next to him along the narrow wall that made up the edge of the observatory. "She wants a whole lot to do with you, Drake. More than a lot, if I'm not mistaken."

"And what makes you think that?"

"Let's just say I suck at social pleasantries, but I spent an awfully long time observing people. And I know what I see when I look at the two of you."

"What's that?"

"Sorry, cowboy, I'm not letting you off that easy. Besides"—she flashed the wicked grin he'd come to associate with her—"I think you already know."

Before he could reply, Ilsa flounced toward the staircase at the edge of the roof, hollering over her shoulder as she went, "Sorry to rush off, but I've got a pair of heels to go break in."

Drake wanted to stay mad. He really did. But the wiggling ass that flashed her good-bye at him was too much to keep him in a dour mood.

Resuming his position at the end of the roof, he let his gaze drift toward the house next door. Brownstones lined the observatory on either side, but the front and back were edged with a half wall that allowed him to look over into the backyards up and down their block. His breath caught in his throat as his sights settled next door.

Emerson stood fully naked, her arms stretched

toward the sky. She moved in long, sensuous motions, her sleek body exposed to his gaze like an offering. His own body tightened in response, the sheer beauty of her striking him on a visceral level he was powerless to resist.

And powerless to ignore.

Fascinated, he stood and watched her. She was so private—so closed off from him in every way except sexually—that the opportunity to observe her without her knowledge was far too large a temptation to resist.

So he simply stood and drank her in.

One enchanting moment spun into the next as she moved through what he could only assume was a prayer. Her voice floated up to him in small snatches as she used her entire body in offering, moving through the ritual that encompassed her worship. Long, slender fingers spread something from a pouch while the muscles of her thighs kept her balance as she moved through a series of complicated poses.

The long column of her throat caught the moonlight as her head fell back and he imagined himself pressing his lips there, drinking in the hot scent of her as it mixed with the light summer breeze that swirled through the air.

On a muttered curse, he took a long drag on his beer, draining the bottle in a desperate effort to cool the raging ardor that filled him.

Gods, how he wanted this woman. His body burned for her in more ways than he could count.

He craved the opportunity to hold her tucked against his heart and he yearned to talk with her at the end of each day, their words full of the everything and the nothing that made up daily life. He wanted her for his partner—that glorious knowledge his every thought, every need, every want was safe with her.

Gods damn it all.

His fingers dug into the concrete ledge of the half wall as he fought the rising emotions that threatened to swamp him like a ship at sea. Desire was a harsh and punishing taskmaster, and it was having a fucking field day with his emotions.

Unlike his fellow Warriors, his Pisces blood ensured he didn't equate getting in touch with his softer side as emotional emasculation. Fuck it all, he was *sensitive* and he still knew how to put his proverbial boots on.

And the damn woman had thrown it all back in his face.

The anger he'd managed to set aside after talking with Ilsa reared up again. Restless and needy, he turned away from the sight of Emerson in her ritual and took long, deep breaths as he struggled to find some of the calm he was known for. The slamming of his heart against his chest slowed and his tight grip on the bottle relaxed as the seconds ticked off one by one.

Satisfied he'd regained some semblance of control, Drake turned and set the bottle on the ledge of the half wall. He'd talk to Emerson later—he had to. These reactions weren't like him and he wasn't content any longer to take the scraps she offered like he was a hungry dog.

He had feelings for her and he had things he wanted to say.

Resolved, Drake reached for his bottle, determined

to leave her to her private moments. As his gaze caught on her beautiful form once more, a slight movement in his peripheral caught his attention.

Cloaked in shadow, a large man skulked along the fence that edged Emerson's backyard. As Drake focused on him fully, the asshole took hold of the top of the fence and pulled himself up to climb over.

Without conscious thought, Drake threw himself into a port. Before he could even hear the bottle in his hand shatter on the concrete of the roof, he'd closed the distance between the Warriors' roof and Emerson's backyard. On a loud battle cry, Drake slammed himself into the large form that dropped into the grass, his only intent to reach Emerson.

Emerson's eyes popped open on the loud shout that echoed toward her from the far side of the backyard. On a scream of her own, she dropped her arms from where she'd had them lifted toward the sky. Two large figures skirmished at the edge of the yard, their grunts evident even from where she stood.

With a muttered oath Emerson moved forward, her fingers already itching with the need to spew fire.

And nearly forgot the sacred circle she stood in.

"Damn it." With a quick, efficient movements, Emerson dissolved the circle she'd created at the start of her ritual and took off for the grunting, heaving mass that knocked against the fence. She caught sight of Drake's large form, the reassuring size of him sending a shot of warmth through her belly.

What was he doing here?

And what the hell—?

She screamed again and leaped toward both of them as Drake rolled his opponent onto his back.

"Drake! No!"

More grunts assailed her and she knew she was risking a hit by a stray elbow, but she waded in anyway. "Drake! Get off of him."

When her voice still didn't register, she did the only thing she knew how.

Extending her hands, she let the waiting heat flow out of her fingers as a stream of fire rimmed the struggling duo in a circle of flame.

"What the—?" Drake looked up, but the movement cost him. A heavy fist slammed into his jaw.

Before he could retaliate, Emerson pulled back the fire and let out another scream. "Magnus!"

The haze of battle filled Drake's green eyes and it was only as she ran toward him and wrapped her arms around his broad shoulders that some of the Warrior dissolved from those orbs. The iron set of his shoulders relaxed slightly under her hands as his breathing slowed.

"Drake. It's okay."

"What the hell is this, Em?" Magnus's loud voice echoed over her shoulder, carried on the night air.

Drake's arms tensed immediately and his hands gripped her waist to move her out of the way. "You know him?"

"Magnus!" Emerson hollered over her shoulder. "Shut the fuck up for a minute and go stand over there."

"Em—"

"Over. There," she shot back through gritted teeth, unwilling to break eye contact with Drake. "Drake?"

His hands still spanned her hips and Emerson was increasingly aware of her naked body pressed against his. That familiar magic—as old as time and more powerful than any other force on earth—settled low in her stomach as wet heat pooled between her thighs.

She *so* could not do this right now.

Drake broke his gaze from her to watch Magnus along the length of the yard. "Who the fuck is that?"

"My brother."

Chapter Three

Drake dragged his T-shirt off and handed it to her so she could cover up. The sight of his bare chest shot a bolt of warmth through her, which she ruthlessly tamped down.

How was it possible, Emerson marveled, she could still melt at the sight of his bare skin? Even worse—how was it the sensation grew more intense the more time she spent with him?

This . . . *thing* between them should have burned out by now. She should have gotten him out of her system.

Of course, if she was really worried about what she *should* be doing, she wouldn't even be in this position because she wouldn't be heading next door for midnight sex with her hot neighbor on a regular basis.

A loud cough echoed across the backyard, interrupting her conflicted thoughts. At the realization she was still naked, she dragged Drake's T-shirt on.

Oh God, it's still warm.

"So tell me, does your brother always skulk around

the back of the house?" Drake bit out the words with military precision.

"Not that I'm aware of. But seeing as how I haven't seen him in four years, what do I know?"

The flippant words came easier than they should have, but damn Magnus. She'd had a long time to get used to not having him around. Four years in which she and her grandmother had worried and waited and lapped up the small scraps he'd offered in the occasional call or postcard from wherever he was at the moment.

"That's a long time to be away."

Drake's warm, steady gaze held hers, and in the depths of his eyes she saw understanding. That steady quiet that told her he saw—and understood—far more than he outwardly let on.

"Come on." She linked her hand with his and pulled him toward the small patio at the back of her house. "Let's go find out what he did with his key."

Magnus sat sprawled on a lawn chair, his posture casual for someone who'd been away for so long.

What had he been doing? And where? With whom?

It wasn't the first time she'd questioned his absence. Realistically, she knew he was a grown man who could make his own decisions, but his complete abandonment had felt unduly harsh.

"He doesn't look like someone who hasn't been home in four years."

Emerson turned to stare at Drake, his words so oddly similar to her thoughts it was eerie. And then the urge to defend her brother rushed her—as it always did—and she resolutely pushed aside her doubts.

"This is the house we grew up in. I'd imagine it would always feel like home no matter how long I was away."

"Still. Makes you wonder what he could have been up to."

"Why are you being so judgy?" Emerson hissed at him, her voice low so Magnus wouldn't overhear their conversation.

"Until we get some answers, I'm not changing my initial opinion."

"Which is what?"

"He's hiding something."

Emerson let out a small grunt of surprise and a muttered "look who's talking" before they moved close enough to be overheard.

"Magnus."

The smug smile dropped from Magnus's face as he stood, shifting from foot to foot. "Who's that?"

"Drake. Our neighbor."

"He was awfully close for a neighbor."

"And you've been gone too long to have an opinion on the matter."

Score.

Her words managed to bank the fire in his menacing stance and his next words had a distinctly petulant overtone. "Doesn't mean I don't have one."

Emerson leaned up and wrapped her arms around her brother, pulling him close. "Shut up and give me a hug."

The last bit of fight evaporated as he pulled her close, his large frame overpowering her petite one. He'd grown in the last four years, she realized as her hands ran over the muscles along his upper back. He'd always been a large man, but the body under her fingers was hard. Unyielding.

Pulling back, she didn't miss the fact that Magnus's gaze was firmly pinned on Drake. Unwilling to answer questions even she didn't have the answers to, she punched him on the shoulder to get his attention.

"What are you doing coming in through the back?"

Magnus turned his full attention to her. "I thought we still had a key back there."

"This is New York. What do you think?"

Confusion filled his dark eyes. "But we did have a key. Mom spelled one years ago so only we could find it."

Their mother's special skill—planting power in inanimate objects—had never carried through to her children. What seemed so simple, Emerson knew, wasn't in actuality and it was something she'd never been able to master.

"Mom's been gone a long time, Magnus."

"Yeah."

As confusion morphed to somber awareness, Emerson saw his years of absence hadn't managed to fill the well of grief he carried.

An hour later, Drake nursed a club soda as he tossed back a handful of beer nuts. Equinox was rocking tonight; he could hear it even through the heavy walls of Grey's office. He still hadn't shaken off those last few moments at Emerson's and was depending on Grey's mission to do something for his shitty mood.

"Hey, sunshine. You ready to roll?" Speak of the devil. Their Aries walked back into his office dressed head to toe in Armani. The sleek look did nothing to hide the lethal set of his shoulders; nor did it soften the look of battle in his eyes.

"Been ready." The ice clinked in Drake's glass as he took a final sip. "You're the one who's been upstairs making time with your patrons."

"Securing a few last bits of information."

"I saw the pair of legs you were talking with when I came in, but if you want to call it information, be my guest."

"You up for this?" Grey cocked an eyebrow as he pulled a gun from a safe behind his desk. "You look distracted."

"Hell yeah, I'm ready." Drake slammed his glass down on the coffee table harder than he'd intended and stood. "Believe me when I say there is nothing I'm more ready for than to kick the shit out of something. And if the fucker deserves it, as I've no doubt he does, that's even better."

One dark eyebrow cocked over eyes the same color as his name, but other than that, Grey held his opinions, as usual. "Then let's go."

Their Aries got him up to speed as they took a car toward the docks. Two of the city's crime families had escalated into an all-out war and Themis had asked Grey to intervene in a likely shoot-out.

"Interesting conflict Themis has asked you to get in the middle of. I know she loves humans, but she's pretty diligent about avoiding their politics. Especially the ones with their own set of rules."

"She's had me involved in this for a while. It seems one of the families recently procured a new weapon and has used it to tip the balance of power."

"What is it?"

"Eris's Golden Apple."

"No fucking way." Drake let the news sink in and realized he wasn't actually surprised. The goddess of discord had several weapons at her disposal, the apple being her oldest and most well known. Her gift as an immortal was the ability to create discord and chaos out of nothing. The apple was a physical manifestation of that same ability.

"It figures, though," Drake added. "We've known she hasn't simply been cooling her heels since buddying back up with her sister last year. It looks like Aidan and Quinn's run-in with her a few months ago was just a prelude. Clearly, she's been up to far more than we realized, including meddling in mob affairs."

Grey shrugged. "Her MO's staying behind the scenes. It's what she does best."

"But why organized crime? Even she can't be delusional enough to want to get involved with that human mess."

"Yeah, but see it from her perspective. What better way to create discord than get the city's major criminal forces all worked up? You get them going, you distract attention from the big show."

"You think this is part of something bigger?"

"I have no doubt it is."

Drake turned over the implications of Grey's words. While Enyo usually went for flashy and theatrical—her role as the goddess of war ensuring she loved to make a scene—her sister, Eris, was far more subtle. And a damn bit more effective when she put her mind to it.

If Grey's suspicions were correct, and Eris was creating discord with the city's major crime families to draw attention from something bigger, what would it be?

And why now?

"So this is what you've been so secretive about? What changed your mind tonight that you brought me in?"

Grey reached for a bottled water, but Drake couldn't help wonder if it was a move to keep his eyes averted. "I've kept my own counsel on this, nothing more."

"Answer my question. Why bring me in now?"

Grey's wry smile had just the slightest hint of cockiness. "Even I know when I need help. Besides, this is going down at the docks. There's no better ally than you, Fish."

"Fuck, not another nickname."

"You've got others?"

Drake pointed at Grey even as he reached for his own bottle of water. "Nice way to shift the scrutiny. Don't think I've missed that there's something else going on here. And why does my Spidey sense tell me it has to do with Legs?"

On a muttered oath, Grey ran a hand through his hair. "She's an ADA. Her name's Finley McCrae and her information has been invaluable on this one."

"That all?"

"Damn it, yes. She's human, Drake. And in a position with access to power."

"For the record, you're human, too."

Grey's lips thinned into a fine line. "Doesn't change the way we live."

Drake opted to ignore the philosophy and shifted toward their potential for casualties. "Do you think she has any sense of what's really going on?"

"No way."

The answer was too quick for comfort. "You sure of that?"

"Damn it, Fish. She doesn't know. She can't know."

"She's highly trained to seek the truth. That's an awfully powerful motivator."

The fine cut of Grey's suit couldn't hide the stiff set of his shoulders. "I've been careful with what I've asked. She thinks I'm nosing around for some property expansion at the pier."

Drake shook his head, unable to suppress the sense of discomfort that rode his back. "Your dick's making decisions, Grey. Whatever little box you've neatly put her into, I suggest you pull her out and give her more credit."

Their ram turned to look out his window at the buildings passing them on the West Side Highway. "I'm using her for information. That's all."

Drake left it alone, unwilling to push any harder. Grey knew how to take care of himself. And if the ram had developed a glaring blind spot, well . . . Callie would suss it out soon enough and give him shit about it.

All that said, Drake was just raw enough from his own evening to poke the lion once more in his den. "You want it to be more?"

Grey pulled his attention from the window. "Come on, we may be human, but immortality has a way of skewing things."

"Doesn't mean she's not willing to cooperate with your stubborn brand of Aries charm as so many other women have blindly done. I don't get it"—Drake forced an exaggerated lift of his shoulders—"but there's no accounting for taste."

"There's nothing going on between us and nothing's going to start. And, for the record, fuck you."

Drake couldn't stop the bark of laughter. Not only did it feel good, but it was nice to be in his own element. Preparing for battle with one of his brothers while slinging bullshit at each other.

Not spying on a woman in his backyard. Or falling squarely in the middle of her family drama he had no business taking part in.

Focusing on the bullshit once again, he couldn't resist ribbing Grey a bit more. "She does have a sweet pair of legs."

The harsh set of the ram's jaw confirmed he'd hit the mark.

"I suggest you keep your gaze on the enchanting Ms. Carano and off my ADA."

Drake had stood beside Grey for a long time and hadn't ever seen him remotely bent out of shape. If this woman had managed to get under their Aries's skin, she was worth another look.

"What the hell's happened to us, Grey? Time was—not that long ago, I might add—when it was just fun. And easy. No strings attached."

"Emerson's putting strings on you?"

"They've sprouted on their own accord."

"Blame it on Brody. He started it."

Drake took another drag on his bottle of water. "Kane and Quinn had no problem following suit. It's like something's in the air. What's happened to us? We were an elite fighting team."

"Speak for yourself. And last time I checked, we were still an elite fighting team, with a few more fighters to the good. Ava and Ilsa have been kicking ass and taking names."

Drake nodded his head. "That's fair."

Ava and Ilsa had embraced their new lives along with their new spouses. And to Grey's point, both had been invaluable in recent battles.

"So what happened with the enticing witch this evening?"

An image of Magnus Carano roving around the back alley behind their row of brownstones reared up in his mind's eye. "I nearly beat the shit out of her brother. Thought he was a thief trying to get in through the fence."

"You catch him on Quinn's equipment?"

Drake couldn't have stopped the heat from creeping up his neck if he'd tried. "I was up in the observatory. Saw it from there."

It didn't take millennia of knowing each other for Grey to smell blood in the water. "And what, pray tell, were you doing up in the observatory?"

"Relaxing."

"Sure you were. So tell me, was she naked? I'll cut your lovesick ass some slack if you tell me she was naked."

The heat flushed again and Drake fought the urge to roll down the window. Shit, the way Grey made it sound, he came off like a fucking pervert. "Why'd you think that?"

"Come on, Drake. Where the hell have you been all these years? It's no secret our neighbors like to go naked under the moon. They have for generations."

"Somehow, I'd missed that bit of news."

"Sucks for you."

"So you going to tell me anything else I need to know about tonight's adventure? Any reason we haven't already ported in instead of taking the limo?"

"Nice deflection, Fish. I'll take that as a yes. You're also off the hook since we're about three blocks from the meet. The limo's a practical choice. We go porting in there and we may fall into something we'd rather observe."

"And that would be awkward."

While their gift of teleportation was one of their most useful assets, they needed to know where they were going to do it successfully. Landing on an unsuspecting enemy or straight into the middle of a wall had a funny way of ruining a stealthy op.

At Grey's direction, the limo dropped them off about three piers down from the one they wanted so they could approach at their own pace.

"You want me in the water?"

"Not yet. Let's see what we can find out up here."

Drake pointed out a couple of thugs standing guard as they got nearer their destination. "Eight o'clock. See them?"

"Yeah. See any more?"

"Nope."

"Probably not trying to draw more attention out here than they need to. Besides, things have escalated so far, they're risking their people if they put too many of them out here and make them targets."

Drake stopped, opening his senses to see if he could catch any other noises. No matter how long he worked for Themis, the things he'd learned in battle so long ago for Alexander still served him well.

And taking a quick moment of calm to assess and prepare properly was invaluable.

"How do you want to handle them?"

"Quietly," Drake said.

"You take all the fun out of it."

"Let's rock and roll."

Grey's eyes sparked with mischief. "Before we do, tell me one thing."

"What?"

"She was naked, wasn't she?"

On a sigh, Drake nodded. "As the day she was born."

Emerson snatched the whistling teapot off the stove and poured steaming water into two mugs. The tisane she'd prepared a few days earlier to sleep seemed like a good choice to calm the nerves she couldn't shake.

When it had become obvious Magnus wasn't going to lose his mood to pick a fight, Drake had kindly excused himself from their burgeoning family drama. She had thought it would make things easier with her brother, but so far, their conversation had only gotten more uncomfortable.

Setting both mugs on the table, she took a seat opposite Magnus and studied his face. Fine lines bracketed his eyes and mouth. They were faint, but visible. It wasn't the lines, though, that had her taking a second look.

It was the hard, unyielding set of his brown eyes that had her nerves jangling again.

What had happened to him?

The large, tough body. The readiness to battle Drake that wouldn't seem to calm. And then the eyes.

He looked like a warrior.

The thought caught her off guard, but as she considered it further, it seemed like the exact right word. She'd lived with a gang of Warriors next door—had even been on a mission with them—and she knew the look.

How had her brother come by the very same?

He'd taken their mother's disappearance hard. They all had, the lack of knowing an unimaginable pain. But it was the resulting changes in him that were unsettling. And it wasn't simply because she hadn't seen him in four years. Realistically, she could acknowledge that time had aged them all.

But this . . . *hardness*? It wasn't Magnus.

She clenched her fingers in the material of Drake's T-shirt where it pooled over her thighs. She'd added shorts but couldn't bring herself to change into another shirt. The smell of him—like the fresh tang of the grass at midnight in August—was a source of comfort as she searched for the right words to deal with her brother.

"Who was that guy, Em? And why the hell did he think he could put his hands all over you?"

"He's a . . . friend."

"You let all your *friends* touch you while you're naked?"

"Stay out of it, Magnus. It's none of your business."

"You're my sister. That makes it my business."

She refrained from beating her head on the table and took a sip of her tea instead. "What's brought you back?"

"It was time to come home."

"Time? It's been time for four years."

"Not for me. Why can't you understand that?" He scrubbed a hand through his hair. "Or at least try to."

She didn't miss the underlying insult. He'd said something similar years ago in the midst of them all dealing with their grief. The moment hit her so swiftly, she could only be grateful she was sitting down.

"She's gone, Em. So don't act like you can replace her."

The blow carried a fierce sting, like a battle-ax to her grief. She'd never even think of trying to replace their mother. No one could.

"Magnus! I'm trying to understand you. You've been gone for three days and the rumors are running hot that you're somehow involved in that mess in the park. Tell me you weren't there. Tell me you didn't have anything to do with the vandalism and the drugs and that homeless man who lost his life."

"If that's what you want to hear, then fine, I wasn't involved."

Oh sweet Hecate, was it possible he actually had been involved? That her fears hadn't been misplaced?

"What has gotten into you?"

"I'm a grown man. I can make my own decisions and go where I want to go."

"You're my brother. My family. I have a right to know if you're involved in things you shouldn't be. Please tell me you're not that stupid."

"Leave it alone, Em. Why do you assume you can fix everything?"

A deep well opened in her stomach. She'd recently dubbed it the "pit of despair" since it had manifested itself the day the police showed up informing them of her mother's disappearance. Not only hadn't it closed; her brother's increasing forays into trouble had only made it wider.

Deeper.

"It's not trying to fix things to care about your family. To want to see them on the right path in life."

As she stared across the table at her brother, she couldn't help but wonder about the path he'd taken.

"The last we heard from you, you were in Europe. Is that where you've been the whole time?"

"Pretty much." Magnus stared down at his tea, then stood and headed for a cabinet on the far side of the kitchen. Before she could blink, he had a large bottle of whiskey out on the counter. Mere moments later, he had fresh ice clinking in a glass and his whiskey poured.

"Looks like you haven't forgotten everything."

"You have a problem with my having a drink?"

"No."

Magnus resumed his seat, but not before downing half the glass of liquor he'd poured.

On a sip of her tea, Emerson tried for a different tact. "I'm glad you're home."

"Not much has changed."

She followed his gaze as it traveled around the kitchen. "You say that like it's a bad thing."

Magnus drained the rest of his glass on a sneer. "There you go, putting words in my mouth again."

"Well, how would you have me take your comments?" Emerson tried to hold her tongue. Knew she'd get nowhere pointing out to him what an asshole he was being, but damn it all if she could stay silent.

"Need I remind you once more? You've lost the right to comment."

"I have every right to comment. What the hell is this place? A museum? Life changes, Em. People change. Times change. And if you don't change with it, you're nothing but a dinosaur."

And just like that, she was a teenager again, desperate to be understood and especially hurt because her siblings couldn't understand her. Or couldn't be bothered to.

"Just because I haven't chosen to go gallivanting around the world doesn't mean my life is stale. This is freaking New York City. I could live here my whole life and still not see everything there is to see on this island."

"It's more than that. Don't you want more?"

"More of what?"

"Just more. More out of life. More out of your talent?"

What was *this*?

That same sense of unease that had gripped her so many moons ago when she'd worried if he was involved in the park incident nipped at her with iron teeth. "I use my talents every day, Magnus."

"For what? So you can go out in the yard at night, dance a few rituals and draw a bit of fire in your hands? You're better than that, Em." He leaned forward, his large body pressing on the edge of the table and his eyes alight with a vivid, evangelical fire. "So much better than that."

"It's a gift, Magnus. It should be treated as such."

"Damn it, Em. Why won't you use it?"

The teeth clamped harder, a vise she couldn't escape. "Use it how?"

"For yourself. For gain, Em. Don't tell me you're so bound up in all that white witch bullshit you can't see you're entitled to some benefits."

The mug shook in her hands and she laid it down on the table before she cracked the handle. "Bullshit? Is that how you see my life? Grandmother's life? Your heritage?"

"And there you go blowing it all out of proportion. Look, why don't I just turn in? There'll be enough time to catch up in the morning."

"Emerson?" Her grandmother's voice carried down the hall as she walked toward the kitchen. "Who are you talking to?"

Emerson wanted to argue and demand answers from Magnus, but the sight of her grandmother's face had her holding her tongue.

"Magnus?" Hippolyta's voice exhaled on a rush as she caught sight of her grandson. "Is it really you?"

Magnus laid his glass of clinking ice cubes on the table and stood, turning bright, welcoming eyes to his grandmother. "Grandma!"

Emerson watched as he swept their grandmother up in a fierce hug, the large lines of his body dwarfing her withered frame. The hardness she'd witnessed earlier vanished as if it had never been as Magnus hugged their grandmother.

Could he really turn it off so easily?

Or were there some people you couldn't resist, no matter how hard you tried?

In a moment of frightening clarity, Emerson thought

back to her evening with Drake a few nights before. He'd asked her to stay and she'd not only ignored the offer, but she'd cut him off at the knees. Despite doing the same for nearly a year now, he'd not grown tired of her or her attitude.

Why was she so intent on pushing him away? Or, more to the point, so afraid of letting him get close?

Mom.

The thought whispered across her senses, that ever-present pain swelling like high tide. She could usually keep it at bay. Could usually let it simmer as a dull ache in the background of her mind.

But no matter where the memory lived, it held her back. Taunted her with the knowledge her mother had abandoned her. Had abandoned all of them.

The pit of despair opened once again and threatened to swallow her whole.

Chapter Four

Drake heard the low whistle and saw Grey motion for him on the opposite end of the warehouse they staked out. With a quick port, he arrived next to the Aries. "You find something?"

"There's a good-sized storage closet on the far side of the warehouse. I saw it when I went around the back. Door's closed and it looks empty from what I can see. Lucky for us, they likely checked it when they entered and would never assume anyone could get past them to get inside."

"And you think the apple's definitely here at the meet?"

"No doubt about it." Grey gave a short nod toward the building. "What I got from Legs, as you've dubbed her, is that the crime boss we want has been sporting a new lapel pin as of late."

"Let me guess. It's in the shape of an apple?"

"You got it. The godfather of the Gavelli family looks

like he's a huge supporter of New York, but we both know otherwise."

"Is the godfather inside?"

"Yep. Surrounded by his men, but at least he's here."

"Just as we'd hoped." Adrenaline spiked as Drake mapped their plan of attack out in his head.

They'd worked out their strategy on their walk from the car. The apple was the goal, but they needed to keep the peace long enough to get what they came for.

Drake kept his gaze focused on the far end of the dock. By his calculation, the few guards the thugs had posted were scanning the area every ten minutes, so he and Grey had a bit of breathing room.

"You still want us to each take one of the bosses?"

"Yep. Get them outside. Whoever's got the pin, snag it and we port out."

"And the inevitable cameras that will capture our sudden arrival in the room?"

Grey shoved his phone back into his pocket after a quick scan. "Quinn's already done some prep work and erased some previous feeds so he knows he can do it. Their high-tech system wasn't any match for him and he's watching from his office."

"Let's do this."

The ram nodded his agreement. "In and out."

Drake followed Grey around the far side of the dock to get visual on the storage room. The grimy window didn't offer much in the way of a view, but he got enough of a hazy outline to know where he was going and avoid falling over anything. With an ease that defied his preference for water, he pushed himself into the port.

After materializing in the storage closet, he moved toward the door to listen to the activities going down in the main warehouse. The phone on his belt started buzzing with a text, but he ignored it in favor of focusing on what was going down in the main room as Grey's form took shape behind him.

Drake cracked the door slightly as a burst of shouts erupted inside the warehouse. A muttered "Oh shit" from the ram had Drake shifting his attention. "What?"

Grey held his phone aloft, his face ashen and his mouth a grim line. "They've got Finley."

"How?"

"Quinn just texted me. He saw it all on the cameras."

Drake reached for his phone but already knew what the text would say.

THEY'VE GOT GREY'S LAWYER. TREAD CAREFULLY.

Well fuck, Drake thought with no small measure of disgust.

There went in and out.

Now you've done it, Finley Jane. You've officially ended both your career and your life by acting like a Lifetime Movie of the Week victim.

Blood pumped through Finley McCrae's body in heavy, leaden waves, the sensation amplified by the pounding in her ears. She was oddly aware of all her senses.

The feel of expensive silk under her chin where the large asshole with the gun held her in place.

The garlicky smell of his breath.

Even the dark hues of the back end of the warehouse shimmered in heavy blacks and grays, the absence of color a stark reminder of the people who operated in the shadowy recesses of human depravity.

They were going to kill her.

Refusing to give in to the wellspring of despair that waited in the wings of her mind, she focused again on the information she'd learned earlier from her colleague Melanie.

A meeting had been planned for over a week between two of the city's biggest crime families, with their respective bosses most assuredly in attendance. Her gaze drifted around the room, confirming the information had been one hundred percent accurate.

Some sort of secret deal was in the works to amass more power between them. Again, she processed what she'd managed to hear before she'd been caught in the basement, just underneath where she now stood captive. Melanie's information had been spot on.

So how had the thug currently holding her and his partner found her, hidden away in a dark corner behind a row of moldering boxes?

Wincing as Garlic Breath tightened his grip on her neck, she fought to keep her calm.

Fought to use the rational mind she prided herself on to figure it out.

Was it a bad tip?

She'd always been obsessively diligent in checking tips, no matter the source. Even the most trusted adviser could give bad information or be set up to give bad information. Worse, she knew even those with the best motivations could be lured with the temptation of something more rewarding.

But Melanie?

Any way she looked at it, Finley couldn't make the facts add up. Melanie was a trust fund baby who had a passion for the law and the justice she and her fellow attorneys brought to the city. She was Ivy League and *magna cum laude* all the way.

It just didn't add up.

Which means, if it wasn't Melanie, who set her up?

The grip on her neck tightened once more, the lack of air instantly pulling her from her thoughts to the pressing matter of her life.

Cold, lifeless hazel eyes bored into hers as one of the mobsters stood over her. "Ms. McCrae, I'm going to give you one more chance to tell me what you were doing in the basement of this building."

Right. Like she'd tell *them.* The last time she checked, crime investigation wasn't in her job description. And while she usually avoided overt behavior that screamed she was too stupid to keep her job—or live, for that matter—she hadn't been able to resist investigating this tip.

Something *big* was going on.

Finley took in the mobster's gaze and abstractly remembered that her grandfather had had hazel eyes. With small flecks of gold and a dark rim around the irises. He'd been warm and fun, with a perpetual smile on his face whenever she was in his presence.

"Now, Ms. McCrae!" A gun jabbed into her stomach and the warm memory of her grandfather faded away as cold, harsh reality replaced it.

She was going to die.

*   *   *

Grey's stomach clenched as he pushed past Drake toward the door. How had she gotten in there?

And how in fucking hell had she gotten past him? She'd been perched on her favorite bar stool in Equinox half an hour ago.

With steady patience and a calm he didn't feel, Grey cracked the door a fraction of an inch and peered into the common area of the warehouse, taking stock of the players.

Although everyone was dressed in matching silk suits and expensive Italian loafers, the sides were clear, almost like an invisible line ran down the center of the room. And while the two sides might be enemies, all the players were aligned in their focus as one of the lower-level goons held Finley in his arms, a gun against her side.

She was dressed in running clothes—what Grey could only assume was her disguise for getting close to the warehouse. The long legs he'd admired in her fitted pencil skirts were even more impressive in runner's shorts, but the skimpy attire made her look even more vulnerable.

Another wave of anger torpedoed his system and Grey took in the stark terror that covered her face like a mask. Her porcelain skin was paler than usual and her bright blue eyes were huge round saucers in her face, telegraphing her terror.

He never should have talked to her tonight. Never should have given her an indication of what he suspected. He'd known the meet was going down and he shouldn't have created the pretense of discussing it with her.

So, damn it, why had he?

Because the moments you spend with her are the sweetest in your day.

"How do you want to play this?"

At the sound of Drake's hushed voice, Grey moved away from the door. "She's the priority."

"Absolutely." Drake nodded

"I want to get her and get out. We can come back for the apple later."

"Where are you going to take her? After you get her out, do you think you can get her mind wiped?"

"Fuck." Grey gripped his hair and tugged. "She's not very susceptible. I already tested it out on her a few months ago, in case I needed to use the Mind Meld."

"Didn't work?"

"Nope. Not in the slightest."

She hadn't bought it, he remembered, as he'd tried wiping the conversation they'd just had. Instead, she'd looked at him with a small smile playing the edges of her lush lips as those bright blue eyes stayed steady as a rock on his.

No hazing, no clouding, no loss of memory. Nothing.

She'd forgotten nothing.

"Let's play it like the Artemis affair."

Drake's laughter was a low rumble between them. "Hurt as many as possible before we port out."

"Exactly."

"And if I can snag the apple?"

"It's secondary, but take the opportunity if you can get it."

"Let's do it. You head for Finley, I'll come in right

behind the guy who's holding her." At his nod, Drake added, "I'll count us off."

"See you back at the ranch."

"On my mark," Drake began. "Three, two, one. Now!"

Both disappeared in a rush, the outer room their destination.

In the blink of an eye, Grey had his hands on Finley's shoulders as Drake disarmed the goon holding her with a swift, downward chop of his hand. The gun at her side clattered to the floor as shouts erupted around them.

The tight troop of men moved forward in a rush and Grey kicked out, satisfied when he heard the crunch of bone as his foot connected with a kneecap.

"Get out of here, Grey!" Drake shouted at him as he dropped the man who'd been holding Finley, then launched himself into a throng of thugs advancing on them. "I see the target; then I'm right behind you."

Grey wanted to argue, wanted to tell his Warrior brother to get the hell out and they'd come back later, but he was distracted by the trembling woman in his arms.

"You?" Finley stared up at him as her mouth dropped open on an *O* of surprise.

"Yeah, it's me."

Tightening his grip on Finley, he threw them both into the port. As their bodies left the warehouse, Grey heard the gunshot.

Drake saw the apple lapel pin the moment they ported into the warehouse. The two sides had clearly demarcated themselves in the room, with the bosses of each family surrounded. The setup was so clear it was almost laughable in its simplicity.

Circle of thugs, kingpin in the middle.

The smug look on Franco Gavelli's face gave him a momentary flash of Magnus earlier that evening and Drake made his decision.

He wasn't leaving without the apple.

Wise? Probably not. Satisfying? Abso-fucking-lutely.

It also hadn't escaped his notice the thug holding Finley was operating under the influence of the Gavelli family. With the capture of a public official, it was clear the apple had done significant harm in a short period of time.

The fact that he'd feel good bashing the self-satisfied look off the guy's face in the process was only a small side benefit.

The whirl of air that accompanied Grey and Finley's departure gave him the opening he needed. Throwing himself into another port as gunfire erupted in a loud burst, Drake heard the resounding confusion in stereo as he reappeared and fell into the center of the circle of thugs. The port was near perfect, landing him within an inch of Gavelli.

The man's eyes widened in his doughy face as Drake reached for his lapels. Hand on the apple, Drake nearly had it when the guys protecting their boss picked up on his intent. The goon to Gavelli's immediate right lifted his gun and from his peripheral Drake could see it was aimed straight at his midsection.

Drake pressed one hand on the boss's shoulder for balance and executed a sharp tug on the pin, satisfied when the silky material of Gavelli's suit gave way in his hands. As his fingers closed over the Golden Apple, he pushed himself into his port.

And as the air whirled around him, the unmistakable sound of gunfire swelled once again in his ear. Drake felt the searing fire in his rib cage as his body floated into the ether.

Emerson paced her room, unable to calm down after the fireworks with Magnus. Four years gone and nothing had changed. In fact, it seemed as if things had gotten worse.

What was it with the whole power play about how shitty her life was?

Her life was fine, thank you very much. She lived a vibrant, interesting life and she liked it that way. She was satisfied.

And what about Drake? her conscious taunted. *Are you satisfied there?*

Before she could even attempt to engage in her daily argument with herself, the air around her grew heavy, like a threatening storm, and the object of her thoughts fell to the floor of her bedroom in a heavy rush.

"Drake!"

Alarm bells went off in her system immediately as she took in the odd way he lay on the floor. Rushing to him, she barely held back a scream as she took in the blood that covered his side.

"Drake! Oh my God. Drake." Pulling at his body to roll him toward his back, she saw where he had a hand pressed to his side, a raw, angry wound gaping under his fingers.

"Hang on, baby. Hang on." Rushing from her room, she hit the hall closet and grabbed a handful of towels.

Could he be fatally shot?

A long, low groan greeted her as she ran back into her room, the sound sweeter than she ever would have believed. She didn't have all the ins and outs of his abilities, but he'd always seemed so invincible—so perfect, really—the idea that he could be hurt like this tore at something inside of her.

Pressing a towel to the wound, she pulled at his hand once she got the proper pressure on it. Another heavy groan drifted from his lips and she linked his fingers with hers, all the while maintaining pressure with her other hand. "Drake, can you hear me?"

"Emerson?"

"I'm here. I—" She broke off at the shock of seeing the towel under her hand fill with blood. "I'm here. What happened to you?"

"Got shot."

He may have been in pain, but she couldn't miss the utter disgust in his raspy voice. "I can see that. But what happened?"

"Helping Grey. Fucker got off a shot before I could get out of there."

"What fucker? Grey shot you?"

"No. The crime boss's goon."

"You went after a crime boss?" Emerson kept her movements gentle as she reached for a fresh towel. She was pleased to see the bleeding was definitely slowing. And it looked less *angry*, somehow . . . less raw.

"Grey did."

"Well, why the hell did you go, too? Do you both have a death wish?"

Drake opened one eye, his green gaze hazed with pain. "That's what we do."

"Do you make it a habit to get shot?"

He opened the other eye. "It's an occupational hazard I usually manage to avoid."

"So what happened tonight?" Emerson heard the tough edge to her voice—reveled in it actually, because it meant she had some measure of control back over herself—and poked at him. "Who'd you piss off? And what could possibly make you think it was a good idea to go after one of New York's crime families? Who was it, by the way?"

"The Gavellis."

"Are you out of your mind?" Emerson almost dropped the towel as she focused on him. "They're meaner than snakes and they've been all over the news for their suspected antics lately. Bombings. Drownings. Even a delightful buried-alive story that gave me the chills the other night."

"Which is the exact reason Grey and I needed to pay them a visit. They've been getting some help."

"Help?"

"From a supernatural source."

"Oh."

Wind knocked from her sails, Emerson focused on tending to Drake's wound. Keeping her movements gentle, she lifted the towel, pleased to see the wound continuing to close. "Will it close all the way?"

"It'll heal—but not fully until the bullet comes out."

When he began moving around to reach for his feet, she clamped a hand on his arm. "What are you doing?"

"I need to get it out."

"With what?"

"My Xiphos."

"Drake." Emerson pushed harder on his arm to keep him still. "What are you after?"

"I've got my weapon strapped to my ankle. It's a really big knife. I can use it to remove the bullet."

"You most certainly will not."

"Why not?"

"It's dirty, for one."

"Look, it hurts more to leave it there."

"I'll get it." Shifting, she scooted back to give herself easier access and reached for his ankle, unstrapping the knife sheathed there.

He wasn't kidding. The blade was wicked-looking and a little less than a foot in length. Holding it up, she summoned fire at her fingertips and let the flames wash over the length of the blade, paying particular attention to the tip.

"What are you doing?"

"Sterilizing it."

"I can't catch a disease from it, Emerson."

She focused on the flame, unwilling to acknowledge his muttered complaints. "Roll to your side."

"It's going to be hot."

"Which means it'll cauterize the wound as I remove the bullet."

"Just do it quick."

Leaning forward, she placed a firm hand on his

shoulder as she pointed the knife at the entrance of the wound. "Hang on."

Emerson heard Drake's sharp exhale of breath and fought to keep her hands steady as she dug for the bullet. *This should be easier.* She continued to probe the torn flesh at his side. *Where was the damn thing?*

"You drilling for oil?" Drake muttered through gritted teeth.

"I'm trying to be gentle."

"I know." Drake's free hand moved up to cover her left one, where she'd shifted to hold it against his chest, and squeezed hers in reassurance.

She felt the quivering in her belly and exhaled on a deep breath. The bullet had to be in there. It was just a matter of finding it. She could *do* this.

"Just focus, baby. You'll get it."

Drake's voice drifted over her, the calm reassurance— and absolute belief in her—a soothing balm to her pounding heart.

She shifted the blade slightly and felt the resistance immediately.

"Got it." Digging the point a hairsbreadth deeper, she felt it as the tip of the blade notched under the bullet. "Hang on to me."

Drake's hand tightened on hers, but there was no other indication of his pain. No other indication of how badly he must be suffering.

On a final rush of motion, she had the bullet out in one smooth move, the now-misshapen metal falling to the floor.

Immediately, his skin began to mend even faster than before. She grabbed a fresh towel and pressed it to the wound, but it was obvious he wouldn't need it much longer.

Drake's big hand squeezed hers. "Thank you."

"You . . . you're welcome."

She still gripped the knife so hard her knuckles were white. She tossed it across the room, where it clattered along the floorboard. As soon as the knife left her hand, uncontrollable shakes gripped her entire body.

"Emerson?"

Her name on Drake's lips sounded very far away as she turned to look at him.

"Emerson? Are you all right?"

She tried to snap out the words "of course," but they wouldn't form. Instead, a wash of hot tears filled her eyes as another round of shakes gripped her shoulders.

Drake struggled to sit up—should he be doing that?—and reached for her. "Come here."

"F . . . fi . . . fine." Her teeth chattered so hard she couldn't form a word. "I . . . I'm fi . . . fine."

"Sure you are." He pulled her close and Emerson wanted to feel embarrassed, but all she could feel was the delicious warmth that seeped into her skin wherever he touched her. Drake shifted back slightly to look at her, those mysterious genie's eyes boring into hers. "Thank you."

An embarrassing hiccup escaped her lips as she said, "You're welcome."

When Drake's arms wrapped around her once again, Emerson did something really embarrassing.

She broke down and sobbed.

Chapter Five

"You want to tell me what just happened?"

"Not really," Grey snapped out as he reached for a crystal decanter on the credenza behind his desk.

"Can I at least have one of those? I don't quite have my sea legs yet." Finley's tone was low, but he had to give her credit. That sexy voice never quavered.

Grey gave the legs in question a quick look before turning back to pouring. He heard the light clink of the decanter against his crystal-cut glass and struggled to keep his hand from shaking as he reached for a second one. "Of course."

He poured her a couple of fingers of bourbon and carried their glasses back to the leather couches on the opposite side of his office. Everything looked exactly as he'd left it an hour before, even if it felt entirely different.

She was here after nearly getting herself killed by a bunch of unrepentant thugs who would have reveled in her death.

Focusing on the fact she was safe, he handed over the bourbon and had to give her credit for the steady blue gaze that never wavered, even as she took a sip of the harsh liquor.

"I had a feeling there were a few secrets here." She glanced around the room. "I can't say I'm all that disappointed to have my instincts proven correct, especially since I suspect that's how you saved me tonight."

"Ms. McCrae," Grey began.

"Haven't we gotten a bit past that? I'm Finley." And to prove it, she moved forward, set her glass on the coffee table with a soft clink and turned toward him, laying a hand on his knee.

Grey hadn't been a teenager since Rome fell, but he'd be hard-pressed to say he'd ever felt so awkward around a woman in the ensuing years. "Finley."

"That's better. Now, what the hell is going on? How'd you know I'd be in that warehouse and how did you and your friend get in like that?"

"I was at that warehouse because you gave me the tip. Earlier this evening. Remember?"

The impatient huff as she exhaled on a heavy breath was unmistakable. "Yeah, but it was the *way* you got in."

"What's that got to do with it?"

"You just . . . appeared."

Deflect. Evade. Lie. He'd had centuries of practice. "We were hiding in the storeroom."

"Between the storeroom and the middle of the warehouse. Don't act like you don't know what I'm talking about."

"Okay, fine. How do *you* think we got in?"

"I'm a logical person, Grey. I have to be. I'm a lawyer. I deal in facts and things that can be seen and touched. Things that are proven."

"And?"

She brushed a lock of auburn hair behind her ear. "There is no logical explanation for how you arrived. You just . . . appeared." Finley said it again as she reached for her glass, her puzzled gaze focused on the amber liquid.

Grey shifted back to his original strategy and sought to deflect the conversation and turn it around. Put her on the defensive. "Are you going to report what happened this evening?"

"Report what?"

"To the DA? To the cops. I wouldn't blame you for either. They may be a slippery bunch of thugs, but they still threatened to kill you." He took another sip of his bourbon. Even as he asked the questions, he knew he could never let her put voice to them.

Couldn't let her face the danger that would come with riling up the monsters that hid in the DA's office.

Finley ran her thumbs over the pattern on the glass. "I shouldn't have been there, so I'm not planning on saying anything. My boss wouldn't be very happy to find out I specifically defied a direct order."

"So why did you?"

"I couldn't miss out on the opportunity to figure out what was going on."

"Gavelli's men know who you are. Now so do Lavano's men."

"Grey, this is New York City. There's not a thug in New York who doesn't know who works in the DA's office. This isn't the first time I was a target. I'm sure it won't be the last."

Grey finished his drink in one large swallow, the thought of her facing that danger alone sending ice-cold fear winging through his veins. Settling the glass on the coffee table, he managed to keep his voice to a quiet whisper. "You were captured."

"It was a calculated risk."

The simmering anger that had roiled in his gut since he looked out of the storeroom and saw her at gunpoint erupted. "Like hell it was!"

Other than those bright blue eyes going wide with surprise, she didn't even flinch at his raised voice. Instead, she leaned forward, the hard set of her slender shoulders proof positive she felt no remorse about her decisions that evening. "Grey, I knew what I was getting into."

"Bullshit. I want to know how you got a tip about Gavelli's meeting and then ended up at gunpoint."

"My colleague Melanie gave me the tip. Gave it to both of us—my boss, Charlie, and me. He forbade me to go. Forbade both of us to get involved."

"So Melanie's responsible for setting you up?"

"But then why would she have told Charlie about it? It doesn't make any sense."

Anger had him in its cold, pointy claws, but he held his voice steady. "It makes perfect sense. She knew you wouldn't be able to resist going exactly where you didn't belong."

"She has nothing to gain. Why would she own up to a tip, tell our boss and then use it against me?"

Grey wasn't ready to let their illustrious DA or his staff off the hook just yet, but she had a point. It would also be an incredibly poor move for her colleagues to suddenly make themselves targets if she'd gone missing.

"Why did you go into that warehouse? People do lots of dumb things."

The dumb comment had her back up, but she didn't rise to the bait. "I had an opportunity and I took it."

"Well, then, Miss Opportunity. It looks like we have a new mystery to figure out."

"What's this 'we,' Grey? This is my problem. And if it is someone in my office, I'll deal with it."

"No, you won't. Not on your own."

She lifted her gaze to his, heat rising quickly in the sea of blue. "You don't have a say in it."

"Fuck if I don't." Grey didn't think—didn't keep the cool head he prided himself on.

Instead he simply acted.

Reaching for her waist, he dragged her forward on the couch, the leather making it easy to pull her slender frame forward. Unable to see anything but her—unable to think about anything but her—he slammed his lips on hers, fusing their mouths in a rush of heat and need and such soul-pounding fear he didn't know if his heart would ever stop thumping against his ribs at triple its normal speed.

The need to consume her simply filled him and he was unable to stop the rush of heat as their tongues met and plundered.

Possessed.

A soft sigh left her throat as she moved against him, her hands closing the distance between them to run her fingers over his shoulders. When she leaned forward and nipped his lower lip with her teeth, Grey felt his heart speed up for a reason far different than fear.

This was need. Raw and yet surprisingly sweet, he knew with harsh honesty it could only be sated by *her*.

Finley.

Grey pulled back, reluctantly dragging his mouth from hers, as he stared into the mysterious blue depths of her eyes. The fear struck again without warning, the image of a gun pressed against her body one he couldn't erase.

Eris snapped her cell phone closed, took stock of her current situation and repressed the urge to scream. Instead, she snagged a towel from the hall closet and headed for her workout room.

Damn humans. They really couldn't find their asses with both hands and a flashlight.

The Golden Apple was the perfect weapon. She'd protected it well since the Trojan War and used it sparingly through the years. It was a powerful tool and it wasn't to be leveraged lightly.

She'd protected it for thousands of years and now it was not only out in the open, but in the hands of Themis's boys.

Unacceptable.

Her two-bedroom home was small by Mount Olympus's standards, but it suited her just fine. One bedroom was for her and the second was for her workout equipment.

What else did she need?

She flipped on some music, climbed on the elliptical and set the resistance on eight. Within moments she was sweating as Lady Gaga blared through the speakers.

Involving herself with organized crime had been a

calculated risk. Realistically, she knew that. But New York's crime families were the perfect diversion for her plans. Get the city's peacekeepers focused on a resurgence in turf warfare and then step in and let the real fireworks start.

The plan had been perfect.

Until one of Themis's Warriors got his hands on the apple. That beautiful little device that channeled all of her abilities into one small, unassuming package.

It had been shockingly simple to create all those many years ago and despite trying so many other things through the years, she was rather fond of her apple.

Who's the fairest of them all?

Who wants the power to rule the city?

It was an easy leap—you simply played on whatever an individual wanted in the deepest part of themselves—and you let good old-fashioned human nature do its job.

Eris jumped off the elliptical and switched to a weight machine. With even breaths she pushed the bars up and down, never breaking her stride as she let her mind whirl through her problem.

Her new weapon was close to ready, but it needed a bit more work. And losing the apple put a serious chink in her armor, so she needed to figure out a way to get it back.

Rogan? Could she use him for that?

A shot of warmth suffused her as she started on her third set of reps.

Who the hell was she kidding? She could use Rogan for just one thing.

Anytime, anywhere.

That didn't mean he'd fuck over his brothers for her. And, if she were honest with herself, that was one area she wasn't crazy about tainting with her job.

She and the Sagittarius had an understanding. A rather delicious understanding. And she wasn't interested in losing it over a problem she could find a solution to all by herself.

Finishing up on the weights, she moved to a mat on the floor and went through a few stretches to cool down. Although the exercises weren't technically necessary when you had an immortal body and a youthful physique that never aged, she found the time well spent and more than a little therapeutic.

Unlike her sister, Enyo, who found solace in self-pity, pouting and nasty, vengeful tricks, Eris found a more inwardly focused approach worked wonders. It allowed her to think clearly and rationally—a skill fairly underdeveloped on Mount Olympus.

Moving to the fridge, she snagged a large bottle of water and downed the crisp, cool drink. The ringing peal of her phone announced a text and she moved across the kitchen to grab it.

YOU FREE?

Rogan.

On another swig of water, she thought about how to play it. A quick "yes"? Or a definitive "no," because she really was becoming far too dependent on the delights to be found in his arms.

Oh, who was she kidding?

Snatching up the phone, she texted back before she could second-guess herself.

SEE YOU AT OUR USUAL PLACE. MIDNIGHT.

Tossing the phone onto the counter, she headed for the shower.

She might not know yet how to fix her problem.

But scratching an itch always helped a girl think better.

"Emerson? You okay?"

A loud sniffle rumbled against his shoulder. "Not yet."

Drake ran his hands over her back in soothing circles as he held her in his arms.

His side still stung, but he refused to let her go. She was so tough around him—so unwilling to show vulnerability of any kind—that the moment had an odd sweetness he was loath to let go of.

"I'm fine now. The wound's already healing."

"You were bleeding all over my floor ten minutes ago."

Drake shifted and reached for her chin, tilting her head up until her gaze met his. "Well, it's ten minutes later and I'm on the mend."

"I pulled a bullet out of you."

"Thanks."

"How can you take this so calmly?" Her gray eyes were wet from her tears.

"It's what I do, Emerson." He pressed his forehead to hers. "I'm fine with it."

"But you always come home bloody and bruised."

"Just how would you know that?"

A sweet blush crept into her cheeks, despite the tanned color of her skin. "Callie's mentioned it before."

"Oh really? What did she say, exactly?"

"She just mentioned your missions take a toll on you. The others, too," she added after a beat.

"We're immortal, Emerson. It's a bit painful at the time, but we regenerate. Callie cooks us a load of food and we get our strength back. It doesn't last."

She scooted back and got to her feet, reaching for the discarded towels on the floor. "What made you think going after a crime boss made any sense?"

He watched the sweet curve of her ass covered in thin cotton yoga pants. It wasn't until she'd left the room and he heard her enter the bathroom that her words reminded him of what he'd removed from the scene. "Did I drop anything when I came in?"

"You mean other than you?" Her voice echoed back at him from down the hall.

"What?"

Emerson padded back into the room on bare feet. "You fell to the floor like a tipped cow."

He couldn't resist. "You've been cow tipping?"

"One of my aunts lived on a farm upstate. We spent summers there when I was a teenager."

Fascinating. He kept the thought to himself, instead opting for, "Now that we've got that settled, where did I fall?"

"Over there. Foot of the bed."

Drake rolled onto his stomach to search the area under the bed. The darkened room made it hard to see, but he shoved his hands under the mattress frame, satisfied when he made contact with the sharp end of a pin.

Snagging it, he pulled it out and held it up in the soft light of her bedside table.

"What is that?" Emerson sat down next to him. "It looks like a pin of some sort. An apple?"

"Yep."

"Where'd you get it?"

"Off the crime boss you were so worried about me going after."

"Your mission was to snag a piece of jewelry?" She reached for it, holding the apple up to turn it in the light, her movements so like his own.

Drake marveled at the delicate lines of her body. The slender taper of her fingers with finely sculpted nails as she held the small piece of jewelry. The line of her neck and the soft hair that lay at the nape.

She was small and feminine, and no matter how hard he tried he could not get this one woman out of his system. In fact, he realized with a start, he had no interest in getting her out of his system. "Are we actually having a conversation?"

"Hmmm?" She turned the pin again in the muted light of the bedside lamp.

"You and me. Is this a real conversation?"

Emerson's gray eyes snapped to his. "What's that supposed to mean?"

"It's nice. Talking to each other. Just like I knew it would be."

"Look, Ace. You're the one who came in bleeding all over my floor. If you're okay enough to give me shit about it, maybe you're okay enough to head home."

The silky tendrils of frustration uncurled in his belly as the moment morphed from tender to tense in the space of a heartbeat. "And here we go."

"You've got a problem with me?"

"Yeah, I do. I can't see why you willingly ignore what's between us. Because when you forget about it, like you just did, you seem awfully comfortable in my presence."

"I regularly get naked in your presence. I ought to feel comfortable with you."

Drake saw the wall—he'd have to be deaf, dumb, blind and dead to miss it—and puzzled at the reasons for it. "That's not the only way I see you."

"Naked?"

"I desire you, Emerson. I won't deny it. But it's not the only reason I spend time with you."

She handed him the apple before moving to fiddle with the knob on her dresser. "Why do you keep pushing for more?"

"Why do you keep pushing for less?" Drake shoved the pin in his pants pocket, not in the least surprised when it pulsed warmly against his hip.

On a smooth move, she dragged the T-shirt he'd given her earlier over her head and had a new one out of the top drawer of her dresser. He couldn't deny that very desire as it whipped through his veins, his gaze drinking her in.

But it wasn't all he saw.

He also saw the harsh set of her impossibly slim shoulders as they fought to hold up her world. The proud tilt of her head as it sat atop a spine stiff with pride. The capable strength in her hands as she pulled on a new shirt, one far more fitted to her frame.

"We don't want the same things, Drake."

The pin pulsed hotter in his pocket and he couldn't help but wonder if their argument somehow fired the item. It was the Apple of Discord and he and Emerson weren't exactly having a pleasant moment.

A necessary one, but far from harmonious.

"Don't we?"

Whirling from the dresser, she stalked toward him. "No, *we* don't. I wanted a no-strings-attached fling. We were agreed on that from the very first. Hell, I've seen you and your brothers. You're the sex squad, for fuck's sake. You don't look like a team of men who are hard up for sex; nor do you look like a bunch of men who have to tie yourselves to a woman to get laid regularly."

"You think that's what a relationship with someone is all about? That the only reason to tie yourself to someone is to get laid? That it's some sort of cop-out? Or consolation prize? Because let me tell you, sweetheart. I've seen my Warrior brothers since they've married their wives. You've got it wrong."

He leaped up and closed the gap between them, ignoring the twinge that still burned in his side from the bullet. "All wrong."

Drake reached for her and pulled her close, even as she immediately started to protest, her voice etching out on a loud squeak. "What are you doing?"

"You're no consolation prize and I'll be damned if you treat what's between us like it is one."

With one hand on the back of her neck, he drew her close. His other hand settled on her lower back, pulling their bodies flush against each other. He covered her mouth with his, the last of her protests fizzling out on a rush of air as she met him eagerly.

The plump cushion of her lips met his in hard, greedy motions designed to take.

To plunder.

And then her clever tongue followed, tangling with his, promising the delights of what always built between them. What her body already knew even as her mind stayed stubbornly separate.

The kiss continued to buffet him on a wild, ruthless ride of the senses. His fingers tightened on the thin material of her pants while with his other hand he reveled in the soft texture of the skin at the base of her neck. Despite her delicate frame, there was strength coiled under her skin and her muscles bunched under his touch.

"Tell me you know there's more between us," he ground out against her mouth.

"Tell me you want me," she pressed back, her lips curving into a smile under his.

"Always."

The moment stretched out as he waited for her answer. And then the phone at his waist rang, breaking the moment.

Ruining the spell between them once again.

"Saved by the bell." Emerson's tone was light, but the humor didn't reach her eyes. "Is that the theme to *Batman*?"

"It's Quinn."

"It suits him." She nodded, slipping under his arm and putting space between them. "Although, you should take better care of your phone. You know, from all that mysterious ringtone sabotage."

"What do you want?" he barked in answer.

Quinn's tone was no less upset. "You were shot, Drake. Where the hell are you?"

"Emerson's."

"You okay?"

"Yeah, I'm fine. Is Grey there?"

"No. And I haven't made contact yet. Did you get the pin?"

Drake patted his pocket, the lapel pin still safely in place. "Yeah. I've got it. I'll be right over."

He shoved the phone back in his pocket and reached for the pin in the other. "I need to get back."

The sexy teasing was gone from Emerson's voice, replaced by a levelheaded coolness that suggested she knew how to handle herself in difficult situations. "What happened?"

"Grey hasn't come home yet."

"Is he hurt?"

"I don't know. He got out of there before me. With someone."

Emerson's eyes widened on that. "One of the thugs went with him?"

"No. A woman. His contact who told him about the meet in the first place. I need to go."

"It's probably for the best."

The words pierced him far more lethally than any battle he'd ever participated in, but he forced himself to stay calm and not take the bait.

Instead, he walked forward and placed a finger under her chin, forcing her gaze up to his. "I just can't agree with you."

Eris ran a hand over the smooth silk of her shirt, the material soft under her hand. Although she never wore her clothes for long when they were together, it didn't stop her from spending far too much time worrying over what she'd wear for her assignations with Rogan.

Gods, she loved Las Vegas and their time there. Humans called it Sin City and the moniker fit.

But to her, it had become so much more. She and Rogan met there with increasing frequency, this strange thing between them growing with the intensity of a wildfire. Like a dream she could escape to. When she was there, staring out over the lights, her body humming from their lovemaking, she wasn't a goddess.

She didn't have a reputation to live up to.

She was simply Eris.

The sensation had grown increasingly heady as the months had passed and their liaisons had become more frequent. Of course, none of it—no matter how enticing—could stop her from her course of action.

Which seriously sucked.

But there was no help for it. She'd been the goddess of discord far longer than Rogan Black had been her boy toy. She had a job to do and she did it well.

If the thought of him as an object made her wince, well then, she was growing far softer than she'd have ever believed.

To prove to herself she could resist him—could still be the person she was born to be—she turned away from the mirror and focused on her current problem. While she had no intention of talking to Rogan about the little report she got back from the docks, she still had a problem and it sat squarely with one of his brothers.

She needed to get that apple back.

When she'd spoken to Gavelli earlier, he mentioned

sending her some video footage to view. Although she
had no doubt the security video from the site would be
corrupted—or simply nonexistent—apparently Gavelli
knew how to protect his own.

That included securing his own footage when he
went to meetings.

Reaching for her phone, she pulled up her e-mail
program and, just as promised, there was attached
video with a very clear image of just who had invaded
their little meet and greet with the Lavanos. As the
short clip played out, she watched the Warriors port
into the room, two large bodies filling the screen and
quickly surrounding the lawyer.

Grey. The Aries. She'd suspected when she saw the
finely cut suit, but confirmed it the moment the camera
captured his features. He poofed out of view and the
camera swung around to the large Warrior stalking
Gavelli. His face was turned away from the camera, but
Eris paused it and expanded the frame.

Damn it, but were they all chiseled out of marble?

Living on Mount Olympus, she'd always had ready
access to fine, fit, healthy male bodies, but these guys
took the cake.

They were perfect.

The paused image had the man in question in profile, the side of his face, neck and shoulder visible in the
frame. His jaw was straight and firm and his neck was
thick with muscle. Her gaze followed the form on the
screen.

Damn, but she had a weakness for broad shoulders.

Hitting PLAY again, she waited to see if she'd catch a
more full-on view. Although she didn't know all of

Themis's boys by name, she had a good sense of who they all were and how they fit in.

His face stayed in profile, but she didn't miss his hand reaching for Gavelli's lapel. One of the goons got a shot off on him, but it didn't matter. A moment later, he was gone.

So he was hurt. Even if it wasn't a kill shot to the head, he had to be feeling relatively shitty right now.

Which means he'd go back to Warrior Central to nurse his wounds.

She glanced at the clock. An image of Rogan flitted across her conscious once more, but she ignored it. With a quick scroll through her phone book, she found the name she was looking for and tapped out a quick text.

As she hit SEND, she again thought of Rogan and the look in his vivid green eyes when he brought her to orgasm. The sheer possessiveness in his gaze never failed to enhance the moment and she always came hard, that instant of connection heightening the experience in a way she simply couldn't ignore.

Heat licked at her belly as her nipples hardened into tight points.

Gods, how was it possible?

How could she have such inconvenient feelings? Especially considering the orders she'd just dispatched.

With a quick glance down at the phone in her hand, she tossed it into the top of her open purse.

She would not think about that right now.

All that mattered was her and Rogan and what they shared in that room in Vegas.

That's all that *could* matter.

Chapter Six

Emerson was surprised to find a rather sizable well of guilt in her stomach the following morning as she laced up her shoes for a run. She'd lain awake for most of the night thinking about her exchange with Drake and the small, petty behavior she'd exhibited. As one minute ticked into the next on her bedside clock, she replayed their conversation on a continuous loop in her head.

And had to admit as she'd risen bleary-eyed to face the day that she'd been exceptionally bitchy to him, even for her.

Not for the first time, she allowed herself to imagine what it would be like if she just let go.

Let him in.

Let herself love Drake.

The idea suffused her with warmth and more than a little bit of terror.

Terror that he'd ultimately go away again.

Just like her mother.

Even if she could see her way past that, Emerson mused, the life of a witch wasn't an easy one. She chose it proudly and freely, but it exacted a price.

Although she never spoke of it—her grandmother kept her emotions under heavy guard—Emerson knew Hippolyta had some serious heartache in her past. Even Veronica, who refused her gifts of magic for a thousand and one reasons, had often argued through the years that Emerson would never find a successful relationship with a man if he thought she could spell him into oblivion if they had a fight.

Not that Drake couldn't put up a damn good fight of his own, her conscience quickly defended him.

With a final tug as she double knotted her shoelace, Emerson stood and resolved to give herself an hour where she thought about nothing but the pounding of her feet on the pavement and the bright, crisp air of morning. All of this would still be here when she got back.

Not to mention part two of her argument with Magnus, which would surely greet her on her return.

Living on the West Side of the city, she normally ran the length of Riverside Park. But the churned-up reminder of what Magnus might have been involved with there before he performed his little four-year disappearing act had her heading for Central Park instead. Although the city's most well-known park was more crowded this time of day, the anonymity would provide a welcome distraction.

Emerson stretched as she waited at the crosswalks while she headed east across West End, then Broadway, then Amsterdam. She'd nearly crossed Columbus—

could see the edge of the park—when the sound of her name broke through her thoughts.

Along with that spear of guilt she'd resolved to ignore for an hour.

"Drake? What are you doing here?" The light turned and she continued moving toward the park, adding another item to her list of bitchy behavior.

If her heart gave a small lurch at the sight of him in a gray T-shirt and navy blue workout shorts, well, that was only further proof she had no objectivity over her hormones when it came to Drake.

She tossed a sideways glance at his narrow waist and powerful legs as he easily kept pace with her crossing the street, and another spear of attraction arrowed through her.

Damn.

No control whatsoever.

"I saw you leave and thought I'd join you."

"Spying on me?"

"Looking out for you. And before you get too suspicious"—he held up a hand—"Callie heard me up and moving around and sent me out for bagels. I saw you as I got back and decided to join you. I will, however, admit to watching your house whenever I pass to make sure things look as they should."

Another brick around her heart crumbled to dust. Even his excuses were logical. And sort of sweet. Unwilling to show she was flustered, she put on her best Ellie Mae voice and batted her eyelashes. "That's right neighborly of you."

"We've always watched out for your grandmother, and her mother before her and her mother before that.

Consider it the side benefit of living next door to a horde of ass kickers." Drake bumped her hip with his as they cleared the crosswalk and moved into the park entrance. "My extra interest in your body doesn't have a damn thing to do with it."

She wanted to stay mad and annoyed and irritated. Wanted to rant and rail that she didn't need looking out for. Or watching over. The knowledge that he did watch over her—that all his Warrior brothers kept an eye out for her and her family—felt sort of . . . *good*.

Emerson stepped off the sidewalk and onto a dirt walkway that led to the jogging path around the reservoir. "You're looking awfully chipper for someone who got shot last night."

"And you're looking rather unhappy to see me that awfully chipper." His broad grin and the pure mischief that filled the green of his genie's eyes didn't suggest the slightest bit of remorse.

"I'm glad you're okay."

"You up for seeing just how okay I am?"

"It's awfully early for innuendo, Ace."

A loud bark of laughter greeted her. "I meant a bit of a race around the reservoir, but if you're up for turning around and heading home I'd be more than happy to oblige you."

The heat crept up her cheeks, but she refused to let him see he'd managed to mentally knock her sideways. Again. "You've got well over a foot on me. I'd never beat you in a race."

"I'll spot you a few lengths."

"You just want to watch my ass."

"I won't deny that."

Emerson shook her head but found the banter went a long way toward improving her mood. "Just run next to me and keep me company. You know. Since you're here and making a nuisance of yourself."

"As you wish."

They flowed in with the rest of the runners on the dirt path that surrounded the reservoir—the large body of water in the center of the park—and Emerson let the moment simply envelop her. Allowed the rhythm of the morning and the soothing slap of her feet on the ground to keep her focused as she took one step at a time.

"That was pretty nifty. What you did last night."

"Nifty?" Emerson turned to look at Drake without breaking her rhythm. "Are you going to ask me for a soda next?"

"I meant what you did with the fire. When you sterilized my Xiphos before removing the bullet."

"Oh."

Yep. There it was. The questions about her talent and her capabilities, just like Veronica said there'd be.

"After thinking about it, I realized I haven't seen you do any magic since that first night I met you. When you helped us in London."

"I don't *do* magic, Ace. It's a gift and I use it when appropriate."

"I didn't mean it as an insult. More as an observation. A curiosity, really."

A runner stumbled in front of them and she focused on paying attention and running around him.

A curiosity? As in freak show, more likely.

"So?" he probed.

Emerson held back the small sigh but knew she couldn't hide the defensive tone. "So what, Drake?"

"Your abilities. I know you're a powerful witch. What you did last year in London to help Kane and Ilsa was proof of it. But what are you truly capable of?"

"Why? Are you suddenly worried I'll put a spell on you?"

"Too late."

The mixture of shock and outrage that filled her stomach in short, sharp jabs had her speeding up. The nerve of him!

"I've done no such thing. As if I need to put a spell on a man to sleep with me."

"Well, that's a relief." He maintained that damn casual, laconic tone that made her want to turn around and beat some sense into him. "Because it feels like you put a spell on me."

"Why's that, Ace?" She couldn't hide the cocky grin that spread across her lips. "You can't get enough of me?"

He held his hands up. "There you go, practically admitting it. You *did* put a spell on me. Bubbled up a witches' brew and made me think it was one of those cold bottles of beer I'm so fond of."

"Blame your uncontrollable lust wherever you'd like. Last time *I* checked, we were two consenting adults who enjoyed each other's company. End of story."

The hands he had up near his head shifted so they clutched his heart. "It really is just about the sex? I feel so cheap. So used."

She laughed in spite of herself. "You're in rare form this morning. But if it makes you feel any better, the only thing that bubbles and brews between you and me are a boatload of hormones."

"Oh, I don't know. When done right, there's an awful lot of magic in that."

She nearly stumbled at the truth of his words, but righted her footing as he steadied her with a hand on her elbow. Dragging the smile from her lips, she readjusted the mantle of sarcasm and self-protection that served her so well. "Look, if you're just here to bait me, maybe I will let you spot me a few yards."

"If I'd known you were so easy to bait, I'd've joined you for a run a lot sooner than this."

She held her tongue, not sure what else to say to him. Their time together was normally so intense—so full of the passion she refused to put a name to—that it was more than a little unnerving to find such enjoyment in sparring with him.

"Come on. Are you going to answer my question and tell me a bit about your magic?"

She bit back the sigh, unwilling to mess up the even breathing she worked so hard to maintain on her runs. "What do you want to know?"

"How do you do it? Where does it come from? Has it grown stronger over your life or can you make it stronger? Build it, like a muscle? I'd like to understand."

"Understand so you can protect yourself?"

"From what?"

She'd hazarded a look at his face and couldn't stop the surge of surprise at the lines that furrowed his forehead. "From me."

"You wouldn't hurt me. Or at least you wouldn't hurt me with your magic."

Again, Emerson couldn't fight the sensation that her world was tilting.

How did he manage to do that? Trip her up with his softly spoken words that should have sounded needy but didn't. Instead, they dragged at her in intense layers of need and want and quiet truth because he wasn't afraid to put to words that he wanted her in his life.

Why couldn't he be content to stay an arm's length away? And why couldn't she keep her footing with him?

When he said things like that it was like riding a roller coaster at the carnival. She could see her broader surroundings didn't change, but her view of them just wouldn't stay constant.

Emerson fought to keep her breathing steady as they continued to run. Pushed through the beginnings of the pain as they moved into what had to be their third mile. "Callie was right about you."

"I figured out a long time ago that Callie is usually right about everything. But what, specifically, do you think she's right about?"

"She said not to be fooled by you. That you only look dreamy on the surface."

Amusement sparked in the green and gold of his irises. "And my still waters run deep?"

"Pretty much."

"I don't know about that. I'm a simple guy. I like simple things. A good meal. That cold beer I mentioned." He shot her a saucy look that nailed her low in the belly. "A hot woman."

Emerson veered off the dirt path to vary up the run a bit. "If that's where women rank on your list, no wonder you're still single."

Drake's stride never broke; he just continued to keep pace beside her as they cleared a stretch of path. A large set of boulders framed the edge of their next turn. "I'll give you the still waters, but—"

Emerson didn't hear the rest of it as his words were replaced by a rush of air that filled her ears. Before she could react, she lost her footing and felt herself fly through the air.

The lazy calm of their run evaporated as Drake went on high alert, scrambling as fast as his legs would carry him.

One minute Emerson was standing next to him, the very next her body was flying through the air to land on the other side of the boulders they'd nearly cleared.

What the hell was this?

Although the urge to port was strong, if Emerson *was* on the other side of the rocks, he could do more damage if he landed on her. Racing to the edge of the rock formation, he kept his body shielded as he looked down the jagged length.

And felt his heart stop as his gaze took in her still form where she lay sprawled on the ground, a man standing over her. Drake would have known it was a Destroyer without seeing the soulless gaze that greeted him, but the static electricity that snapped and snarled off his form confirmed it.

Destroyers always traveled in pairs, and under normal circumstances he'd bide his time to get the lay of the land. But there was no way he was leaving Emerson there. Without another thought, Drake pushed his body into a port, re-forming next to her and leaping on the Destroyer the moment his feet hit the ground.

Momentum and sheer, white-hot anger gave him the advantage as Drake slammed the asshole's head into the rocks. Streams of static electricity flowed through his hands and up his arms, but Drake wouldn't release his grip.

Wouldn't let go as he slammed the Destroyer's head a second time.

The head was the key, Drake knew, and the force of his blows had the body in his hands going limp, the electric charge cutting off abruptly. The kill was quick and had the husk of the Destroyer's body disintegrating as its life force drained away.

Drake tossed the body aside and sank to his knees to gather Emerson into his arms. As he reached for her, the air grew heavy beside him.

Well, fuck it all. There went his plans to port them both out of the park.

Turning so that he had Emerson behind him but protected with the rocks at her back, Drake faced his attackers. And was surprised when the object of his attention danced like a mad toddler before him.

"Deimos?"

A small pout touched scaly lips as Enyo's nephew let out a low growl. "It's Phobos, asshole."

Drake desperately wanted to shift away from the threat, but the same barrier of protection the rocks created kept him and Emerson firmly in the sphere of Phobos's life force.

Which meant Drake would risk possibly pulling the

demonic god into the port right along with them if he attempted it.

They were trapped.

Forcing bored calm into his words, Drake reached for Emerson's thigh, reassured by the feel of her as he stared up at that visage that was perpetually tinged with madness. "You and your brother are both interchangeable as far as I'm concerned. Speaking of the vile little fucker, where is he?"

Irritation bloomed in concert with the insanity, but the taunts did nothing to make Phobos lose focus. The only sign of anger was his increasingly agitated hopping from foot to foot. "We're hardly interchangeable."

"Could've fooled me."

Drake tightened his grip on Emerson's leg in hopes he could bring her to consciousness, but she still didn't stir. He wasn't sure what would have placed attention on her—especially not the attention of one the demon twins—but he was going to find out.

Although not technically demons in the most descriptive sense, the gods of dread and fear were the closest thing they had to actual demons on Mount Olympus. Add in their fierce devotion to their aunt Enyo, and Drake and his brothers had met up with them on more than a few occasions.

"What do you want? Or should I say, what does Enyo want?"

Phobos emitted a sharp giggle. "Aunt Enyo's not the one who sent me."

"Who did, then?"

"Unh-unh-unh." Phobos waved a finger. "Like I'd give you those details."

"If you won't tell me who sent you, tell me what you want."

The worthless piece of shit's eyes shifted determinedly toward the ground. "She's awfully pretty."

Drake shifted to shield her from that lascivious gaze as he kicked out a foot at Phobos to get his attention. "What. Do. You. Want?"

"You've got something that doesn't belong to you."

The apple?

What would Phobos know of it?

"What are you talking about?"

"Playing dumb isn't going to help you, Pisces." The air crackled again as three Destroyers moved up to form a half ring around Phobos.

Drake tried one more squeeze on Emerson's leg, angry at himself as he knew he'd cause a bruise but desperate to wake her. "It's not playing dumb if I don't know what you're talking about."

Phobos took another step forward, his thugs closing ranks behind him. "Oh, but I think you do. Where's the apple?"

The air crackled with static electricity as Drake felt the slightest movement behind him

Was Emerson conscious again?

Her leg quivered under his hand in the slightest movement, and he unclenched his grip just as the Destroyer on Phobos's left reached forward and emitted a stream of voltage strong enough to reanimate the dead.

Drake fully released Emerson's leg as he took the hit, unwilling to allow her battered body even a bit of exposure to the current. Clenching his teeth, he fought through the pain, using his own life force to fight it back.

And then the world around them exploded as fire crackled from behind him, traveling like a live wire back toward the Destroyer's extended hand.

"What the fuck?" Shouts erupted in front of him as the Destroyer who'd been supplying the power reached for his head—which had suddenly erupted in flames—and fell to his knees.

The other two Destroyers fell back in self-preservation, and it was their retreat that gave Drake the break he needed.

"You want to get us the hell out of here?" Emerson hollered at his back.

"Hang on."

Reaching for her hand, he mentally counted off Phobos's steps as the god shifted back to holler at his minions. Three . . . two . . .

Now!

The world around them evaporated as he and Emerson were spun into the ether.

Finley rubbed at her forehead in time with the screaming chorus of jackhammers that had taken up residence there.

What had she been thinking?

Cracking an eye open, she saw the empty bottle of Screaming Eagle on Grey's glass coffee table and remembered exactly what she'd been thinking.

The gun and the warehouse. Grey's sudden arrival and their equally sudden departure. His lips and that kiss.

Even an entire bottle of one of the world's finest wines couldn't erase the rich taste of him or the sweet memory of what it felt like to kiss him.

She'd let her guard down. Guzzling down bourbon

followed by wine on an empty stomach and a blood-stream full of adrenaline hadn't helped the matter.

God, but the man was infuriating, keeping her here and acting like he knew better. The thinly veiled implication that she was his prisoner, despite the plush surroundings and fancy liquor. She'd bet every last ounce of instinct she possessed that he wasn't a bad man, but it didn't change the facts.

She was stuck here.

Ignoring the confusing thoughts of a man who was far too compelling a mystery, she shifted gears.

Had she really been set up?

Despite Grey's insistence she focus there, nothing about it made any sense. Her boss had nothing to gain by feeding her to the wolves, and Melanie had a large case to prosecute that would benefit from whatever could have been learned in the warehouse.

It just didn't add up.

Frustrated at the lack of movement, she struggled to sit up, the shift not nearly as difficult as she'd expected it to be. And was immediately forced to rethink her cocky self-assurance as the room began spinning.

"You okay?"

She squinted at the cheery voice that greeted her from the office doorway as the subject of her thoughts materialized. "Unless you have some magical hang-over remedy behind your back, you can go right back out the way you came."

"I actually do have something for you." Grey moved into the room, a glass of water and a bottle of aspirin in his hands. "It'll hold you until we get some food in you."

Her stomach growled at the thought of food—

something that was greasy and came out a window, preferably—but even the insistent roll of hunger couldn't blunt just how good he looked this morning or the fact that her hormones had sat up and taken notice the moment he stepped into the room.

His long legs and trim waist were covered in black slacks—did the man wear anything else? A gray silk shirt hung on his broad frame, the tails untucked. The look was far more unkempt than he usually wore, but she found the contrast enticing.

She also found the slightest bit of evidence that perhaps he wasn't completely perfect each and every minute of the day oddly endearing. Their fingers brushed as she took the water and aspirin and a bolt of awareness shot through her.

Damn, but she didn't need this.

Attraction wasn't often convenient, she knew, but it didn't usually produce such raw dread in the pit of her stomach.

She liked men. Had enjoyed their company since she'd been allowed to date in the eighth grade. And truth be told, she'd had a man on her arm in the ensuing twenty years pretty much nonstop.

None of them had ever filled her with such supreme confusion.

Or such raw attraction that she had moments where she wondered if she could even stand on her own two legs.

After swallowing the aspirin and downing the glass of water, she looked up at him. "You want to tell me what happened last night?"

"We discussed it last night."

"No, you neatly avoided my questions last night. I won't be so easily distracted again."

"You sure about that?" Grey took a spot next to her on the couch, the warmth of his body a swift reminder she wasn't immune to him and that she'd need to stay on her guard.

Unwilling to be baited, she shifted and put a few inches between them. "Yes, I'm sure. Now. How about some of those answers you've no doubt got hidden up your sleeve?"

"I do have answers, but I can't give them to you. I just have to ask that you keep what happened last night to yourself."

"What if I decide I can't do that?"

He shifted again but didn't touch her. Instead, his gray eyes bored into hers, his gaze absolutely unwavering. "You have to."

"Grey, I've spent my professional career committed to the truth. I can't sidestep that just because some thugs put my life in danger last night."

"It goes way beyond that and you know it."

"Then help me understand."

"I can't."

"Can't or won't?"

"Does it matter?" Steel threaded the notes of his deep voice, punctuated with a distinct undertone of stubborn tenacity.

"I won't stop until I get the answers I'm looking for."

"Finley, you want answers that fit neatly into the world you live in."

"And this . . . situation?" She searched for the right word until she could find a diplomatic solution.

"Does not fit into the world you live in."

"That's why you did that fancy jump through space and time?"

When he remained silent, she added, "Are you trying to tell me you're not really human?"

Her stomach did a slight pitch and roll as she said the words, suddenly afraid of the answer.

What if he *wasn't* human?

"Hell no."

She held back a smile at his affront, but wouldn't let up with the questions. "Then help me understand. You can trust me."

"You sure about that?"

"Of course."

"You can honestly tell me what we discuss isn't going to find its way back to your boss? Or into one of your files?"

The hangover was fading away to be replaced by increasing frustration and not a little bit of anger at his unwillingness to listen to her. "I don't lie, Grey. I won't make you false promises, but I can understand the line between information that can help and information that can get someone killed. You can trust me to separate the two."

"Gods help me if you can't."

"What's that supposed to mean?"

Grey extended his hand, palm up. "Take my hand."

Finley extended hers in return, the sharp jolt as their fingers entwined shooting through her stomach in a sparkle of fireworks.

"Hang on."

Before she could reply, the room disappeared from view on a rush of air.

Chapter Seven

D rake took another bite of syrup-covered waffles—not so much because he wanted it, but because he knew his strength depended on it—as he stared across the kitchen table. His gaze hadn't left Emerson's for more than fifteen seconds at a stretch, while Callie fluttered and forced food on both of them.

"I'm fine, Drake. You don't have to keep watching me like I'm going to disappear," Emerson grumbled as she picked at half of a bagel.

"Bad choice of words, seeing as how you did disappear from my sight an hour ago."

"She's not going to disappear in this house," Callie said, swatting him on the back of the head before laying down a freshly filled platter heaped with more waffles and several pieces of French toast. The fresh platter dwarfed the heaping pile of bagels he'd brought home earlier, which sat at the opposite end of the table. "Let the woman eat."

Even as he made a show of rubbing the back of his

head, Drake didn't miss the small smile of gratitude Emerson shot Callie. "I'm fine, Drake."

He reached out and brushed a finger over her left cheekbone, the bruise that swelled under his touch sending a renewed rush of anger hurtling through his system. "He laid a hand on you."

"I was there, Drake." Emerson ripped another piece, color rising in her cheeks. "I'm not helpless and I'm fine now. Can we just drop it?"

Quinn's heavy voice boomed outside the swinging door, announcing his arrival. "What the hell happened?"

"That's what we're trying to figure out," Drake grumbled before reaching for another waffle.

"Well, who was the target?" Quinn pressed as he reached for his own plate. "You or Emerson?"

"It was me." Emerson's gaze grew thoughtful. "Or at least I thought it was me. But maybe you're right. He did ask Drake about the apple."

"Is Grey back?" Drake reached for more bacon. Despite his lack of hunger, Callie had figured out—as usual—the perfect food to keep them fueled. "Have you even heard from him?"

"Other than a text that he's fine, I've got nothing."

"Convenient," Drake added drily.

"Or very inconvenient. I don't think he's shaken the lawyer loose yet."

Drake didn't miss the avid interest that filled both Callie's and Emerson's faces as each leaned forward eagerly.

"What lawyer?" Emerson was the first to get the question out.

"The op last night was a mess from the get-go and Grey's source of information was captured."

"He's probably been busy wiping her mind," Quinn added around a mouthful.

"Doubtful." Drake shook his head. He quickly got the rest of them up to speed on their Aries's challenges with his informant.

Quinn's gaze sharpened, his security skills veering onto high alert. "You think she's still aware of what's going on?"

A heavy thud reverberated around the room as Grey materialized before them with a slender woman in his arms.

Drake didn't miss Emerson's raised eyebrows, but it was Callie who spoke first.

"I'd say that's a big messy yes."

Magnus slipped into the warehouse, the dim lighting no match for his recently heightened senses. Everything was different now, he thought as he ran a hand over his shoulder blade, even his fucking eyes.

The layout matched his intel, so he allowed himself a moment to relax as he waited for his target. A few oddly arranged folding chairs sat in the middle of the room and he took one, stretching out his long legs.

He hadn't intended to become an assassin, but oddly, the job suited him. He enjoyed the way his large body easily provoked fear in his targets. Add to that the unexpected side benefits and he couldn't complain.

What he hadn't banked on was the way the kills fueled the fever inside of him. All that horrible anger that gripped his nerve endings and wouldn't let go no matter how hard he tried to leave it behind.

Memories—still so vivid in his mind's eye—rose up, their cadence familiar, their moments bitter.

His mother's voice, full of promises for a better life.

The realization as all her carefully laid plans came crashing down around her.

And the moment—that hideous moment—when she'd vanished through the portal, her form and her soul lost to the other side.

Even now, all these years later, he couldn't escape the anger and the hatred that boiled in the very darkest parts of his soul.

As he gave the anger free rein, allowing it to roil and churn through his system while he prepared for the kill, his mind drifted past those last images of his mother to more recent images.

Emerson.

His little sister had always been independent— always convinced of her choices—but she'd changed with them in the time he'd been gone. Had grown harder, somehow. Her absolute defense of her pure magic practices, for one thing. He knew how she felt about the darker side of magic, but the loathing he'd seen reflected in her gaze when he'd dared her to think bigger had been a surprise.

Didn't she ever wish to toy with the dark side?

And then there was her relationship with their neighbor. The big man next door made him itchy, his laconic gaze and easygoing smile too easy. Too casual. Magnus didn't trust him and he most certainly didn't trust the man's influence on his sister.

A heavy scraping at the sound of the door being unlocked caught his attention and Magnus sat up fully in his chair. Thoughts of things he couldn't control fled in the face of the one thing he could. A light flared in the small entryway at the far side of the room, but he stayed where he was, unwilling to leave his seat.

He didn't need to in order to accomplish his task.

Another light flared, this time over his head, and two men crossed the room deep conversation, both ignorant to his presence. With deliberate slowness, Magnus pushed back on his chair, allowing the metal to echo gently on the floor.

The two men scrambled in alarm, drawing guns from their waistbands, but he was on both of them before they could get off a shot.

Emerson took another bite of her breakfast, curious at the drama playing out around her. She'd diligently avoided becoming too enmeshed in the politics of Warrior Central, but even she wasn't immune to the big shit-storm that had just arrived in the kitchen.

There was no doubt the woman attached to Grey was a mortal.

While Emerson knew she fit in the same category, her skills had always made her far more receptive to the unexplainable things in life most people didn't understand.

And didn't want to.

She'd spent most of her life keeping her skills a secret from everyone she met. While she intuitively understood most people weren't broadminded enough to accept someone who could conjure elements, it had always hurt to hide such an important part of herself from the world.

Add to it the fact that witchcraft had a relatively shitty history in the timeline of human events and she'd always found it far easier to close herself off.

Without warning, Magnus's words from the evening before hit an uncomfortable chord in her mind.

Life changes, Em. People change. Times change. And if you don't change with it, you're nothing but a dinosaur.

While her brother's mysterious behavior and harsh judgment didn't make for a great welcome home, his words had churned something up she couldn't shake. And no matter how hard she tried, she couldn't quite discredit the feelings.

"You okay?" Drake's whispered words floated over her, drawing her attention back to the kitchen and the sudden realization a fight was brewing between Grey and Quinn.

"I am. But"—she pointed toward the woman standing next to Grey—"she looks like she's had her fill."

Slipping off her chair, Emerson moved toward the doe-eyed woman who clutched Grey's hand. "Come on and sit down."

"They look pretty angry."

Emerson waved a hand, conjuring a breezy attitude she didn't quite feel. "They're just barking at each other. It's a pretty regular occurrence."

"I don't even know what I'm doing here."

Grey broke off his argument with Quinn as his gaze snapped toward the woman. "You refused to cooperate."

"You kidnapped her?" Emerson felt the shock

straight to her toes. Grey had always seemed like the levelheaded one.

"No."

Emerson turned toward the woman. "Did he?"

"Not exactly. But he's not crazy about letting me leave, either."

Grey's normally cool head and even cooler voice rose a notch as he watched them take seats at the raised butcher-block table. "Look, Finley. If you were more susceptible, this wouldn't be an issue."

"Susceptible?" Finley's mouth dropped. "What the hell does that mean?"

"It means you're too smart for your own damn good."

Before she could say anything, Drake stepped between his Warrior brothers. "You two need to calm down. Quinn. I'm sure there's a very good reason Grey brought her here."

"There is," the Aries quickly added.

"Then out with it."

Callie set a plate and cream cheese in front of Finley and pointed to the bagels. "Eat. You look about to fall over. And you can ignore the 'susceptible' comment. None of the women in this house are what anyone would call shy and retiring." She shot Grey a dark look. "Or susceptible."

"You're not helping, Cal," Grey shot back as he took a seat on the opposite side of the table.

As the testosterone continued to roll through the room in crashing waves, Emerson piped up. "Look, could someone do a quick recap for those of us trying to catch up?"

"Only if you tell us how you got a shiner," Quinn interjected.

Drake got everyone up to speed on their park incident while Quinn fired a series of questions. "Phobos asked about the apple? How's he involved in this? Did Eris borrow him from Enyo?"

"No idea."

Emerson tried piecing the names together. She knew Enyo from the incident last year with Kane and Ilsa, but Eris was a new one. "Who's Eris?"

"Wait." Finley spoke up, her interest clearly piqued. "Enyo and Eris are characters in Greek mythology. Are you somehow suggesting they're real?"

"Yes." Grey's tone was firm.

"But it's not possible."

The implacable tone didn't let up. "A lot of things that have happened to you in the last twenty-four hours haven't been possible, but they happened."

"This is why you brought me here?" Finley looked around the table at the assembled group. Emerson was pleased to see the level of fright in her eyes had diminished, with rising anger rapidly taking its place.

"Until we figure out what's going on, I want to keep an eye on you." Emerson knew all of the guys could be hard-asses when needed, but Grey's attitude was unrelenting.

Before any of them could interject, Grey added, "And before you all make me out to be the bad guy, Finley should be frightened. You all should. There's some serious shit brewing and I'm convinced the apple's only the tip of the iceberg."

"Eris won't rest until she has it back." Drake's green

eyes were thoughtful. "The incident in the park this morning made that abundantly clear."

Quinn spoke, his voice far calmer than his earlier shouting match with Grey. "Then we need to draw her out. Just like we've done to her sister."

Eris handed Phobos another towel as he dabbed at his face. The burn marks were healing, but it did nothing for his attitude, which was getting more riled by the minute.

"She burned me, Aunt Eris." That incessant shifting from foot to foot was worse as his body healed, the nervous motion even more annoying than usual.

"I can see that. But you still haven't told me who you think she is." Eris had her suspicions—her sister had mentioned a witch who had paired up with the Warriors last year—but she hadn't realized the woman had stayed so chummy with the guys. Or one guy in particular, based on her nephew's report of the woman who tossed fire having been out running with the Pisces.

Could it really be that easy? The witch *next door*?

"I don't know, but she's got some power behind her."

"Did you get any information on the apple?" In the midst of planning her assignation with Rogan it had seemed like a good idea to send Phobos to deal with the situation. Now she was paying for her folly.

"No. The fish played dumb."

"He's the Pisces Warrior."

More hopping. "He's a smelly, oily fish to me."

She held back the sigh, knowing full well it was her

own fault the morning hadn't been a success. Maybe it was time to bring out her new weapon. Although she was loath to use her new toy too often, the old tricks in her arsenal were increasingly ineffective as the Warriors fought with the spoils of technology and the basic battle benefit of knowing thy enemy.

It had been like this more and more over the last century and a half. Technology had added a new dimension to their battle that neither side could have anticipated.

On one hand, her ability to create discord was easier than ever. Internet viruses were a personal favorite, but even some basic innuendo and rumor could cause untold problems as it flew through the human world like wildfire.

Of course, it also gave the Warriors a distinct advantage, as everything could be tracked and accounted for.

What a dilemma.

Phobos had shifted to pace the room, the mumbled sounds of "smelly, oily fish" rumbling from his chest at regular intervals.

"He likes her, you know."

Eris looked up from her own pacing to stare at her nephew. "What's that?"

"The fish. He really likes her."

"Well, of course he does. He's a man and she's a woman."

"Not just the sex kind of like, Aunt Eris. He looooves her."

Now this was something she could use. "What makes you think so?"

Phobos stopped and cocked his head, not all that

unlike a snake when staring down its charmer. "He looks at her like he loves her. And he touches her like he loves her. And he protected her."

"He's a protector. That's his job."

"I know what I saw. The smelly, oily fish has a girl-friend."

Eris watched Phobos resume his maniacal dancing around her living room, the towel still pressed to his face, and let a new idea spin its web in her mind's eye.

"You don't need to walk me home. I live next door." Emerson stood in the front foyer of the Warriors' brownstone, full of that awkward feeling one gets when finishing up a first date. She didn't know what to do with her hands, so she kept folding and unfolding them, then finally gave up and made fists at her sides.

Why was she so nervous all of a sudden? And what was there to be nervous about?

She'd been sleeping with Drake for almost a year. She knew what each and every luscious inch of his body looked like and had bared hers in return.

There was *nothing* to be nervous about.

"No one thought we'd be attacked in broad daylight in the park, either. Humor me." He reached for the door, any sign he felt as awkward nowhere in evidence.

"Seriously, Drake. It's like a fifteen-second walk to my front door. You can stand here and watch me."

Drake ignored her, just planted that Zen-like smile he was so damn good at and took her elbow. They descended the heavy stone steps that flanked the front of Warrior Central and, in less than her estimated fifteen seconds, ascended a matched set on the front of her house.

Before she could react, Drake had her pinned against her front door, his lips covering hers with heat and need as the morning air swirled around them.

Emerson wanted to protest—wanted to push him out of her personal space and draw a few deep breaths to center herself—but instead found herself kissing him back, her hands fisting in the soft material of his T-shirt where it bunched at his waist. On a sigh, she gave herself up to the power of what lived and breathed between them.

What she was helpless to resist, no matter how many times she told herself she should walk away.

Hands firm on her body, his fingers played at the top of the waistband of her shorts, the light scrape of his nails on her skin sending rivers of pleasure coursing through her nerve endings. Drake's lips moved over hers, urgent and unyielding as he plied her tongue with his. The kiss was hot and carnal and utterly possessive and she was rapidly losing brain cells.

Lifting his head, the gold that mixed with the green in his eyes dominated. With gentle fingers, he traced the line of her cheekbone, his gaze following the path of his touch. "I'm so sorry they hurt you."

Emerson swallowed around the lump that had formed in her throat. "Like I told you, I'm fine."

"There's a mark on you."

"It'll heal. I'll put ice on it," she added with a wry smile.

His large body still loomed over her, covering her from view of the street.

In protection?

Possession?

Regardless of the reason, she found she couldn't resist the deeply feminine yearning caused by the nearness of his body. Couldn't stop the need that gripped her low in the belly as desire quickly replaced every other feeling—every other thought—inside of her.

"Come up—"

The thought—to invite him upstairs—was cut off by the opening of the door at her back. If she hadn't been holding on so tightly to Drake's waist, she'd have fallen back through it.

"Isn't this sweet?" Magnus drawled.

"Your timing is impeccable," Drake added, his normally easygoing tone as hard as the acre of chest under her fingers.

"I'd say I'm right on time. Especially since my sister's put herself on display for the entire neighborhood to see."

"It's none of your business, Magnus." Even as she said it, Emerson slipped from Drake's arms and took a few steps back. "I'm not fifteen."

"You're acting like it, making out on the front porch."

"Just how long were you standing there spying on us?" She whirled on him, unwilling to continue the fight with her back to her brother.

"I wasn't—" It was Magnus's turn to break off midsentence as he caught sight of her face. "What the hell happened to you?"

Before she could stop him, he'd squeezed past her and was on top of Drake, the two of them perilously close to the edge of the steps.

"Magnus!" She hollered his name a few more times to get his attention, to no avail. "Magnus! He didn't hurt me. Would you just listen to me?"

The two men continued to battle on the small area of the front stoop, their well-matched footing keeping one from getting the better of the other.

With a move reminiscent of their backyard battles as children, Emerson waited for the optimal moment she knew would come as the two men continued to trade position in the small area. On a heavy grunt, Drake went in low with a shoulder to Magnus's stomach and it was that move—and her brother's clumsy stumble on his back foot—that gave her the opening she needed.

She flew onto his back, wrapping her arms and legs around him like a maniacal monkey who wouldn't let go. "Leave him alone, Magnus! Drake didn't do this to me."

Her brother continued to struggle, but Drake stood down, taking a few steps backward to give her brother room to calm down.

"Em! Get the fuck off of me!"

"Not until you listen." She was tempted to slam a hand to his ear to cuff him, but held back at the last minute. "I'm okay. Drake didn't hurt me." When she felt his back muscles relax slightly under her thighs, she added, "Are you calm enough to let me explain?"

"Yeah." He patted her ankle. "Come on. Get off, okay?"

She slid from his back, but kept a hand on his chest to hold him still.

"Em. Come on. I'm done."

"Then say you're sorry."

"Are you kidding me?" Magnus's mouth dropped in a shocked *O* of surprise.

Drake came back up the stairs, his hand extended to Magnus. "Come on, Emerson. It's fine. I'd have done the same."

She watched the male byplay as a series of self-righteous emotions flitted across her brother's face until resignation took the place of all of them. He extended a hand. "Sorry."

She watched as the two men clasped hands, but it was Drake's words that stopped her cold. "I wouldn't hurt her."

Magnus nodded and went to pull his hand back, but Drake's grip stayed firm.

"Ever."

Chapter Eight

Drake left Emerson's house and retraced their morning run, his body hard and uncomfortable. The feel of her in his arms was still imprinted on his nervous system and he could only hope the walk—and the focus on figuring out why they were attacked—would do something to calm him down.

Fuck, but he wanted to go destroy something.

The attack that morning had left him with far too much to think about and any way he twisted and turned the facts, he had only more questions.

The apple and Phobos's sudden appearance.

They had to be related.

But Emerson wasn't involved, so why was she the target?

He entered the park and the area where they'd met up with Enyo's demonic nephew. Central Park was far more crowded now, late morning, than it had been when they took their run. The city's refuge was one of its most well-used recreational areas.

Yet Phobos had selected the park in broad daylight to launch his attack.

Although humans were sometimes collateral damage in the endless fight between Mount Olympus's immortals, all of them—regardless of their goals—knew getting onto humanity's radar wouldn't benefit any of them.

So they fought in the shadows, the power plays of the gods kept as far away from human knowledge as possible.

Drake slowed as he neared the rock formation, his gaze scanning the path leading to it as well as the grass surrounding the area. Although the entire park was open to public view, the way the path twisted through here did offer a bit of seclusion, especially if the actions of the attacker were swift and decisive.

Which they most definitely were this morning.

"Well, well, well. If it isn't the oily fish man. Back to the scene of the crime?" Phobos came around the edge of the rocks, his smile the sort of maniacal leer that filled children's nightmares. The burned skin on his face was a vicious red where it stretched across his cheeks, still healing from Emerson's earlier handiwork.

"I could say the same for you."

"Your girlfriend burned me." The leer downshifted into a definite pout.

"She's not my girlfriend."

"You're a *lying*, oily fish man." Phobos moved forward, his eyes shifting with calculating curiosity. "Very interesting."

Drake kept his attention fully locked on Phobos while he allowed his senses to reach out and probe the surrounding area. The joined fish on his back twitched their tails on high alert, but other than the threat standing before him, Drake couldn't find anything waiting in the wings.

Which really was too bad.

Phobos shifted from foot to foot, but kept his distance. "Since she has the power of fire, I say she's a witch."

"Fine"—Drake shrugged—"say it."

"Yep. And she's your girlfriend, too. I know people having sex when I see it. You've got that look in your eye each and every time I bring her up. And you definitely had it in your eye before."

Uncomfortable with the course of the conversation and just how close to the truth Phobos actually was, Drake shifted strategy, wondering if he could use the moment to his advantage and get the little worm talking. "She's a beautiful woman. A body like that, a man looks."

"It's the sex look." Phobos nodded his head knowingly, far from put off by Drake's nonchalant agreement. "My aunt thinks I don't know about those things, but, oh boy, do I."

Not for the first time did Drake have to acknowledge the beings that populated Mount Olympus were just as deranged—just as fucked up—as humans. They simply had more inherent power at their disposal.

"Clearly you've made a study of it."

"She thinks I don't know, but I do." He hopped again. "I do, I do, I do, oily fish man."

"So tell me why Enyo sent you. What does she want?"

A sharp peal of laughter rang out as the crazy little fucker doubled over at the waist. "You think you know so much."

Gods, this was a pointless waste of time. Phobos was a tool—literally and figuratively. He didn't know anything beyond the orders he'd been given.

The temptation to port home was strong, but Drake decided to wait it out a little longer. "Since you're the one who walked away with your ass kicked this morning, I'd say I'm not doing half-bad."

"This morning was only the beginning. She knows you have the apple and she knows what you value. You won't win."

"The apple isn't Enyo's. She's got enough of her own tools without worrying about her sister's apple."

Phobos shrugged, standing stock-still. "Suit yourself."

"So where'd you get the shiner?" Magnus stretched his legs out in front of him where he took a seat at the kitchen table, looking for all the world like the lord of the manor.

"It's a mouse," Emerson said with no small measure of disgruntlement as she hunted up a bottle of Gatorade in the fridge.

"So if our neighbor wasn't the one to put it on you, which you adamantly informed me as you wrestled me on the front stoop, how'd you get it?"

"A little incident in the park this morning."

Magnus sat forward at that. "What happened?"

How, exactly, did she explain being set upon by a paranormal predator and his goon squad? Although her grandmother knew the men who lived next door were a band of immortals, the knowledge hadn't extended to her brother. The less she shared with him on that score, the better. "Nothing. It was nothing."

"If you think I'm going to drop it that quickly, you've got another one coming."

"Why?" She slammed the Gatorade on the counter. "I've told you it's nothing, but you don't believe me. Yet when the situation is reversed, you won't answer any of my questions."

"So it's quid pro quo? I can't be concerned about my sister?"

"No, Magnus. I just want some answers. Something that explains where you've been for four years."

"Here we go again." Those dark eyes rolled in an almost exact imitation of their sister, Veronica, when she didn't want to discuss something.

Undeterred, Emerson pushed him. "What happened to you? You look like you've been hanging with the WWE. What did you do? How did you earn money? Did you date anyone? Who have you been?"

"I finally found a sweet gig, Em. Someone who appreciates my talents and has found a way to put them to good use."

She rounded the kitchen counter and took a seat opposite Magnus at the table. "You make it sound like you're a mercenary."

He hesitated—for a fraction of a second—before meeting her eyes. "I'm useful, Em. Can't you be happy for me? Be happy that I've finally found some purpose."

The pleading note in his voice pulled her up short,

and whatever she'd thought to say evaporated in the moment. His eyes were filled with an odd, desperate sort of need she hadn't seen since those dark days after they'd realized their mother wasn't coming back.

He was the little boy lost. He'd always been that way, but it had gotten worse after their mom had disappeared, and it was clear he'd never really found his way.

Until now.

She knew about those dark spaces inside. Knew the holes that were left by those who were already gone. Holes that didn't fill, no matter how badly you wished them to.

Or how many years passed.

"You're doing something you enjoy?"

"Yes. I really am."

"But you can't talk about it?"

"Not yet." He reached over and fitted his palm to hers, the calluses on his fingers rubbing roughly against the top of her hand. "Just give me a bit of time. Time to settle. Time to get my life set up again."

She wanted to question him further, but her instincts had her staying silent.

Magnus was home.

Why couldn't that just be enough?

Grey turned the apple over in his hands as he sat in Quinn's office. The pin was small and rather innocuous, hardly something that could bring down a powerful group of humans. Yet it had, several times in the past when Eris had chosen to brandish the weapon.

His own temper felt heightened somehow as he held

it, but Grey also couldn't discount this weird anxiety that had gripped him since pulling Finley from the building.

He shouldn't have done it.

And even as he thought that, he knew he couldn't have left her behind.

"You can't keep her here, Grey." Quinn tapped a few keys on his computer as he watched his security monitors. Despite the technological multitasking, Grey knew the bull was completely focused on the conversation.

"The hell I can't. She's in danger, even if she won't accept it."

"Keeping her here isn't the solution. She's a mortal."

"Ava was one, too. That didn't stop Brody from dragging her here when things got tough."

"It's not the same and you know it. Finley works for the DA's office, for fuck's sake. She can't know the depths of what we are."

"I can't let her go back into a situation where I know she's a target."

"The DA's office and organized crime have a long history." Quinn tapped a few more keys. "I'm sure they can arrange protection for her."

"Who's going to protect her from the DA?"

Quinn looked up at that, his quick mind hitting the mark immediately. "You think the DA set her up?"

"Less him and more likely someone in his office. Those goons shouldn't have known who she was."

"She did go walking into their meeting." The bull leaned forward in his chair, taking a closer look at the screen. "She put herself in danger."

"After being set up with information that wasn't accurate."

"But she gave you the information things were going down at the warehouse." Quinn hesitated briefly before adding, "You sure she's not setting you up?"

The harsh retort was on his lips—and was almost out—before Grey pulled himself back. He wouldn't rise to the bait.

Nor was he willing to pick a fight with his Warrior brother just because Quinn had the stones to ask him the hard questions.

"I don't think she's setting me up. The fear in her eyes was too real to fake. Besides, she was snagged too quickly. Like someone knew she'd be approaching the warehouse."

Quinn nodded before giving him a small, rueful smile. "I saw it all on camera and I don't think she set you up either, for what it's worth. But I had to ask."

"We've run through that tape six times. Nothing's sticking out."

"I made you a copy anyway." Quinn pulled a thumb drive from one of his machines and handed it over. "Look at it with fresh eyes. See if you can find anything after you think about it."

Grey took the drive, but knew he could watch it another hundred times and not turn up anything new. They'd watched for clues, but the information they needed wasn't on that video.

"Let's put her up somewhere. Callie's got some resources. We can get her in a safe house and keep her there until you can gather some more information."

"I want her with me."

One dark eyebrow quirked at that news. While the urge to drag back the words rose up in Grey's throat, he held back. It was the truth, damn it. He didn't want Finley out of his sight.

Quinn's voice was speculative when he finally spoke. "That's a new one for you."

"She's in danger, and I'm not changing my mind."

"How does Counselor McCrae feel about it?"

"She doesn't have a choice."

A heavy bark of laughter filled the space between them. "Oh, this is going to be fun. If there's anything marriage has taught me its that women have a funny way of providing their thoughts on matters they don't have a choice over. And gorgeous women with brains . . ." Quinn laughed again. "Watch out."

"Until I figure out what's going on, she's going to have to find a way to accept it."

"I can get into her computer. Delete all evidence of her files and whatever her coworkers have as well. We'll keep an eye on her for a few weeks." Quinn looked up, paused. "You really can't wipe her mind?"

"I told you, she's completely immune to it."

Quinn's loud burst of laughter echoed around the heavy equipment in his office. "That's rich. The Fates have some fucking sense of humor."

"How do you figure?"

The shitty grin spread even farther before Quinn matched it with a sly lift of the eyebrows. "You really need it spelled out for you?"

The shame of it all was that he didn't need it spelled out for him. It had already announced itself with all the force of a tornado. He was nursing an unnecessary—and completely idiotic—crush on Finley. And fuck him if he had any idea what to do about it.

Quinn stood from his rolling leather chair and offered up a quick backslap. "I guess there's only one other question. Do you think she can be trusted with the truth?"

Grey leaned forward and watched the feed from the kitchen, where Finley sat talking with Callie. "I wish to hell I knew."

Emerson twisted in the late-afternoon light, inspecting the shiner—no, the mouse—in her bedroom mirror. The bruise was a small one and could easily be hidden with a bit of artfully applied makeup. It wouldn't last long and would heal even quicker once she made the poultice her grandmother used for everything from poison ivy to a toothache.

In the meantime, she decided to enjoy it. She'd be lying to herself if she didn't admit to feeling like the slightest bit of a badass as she twisted and turned and preened at her battle scar.

What she hadn't expected was Drake's fierce reaction to the attack.

Of course, if she were being completely honest with herself, she had to admit his innately protective nature probably had more to do with his reaction. They *were* attacked. It was only natural his Warrior nature was going to jump straight into a fight.

"He loves you, you know."

Callie's words from the other day reared up in a loud reminder, cutting off the excuses.

When had her casual affair become so complicated? And why was she fundamentally unable to separate her head from her heart?

On a sigh, she resolved to put it firmly out of her mind. Until her gaze alighted on the hand mirror on top of her dresser.

Suppressing the overwhelming urge to scry on Drake just so she could ogle his ass, Emerson deliberately moved away from the dresser to make the bed.

Why did she keep going back to the same place when it came to the subject of Drake?

She didn't do love. She'd made that decision a long time ago, when even her family—people who knew and understood who and what she was—couldn't accept her.

There was no way a man would.

Oh sure, Drake liked the sex—who didn't?—but he wasn't going to be interested in the long haul with a woman who could shrivel his balls with the snap of a finger.

And no man, Emerson knew, no matter how powerful his physical presence, would ever trust a woman who innately wielded as much power as she did.

A loud rush of air had her whirling around, a pillow still clutched in her hand as the very object of her thoughts arrived in the middle of her bedroom.

"What the hell are you doing here?"

"I wanted to see you."

"So you just"—Emerson broke off, searching for the right word—"popped into my room!"

"I never pop."

She almost laughed at the pure masculine affront

that lined his face, but held it back in favor of giving him a hard time. "Could have fooled me, Ace."

"Besides, I had no interest in going another round with your brother, which would have inevitably happened if I came in the front door."

She wanted to argue with him but knew it was a useless exercise. Magnus had a bug up his ass about Drake, and she suspected she wasn't going to break up the testosterone-fueled dick duel the two of them had going.

The fact that Drake was man enough to walk away was a pleasant surprise.

His words pulled her from her thoughts. "I need to talk to you. I went back to the park."

"Why?"

Drake moved in close, his large body overpowering hers as he lifted a hand to her face. With a whisper-light caress, his finger traced her cheek. "That little demon put a mark on you. I wanted to know why."

On a heavy gulp, she kept herself from lifting her own hand and covering his. "Did you find him?"

"Aye."

She couldn't move for a moment, the strength in his fingers and the feel of his large hand warm against her cheek a sensual feast. For one small moment, she wanted to savor the way he made her feel like a most precious treasure.

Emerson reveled in the moment until his words penetrated the sensual haze his slightest touch could evoke. "Wait a minute. Yes? As in yes you found him?"

"I did. He's not all that smart."

The moment broken, Emerson stepped back as she

imagined all sorts of things befalling him. "The same could be said for you to head straight back to the same place."

"I've dealt with Phobos before."

She was interested despite herself. "Who is he?"

"The god of fear. He's a god in his own right, but Enyo sort of pressed him into her service a long time ago."

"You think Enyo had something to do with this morning?"

Drake took a seat on the edge of her bed, the incongruity of that large form sitting on a bright yellow afghan her grandmother had knitted for her years ago not lost on her. "That's what I can't figure out. She's laid low the last several months, but there aren't any of the usual signs to suggest she's ready to come out of hiding."

"Signs?"

"The Destroyer attacks increase and there's this general feeling of going on high alert when Enyo starts cooking up one of her schemes. I can't explain it much better, but after several thousand years of fighting each other, we've sort of figured out each other's tells."

The truth of his words struck with blunt force and she made herself busy tidying up the papers she had lying on her small desk in the corner of the room. "You've really been at this for a long time."

"A very long time."

"So this time and place is just a blip for you." *I'm a blip for you.*

"It doesn't feel like a blip when you're in the moment. It feels very present and very real."

Emerson kept her hands busy, organizing papers and stacking the normal disorder of her desk into neat piles. "But you're immortal. This day will fade. Will blend in with all the others."

He was behind her before she could register his movement, his large hands covering her shoulders as he bent his head to the curve of her neck. "The days with you will never fade, Emerson. Never blend. I remember all of them." His lips brushed lightly against the tender skin of her neck as his warm breath sent shivers coursing down her spine. "Every. Single. Moment." He punctuated his words with kisses.

Her knees buckled, but it didn't matter. He was there. Holding her up.

Holding her steady.

"It can't change who you are. Who I am, Drake."

"I wouldn't want to change you." More kisses rained over her skin. "Ever."

"But we're so different. There's just no middle ground. Your immortality is just one piece of it." An easy piece to focus on, truth be told. If she was pointing at him, she wouldn't have to expose her vulnerability.

Wouldn't have to watch him walk away, which he'd inevitably do.

"We're not that different." His hand slid down, over her breast to rest on her stomach as he pulled her back against his body. She felt the solid wall of him, punctuated by the hard length of his erection that pressed into her spine. At the answering tug between her legs, she had to acknowledge that on this point they weren't far apart at all.

What lived between them was a special brand of magic all its own.

"Come on. You know as well as I do it's complicated."

Ignoring the rush of need and want, she squirmed in his embrace. But he remained gently immovable.

"Still finding excuses?"

She closed her eyes on his question as his tongue traced the lines of her ear, the pure pleasure of his lips and hands and body in sharp contrast to the reality of their situation.

The reality of just how far apart they were from each other.

"The truth isn't an excuse."

Damn, but the woman could argue with the tides that they weren't going to crash to shore. Drake maintained his hold on her, unwilling to let her go just yet. Unwilling to break the sensual feast she presented to his senses.

She calmed him and excited him, all at the same time. When he held her the raging waters receded and he could take quiet, easy breaths.

Even as she infuriated the hell out of him.

Like the joined fish that lived under his skin, marking that he was in service to Themis, he was bound to Emerson. And he took an odd sort of solace in her words. If she thought about his immortality, then she did a lot more thinking about the two of them than her outward behavior would imply.

With the innate patience he was known for, he decided to dig for the truth underlying her words. Immortality was an easy thing to focus on, but it also smacked of a convenient excuse. "You've got a longer-than-average life span, if I'm not mistaken."

"Yes." She tried to move out of his embrace again,

but he stayed firm, adding another layer of kisses to the soft hair at her nape, satisfied when he felt her shiver.

"How long?"

"If I'm lucky and I take care of myself, probably around a hundred and twenty-five. Maybe a bit more, especially as modern science keeps extending everyone's lives."

"That's a long time."

"It's a long time for a human. It's still a blip on the radar for an immortal." When she shifted—her intent telegraphed in the stiff lines of her body—he let her go.

And they'd fall back on their usual positions and battle instead. He turned away from the desk to face her where she now stood in the middle of the room. "And this is why you've kept your distance from me? Why you won't give in to what's between us?"

"Yes."

She hesitated with the briefest of pauses. He'd likely have missed it if it weren't for the fact that he drank her in when they were together. "You sure?"

"Of course I'm sure. You're going to live forever and I'll be an old woman in the blink of those bedroom eyes of yours. You live in the moment, Ace? Then take a bit of advice."

"I don't know if I should. You being so young and all."

Heat crept up her neck and her hands fisted and clenched, but she didn't falter.

Didn't waver in the slightest.

"Take what's offered and pull your damn emotions out of it."

"And if that's not enough for me?"

"Then maybe it's time we parted ways."

"You're not getting rid of me that easy." Drake fought the acid that chewed at his stomach with all the finesse of rusted metal.

"Look. We've had a good ride, but it's done. Things have run their course."

The wall built around her with stunning speed, the soft, pliant woman in his arms mere moments before evaporating behind a shell that hardened with lightning speed. "You're a shitty liar, Emerson."

"I'm doing what needs to be done."

"You're running away. There's a difference."

The stormy gray of her eyes turned darker under the slash of her eyebrows as his words hit home. "You need to—" Her words cut off as a loud crash echoed outside her room.

Drake didn't think, just moved, hollering over his shoulder as he went. "Stay in here and don't come out until I tell you."

He moved into the hallway. Although their homes weren't identical, the structures had a similar layout and he followed the narrow hall toward the staircase. His first thought was for her grandmother. Had she fallen?

The thought was discarded as his initial scan of the hallway didn't turn up anything, nor did a look down the stairs. Footsteps sounded behind him and he whirled, catching Emerson as she flew into his arms. "Is it my grandmother?"

"I told you to stay in your room."

"Is she hurt? I need to go downstairs."

"No. It had to be something else. The sound was up here." He was already dragging her back down the hall when another thud reverberated through the hallway, rattling the walls.

"Magnus!"

Before he could get a hold on her, Emerson hot-footed it toward a closed door. He raced after her, but wasn't quick enough to stop her from opening the door.

Her scream echoed back at him in the close confines of the hallway.

Chapter Nine

Emerson heard the screams and finally realized they were coming from her. Echoing through her head, rattling around in her mind as she tried to make sense of what she was seeing.

It wasn't possible.

Where did it come from?

Without thinking, she started into her brother's room before Drake dragged her back to the hallway.

"You can't go in there."

She started to protest until Magnus stared up at her from his place on the floor, his dark eyes awash with an unholy light that had her taking a few steps back anyway. "Magnus?"

To her ears, her voice sounded very small and far away.

"Em?" The malice in his eyes receded slightly as he focused on her. "Em, get out of here!"

"Magnus? What are you—"

Words simply evaporated as she focused on him.

Dark ink covered the upper part of his torso, the tattoo clearly depicting a large serpent that wrapped and coiled around his body. Her gaze followed the ink that wove around both shoulders and down each of his biceps.

And it was moving.

The ink was matched by a large snake that writhed at his feet, its thick body unfurling as the head rose before her, poised to strike.

The snake lurched forward with whip-fast movements. Emerson braced herself for the strike, but Drake threw himself toward her, cradling her in his arms as he took the animal's blow to his back.

Drake felt the reassuring curves underneath his hands, satisfied he'd blocked the threat, even as the muscles in his arms grew increasingly numb. "You okay?"

"I'm fine. What about you?"

"I'm fine." A slight slur tinged his words and he swallowed hard, trying to get his mouth under control.

Emerson clambered out from underneath him before he could stop her and he heard the loud shriek as soon as she turned back around to face him. "Oh my God! You've been bitten."

A heavy thump echoed from Magnus's room, but at least her brother had had the wherewithal to close the door after the snake had struck. "I'm fine."

"You're bleeding." She sprinted back toward her room and reappeared moments later with towels.

He reached for her hand, oddly satisfied with the turn of events. Five minutes ago she was giving him the heave-ho and now she was ministering to him again.

Funny how quickly she forgot all her protests as to why they shouldn't spend time together when he was bleeding. "I'm getting the strangest sense of déjà vu."

"Hold still and let me look at things." He felt her fingers probe at the shredded T-shirt that still covered his back and then the press of the towel again. "It looks pretty bad, Drake."

"It's not the first time. It'll heal. Just give it a few minutes."

"But you were attacked by a snake. We need to get you help."

Drake wanted to protest—wanted to argue that he'd be fine as soon as the poison worked its way from his system—but the words wouldn't form. Instead, all he felt was an increasing sense of numbness in his head as his limbs grew cold.

The hallway shimmered in front of him, and despite the bone-numbing freeze, Emerson's hands were hot against his skin, branding him wherever she touched.

"Drake?"

He dragged his eyes open, the lids so, so heavy, her hands burning him again where she touched his face. "Hmmm?"

He heard her words from very far away as she gripped his chin. "Stay with me, Drake."

The words were so sweet—and he wanted nothing more than to do that . . . if he could just . . . keep . . . his eyes open . . .

"Drake!" Emerson watched in horror as Drake's eyes rolled up in his head, his body going limp in her arms. What the hell had Magnus done to him? And why wasn't Drake's natural healing ability kicking in, just as he'd said it would?

Shifting away from him, she dragged on his arms to lay him out, then did the same with his legs. She had no idea if it would help or hurt his circulation, but staying curled up and hunched over couldn't be good for him.

Think, Emerson. Think.

Clearly whatever her brother had wielded had some property that was dangerous to Drake. What could she possibly do to counteract that?

Rolling him, she focused on the bite again. The wound was raw and gaping, and small, dark striations flowed out of the site of the bite, the venom's ravages swift and immediate.

She quickly ran through a number of poultices in her mind but discarded each just as fast when she realized she simply didn't have the time. She had to get the poison out.

Frantic, she searched her mind for something. She'd trained at the knee of one of the century's greatest witches. Surely she could think of something.

Anything.

Think!

Her gaze alighted on his leg and she remembered how she'd used the Xiphos to remove the bullet. Would it work? She didn't have time to debate it.

Emerson reached for the knife, unstrapping it from his calf and examining the blade in her palm. She ran a stream of fire over the length to resterilize it, then pressed the tip to the raw, vivid red flesh around the bite. With tentative motions, she probed around the wound, curious to see the black lines of the poison actually moving away from the tip of the blade.

Drake moaned at the contact, but his limbs didn't move. The lack of movement scared her, and she pressed harder, her explorations more deliberate.

There wasn't much time.

She lifted the knife and ran another stream of fire over it, then pressed the tip once more to the wound. The result was the same, the black lines under Drake's skin actively moving away from the blade.

Was it her magic?

Focused on her task, Emerson felt the knowledge pulse under her skin. It had to be the magic.

Drake moaned again, pulling her from her thoughts. His cry was more feeble now and, as if sensing the weakness, the poison had spread farther, faster, the black lines covering the width of his upper back.

With renewed purpose, Emerson focused on the knife. She knew what she had to do.

She'd burn the poison out.

Shifting, she straddled his back, both for support as much as to hold him still. She positioned the tip of the Xiphos at the entrance to the wound and took a deep breath. Lifting her free hand, Emerson focused a line of fire down the shaft of the blade, forcing it toward the tip.

Drake's body jerked underneath her and the poison immediately drew away from the wound site, spreading farther over his back. Satisfied by the results, she forced more fire, unwilling to leave the poison anywhere to run.

Drake moaned again, his body tensing and writhing underneath her hips, but she refused to lose focus.

Refused to give the poison another moment to do him harm.

Heart pounding, she drew on her magic, pulling it from the deepest part of herself.

Soul-deep magic.

She wouldn't lose him. Not like this.

The black lines of poison slowly receded as she continued to push the fire into Drake's skin. Where it had first looked to be running from the blade tip, the black color was now fading as more of Drake's natural skin tone returned.

Dialing back the fire to a light, steady pulse, Emerson was satisfied to see the ragged red flesh around the wound change along with the retreating poison. The skin around the bite began healing, knitting itself together, the angry red fading into pink.

"Emerson?"

Drake shifted underneath her, and she nearly cried in relief when she saw him flex his hands. Pulling back on the fire altogether, she lifted the knife from the wound and shifted to sit beside him, her legs crossed under her.

"Hey there, cowboy. How are you feeling?"

"Sort of shitty, but about a million times better than a few minutes ago. What happened?"

Emerson pushed a lighthearted note into her voice she most definitely didn't feel. "First you take a bullet. Now a massive snakebite. You're like an accident waiting to happen."

"This was more than an accident." His green eyes grew dark with speculation, even as the pain receded with each passing moment. "Although I can't say I'm complaining about having your hands on my body."

Emerson felt the tension break as he added a leering eyebrow wiggle for good measure. "God, you are a cocky bastard."

"I'm the boy next door."

Drake struggled to sit up, but she reached for him, keeping him in place. "Ass next door, is more like it."

"That's Quinn's nickname. Well, ass *hat*, actually. But I'm everyone's favorite. It's my nice, quiet demeanor and helpful personality. Everyone likes having me around."

She snorted but didn't say anything else, just continued to dab at his back with the towel.

"Everyone except you, I mean."

More long moments passed, the only sound the soft scrape of the towel against his skin. When she finally did speak, it was in a near whisper. "I like having your around. I like it too much."

"You what?" Drake rubbed a finger in his ear. "I'm not sure I heard you."

She dabbed again, uncomfortable with the direction of the conversation. "You heard me."

"I'm not sure I did."

Before she could answer, a large hand reached up and covered her ass. "Drake!"

"I learned a long time ago, there's no such thing as too much when it comes to the things that matter. You matter."

Her hand stilled and Drake twisted to look at her. Emerson knew she couldn't have stopped her next question if she'd tried. "Do you really believe that?"

"I wouldn't have said it if I didn't."

"No, I guess you wouldn't." She shook her head

slightly before refocusing on his injury. "You doing okay?"

He held up a hand and wiggled his fingers. "My hands and feet aren't numb any longer."

"The site's not as red anymore and the puncture marks seem to be closing."

He wiggled his fingers again before reaching for her. "Come here and I'll show you just how much better I'm feeling."

She squirmed away, but he was faster. His strong, capable hand closed around her wrist and pulled her toward him. His lips played with hers and she felt them curve in a smile. "You totally healed me. Do you know how hot that is?"

"Hot?" she murmured back, her thoughts not quite able to catch up as the sexy feel of his body pressed to hers scrambled her senses.

"Incredibly," he murmured, sliding his lips over her cheek before whispering in her ear, "I love what you are. I love the power that's inside of you."

His words were so unexpected, Emerson felt the tight bands around her heart open without warning. "You think so?"

"I know so." His lips kept moving—across the sensitive flesh of her earlobe, then down the line of her neck.

She reached for him, enmeshed in the sexy heat of the moment and the heady rush of his words. Before she could reply, another heavy thud echoed from behind Magnus's door, drawing their attention.

With dawning horror, Emerson dragged herself back from the brink of desire. Instead, she was forced to admit the danger was far from over. "Oh God, Drake. I'm so sorry."

"Why are you sorry?"

She slid from Drake's arms, putting some distance between them as she fought to think. "My brother did this to you. Or a pet he had no control over did it." What the hell was with that tattoo and the snake and that weird, worshipful way Magnus stared at it?

"Was he practicing magic?"

"No." She shook her head. Then she stopped herself, wondering why the answer came so easily. "I don't think so."

"But is it possible?"

Her gaze drifted to the door. "It didn't *feel* like magic. That's the best way I can explain it."

"But your brother's a witch, too?"

"Yeah."

"I need you to go down to your room and shut the door until I've had a chance to deal with this."

"I need to talk to Magnus."

"No, *I* need to talk to Magnus. You need to sit in your room and wait until I'm done." Drake sat up and reached for the Xiphos.

The light of battle burned in her belly while the acid of her brother's betrayal fed the flame. "Like I'm the little woman, waiting for her big bad man to protect her?"

"Pretty much," Drake agreed cheerfully as he re-strapped the blade to his calf.

Without thinking, she channeled that anger. Flames rose up around them immediately, a tight, hot circle of light. "You really don't want to press me on this."

Drake shrugged as he stood up. "Since your brother's gifts are most likely as strong as yours, I can't see how your little light show will do anything against him."

"A little light show? I'll have you know I'm far stronger than my brother."

"You just told me he wasn't practicing magic."

"He's practicing something, and I'm not going to sit in my room like a fucking useless bump on a log. When that door opens I'm going through it with you."

"Like hell you are." Before she could say anything further, Drake had her wrapped in his arms as the hallway vanished around them.

Finley heard the heavy footsteps before the swinging door flung wide on its hinges. Grey walked into the kitchen, his designer suit fresh and crisp. He'd also managed to snag a shower, the cap of his dark hair gleaming in the overhead lights.

He looked amazing.

And now that he was finally here, she could begin her arguments to get herself home.

Although she was more than grateful to Callie, Ilsa and Montana for their time and attention, she wanted to go home. Wanted to touch her own things, wear her own clothes and curl up in her own bed.

She didn't miss Grey's unerring gaze as he moved through the door, unleashing an involuntary shiver down her spine.

How did he always manage to make her feel like she was the only woman in the world?

Finley glanced down at the pink baby doll T-shirt

and sweatpants Ilsa had given her earlier. Although she had similar items at home, she felt deliciously exposed here in front of him, with her breasts on display and the word "Juicy" emblazoned across her ass.

Her thoughts over the last months had been increasingly distracted with images of the mysterious Grey Bennett and if there was anything the last twenty-four hours had taught her, it was that it was a very bad idea.

Even if he *looked* like a very good idea.

"Where the hell have you been all day?" Callie's irate holler pulled her gaze off Grey and on the small spitfire that, from what she'd been able to figure, ran the house with iron-clad control. In awe she watched as Callie marched straight up to Grey, her fist shaking as she dressed him down.

"Working through some things with Quinn." Grey's relaxed demeanor and laconic voice never changed. Finley wasn't sure if he was holding back anger or had simply developed an immunity to Callie's tactics.

"And you couldn't even be bothered to come down here and give this woman some updates?"

He shrugged and she fought the urge to sigh at how the motion drew the eye toward his broad shoulders. "You and the girls have been chewing her ears off all day."

"So you had time to spy from Quinn's computers?"

Grey shook his head as Callie tried to box him in. "Yes, I spent the day in the security center, which you damn well know. And since I knew Ms. McCrae was in good hands with you, Ilsa and Montana, I didn't spend time worrying about entertaining her. Instead, Quinn and I spent the day trying to figure out who the asshole was who set her up."

"Did you get anywhere?" Finley stood up from the large table that took up the center of the room and walked toward him. She kept her voice measured—what she thought of as her well-honed lawyer tone—but even she heard the hope that ringed the edges of her words.

"Not yet."

"Look, Grey. Everyone"—she nodded to Callie and the women in turn—"you've all been incredibly kind to me. But I need to get out of here and back to my life. I've got several cases I'm working on and I need to get back to it. Back to my job."

"I'd rather you stayed here."

Finley saw the tight line of his lips and realized, with absolute certainty, those words had cost him. "I need to get back to my life."

"To the people who set you up?"

Ilsa let out a low whistle and mumbled, "Here come the fireworks," but opted to say nothing else.

Montana took a more proactive approach as Finley felt her move up to provide support at her flank. "Grey. Come on, surely we can put some detail on her until we figure out what's going on."

"There is no other way. She's in danger and it's not a danger the average human bodyguard can deal with."

Montana reached for her hand and squeezed. "Well, you don't have to scare her with it."

"Why not? You should know the feeling. You lived with it more recently than anyone else here. She's become a target, Montana. I won't shirk my responsibilities to keeping her safe."

"No one's shirking anything." Finley interrupted the brewing battle. "But I can't just leave my job, Grey. I've worked too long and too hard to get it. If you think the situation's that dire, I've got internal resources outside my immediate superiors and coworkers. I can get help and I can get protection."

"No."

As he dug in, the need to stick to her guns only grew. With a small smile, she turned toward the women. "Callie. Montana. Ilsa. Could I have some time with Grey?"

A few murmured "of course's" later and the kitchen was devoid of everyone but the two of them.

"Why are you so insistent on this? And why do you care this much? I'd think you'd be glad to find a solution that got me out of your hair."

"I'm not looking for an easy solution. I'm looking for the right one."

"Well, keeping me here isn't it."

"I think it is."

Frustration coursed through her in the same heavy, pounding waves of the bass music at his club. She'd never had any doubt Grey Bennett was a powerful man. Although it would have been easy to dismiss him simply as a New York club owner, his demeanor had always suggested more.

But she'd confirmed it when some light digging on him turned up nothing. Not even a driver's license.

No one could live that far off the grid, no matter how hard they tried.

Being that unavailable meant you proactively worked at it.

Although it had taken her a long time, this case with Gavelli had given her a reason to talk to him. And once she'd been seen befriending the club's owner, others were a bit easier around her. The bartenders were friendlier and the cocktail waitresses were a little freer with the small details that seemed like nothing but added up to some really large clues.

It was clear nobody knew the whole story—nor did they even know a whole lot—but it was the stray comments she'd begun to weave together into something more.

Mr. Bennett's irregular travel schedule. His odd hours. The limited-access areas in the club.

And the regular comings and goings of a group of very large men who frequented the club and the inner sanctum of Mr. Bennett's office.

The only reason she got that last bit was because several of the waitresses had their eyes firmly clamped on Mr. Bennett's friends. And the first rule she'd learned, all the way back in the sixth grade, was that no one was quicker to share a wink and some gossip than a woman in the throes of a hormone rush.

What she'd also discovered, despite her very best efforts, was that she was deeply, horribly and utterly obsessed with Grey Bennett.

And that's when she realized that perhaps she was playing this all wrong. She'd been so focused on getting away. Maybe she needed to change her tactics and focus on getting close. And getting some answers.

Her gaze stroked over his body, the rich fabric of his

suit doing nothing to hide the barely leashed power underneath. Finley felt the pull down deep inside, that feminine curl of need low in the belly, just before it settled between her thighs.

"You can keep a watch on me, but I want to go home and I want to go to my job. I'll check in. I can meet you or any one of these people you share your life with who you think can protect me."

"It's too dangerous."

The fear from the night before struck with swift force. That moment she'd stood in the goon's arms, realizing what a bad decision she'd made. Was she making another one? Even as she thought it, she refused to back down. Refused to live her life on anyone else's terms. "It's my final offer."

The subtle lines that bracketed Grey's eyes softened along with his voice. "Why do you need to do this so bad?"

"It's who I am. I work for justice and I finish what I start." When he didn't answer, she added, "I have to do this."

"Stubborn," he muttered, taking a step toward her.

She forced herself to keep her gaze firmly on his, even as she wanted to look her fill of his broad chest and the power that hovered around him like an aura. "Clearly you're familiar with the trait."

He didn't reply, the moment heavy with unspoken needs as the memory of their kiss the night before swirled around her. In her mind, the memory wrapped around them both, and she could almost believe she was right as he took another step closer.

"Who are you, Grey Bennett?"

"I'm the man who's going to find out who set you up and kill them."

"Kill them?" The luscious buzz that coursed through her body was immediately doused at his words. The gray of his eyes had gone a dark, steely hue and she couldn't repress the shiver at what he implied.

"You can't kill anyone! And certainly not on my behalf."

Grey moved forward, up into her space. The corded muscles of his neck stood out in harsh relief. His breath was warm on her face and that thrumming low in her belly started again at the realization she needed only to lean forward a hairsbreadth to kiss him. "Try me."

He was so close—and what she *wanted* was so close—all she had to do was lean forward and take it.

Take the moment and satisfy her curiosity.

A rush of air exploded in her ear as a loud crash hit behind them. Finley felt her world tilt as Grey snatched her up in his arms and dragged her to the far side of the kitchen.

When they came to a standstill, she looked over Grey's shoulder, shocked to see Drake cradling Emerson in his arms.

Rogan watched Eris slip from the bed and pad toward the bathroom. The sounds of the shower started almost immediately and he briefly toyed with joining her before he acknowledged he needed to get going himself. Grey and Drake had walked into a shit-storm the night before and he knew they needed his help.

Even as the urge to stay pulsed with a steady throb in his veins, he dragged himself out of bed and crossed the room to his clothes. There was absolutely nothing healthy about what went on between the two of them, and the closer he got to her, the more he put his family at risk. But like a drug that hooked after one taste, he couldn't stay away from Eris.

She fucking *owned* his ass.

And while she might be known as the goddess of discord in the rest of her life, he'd never felt this *content* in all of his.

He was already thinking about how quickly he could get back to Vegas—back to Eris—as he spied his jeans. Bending down to snag them, he slammed his shoulder on the small table the hotel had placed there, presumably for decoration.

Fuck. Not only did the woman make him mindless, now he could add clumsy to the list.

He picked up her heavy purse where it had fallen to the floor—what the hell did an immortal need with a loaded handbag?—and dropped it back on the table. A loud ping caught his attention, and he spied her phone still on the floor and lying along a back leg.

As he reached for it, the text that had caused the ping still showed on the phone's flat screen.

Rogan read the display, everything inside of him going cold and numb with the reminder of who she really was.

THE PISCES SAW ME AND KNOWS WHO I AM. I'M GOING AFTER HIM.

Chapter Ten

"**D**rake!" Emerson clung to his midsection as her feet took purchase on the ground. He'd done this . . . *this thing* . . . midargument at her house and she hadn't quite caught her breath. "What the hell'd you do that for?" She ran a hand through her hair, dragging on the spikes as she puzzled through what they'd just seen.

Her brother. And that weird thing with his eyes. And the snake.

Oh God. Magnus had turned a snake loose on Drake and then just vanished.

"I wasn't interested in waiting around to find out if your brother was going to reappear with his big, fat snake in tow."

"Somehow I don't think that's a friendly euphemism." Finley moved forward to take a seat at the over-sized table that dominated the kitchen, her smile gentle as she added, "Or a reference to He Who Must Not Be Named. Come on. Sit down."

Emerson smiled back, calming for the first time at the attempted humor. "It's not. He was bitten by a snake."

"Who was?" Finley and Grey asked in unison.

Emerson pointed at Drake, who looked surprisingly well—not to mention melt-your-self-control sexy— where he stood near the table, reaching for a banana. "Him."

"You fucking idiot," Grey muttered. "How the hell did you have enough energy to port the two of you over here?"

"We had to get here. It was that simple."

"Yeah, well, the laws of physics weren't in your favor on this one. You're lucky you both got back in one piece."

Drake ignored him and tossed a pointed look across the table. "Ms. McCrae's still here, Grey?"

Finley's avid gaze took in all of them and Emerson heard Drake's subtext loud and clear: *Should we be talking about this in front of her?*

"Yes, and if I have anything to say about it she's not going anywhere."

"And if I have any say in it, I am," Finley shot back.

Although still shaken by her brother, Emerson couldn't deny her interest in what she and Drake had interrupted in the kitchen. It was obvious Grey was deeply conflicted about what the woman was doing there. And equally obvious that he didn't want to let her leave.

Finley spoke first. "Look. Something's going on in here and I've no doubt it defies the laws of nature and pretty much everything else my rational, lawyerly brain has believed in my first thirty years of life. So what I'm asking is if one of you will take pity on me and tell me what the fuck that is."

When everyone just stared at her, she added as an afterthought, "Or at least tell me about the really big snake."

"Fine, tell us." Grey sighed, nodding, and Emerson thought it was even more curious to see just how tightly he focused on Finley. She'd only met the man on a few occasions, but her impression of him was that he didn't do relationships. The careful way he looked at the lawyer had her rethinking that opinion.

"He was attacked by a snake. At my house. By my—" Emerson's voice broke off as the reality of the words hit her. "By my brother."

"What was your brother doing with a snake?"

Finley's immediate curiosity only reminded Emerson of all the things she didn't know about her brother. And all the fears she harbored for what he'd possibly become.

Was Drake right? Was Magnus involved in some sort of dark magic?

She'd felt dark magic before—the insidious way it teased and taunted the senses. The promise offered by that abuse of power was a heady rush, like standing on the edge of a precipice with the absolute certainty you could fly.

And Magnus had made that strange comment the first night he was back about using her powers to her advantage.

But she just didn't *feel* it.

Of course, he was her brother. Was it possible he

could mask it from her? And her magic *had* worked to remove the poison.

Maybe the real truth was that she just didn't want to see him in that light.

"I don't know. All I do know is he had this enormous snake on the floor in front of him in his room. It matched the tattoo that covered his shoulders, which I didn't even know he had."

"You didn't know your brother had a tattoo?" Finley probed.

"He's been gone a long time."

"And has now made a sudden return, reptile in tow?"

"He's always lived slightly on the edge, and it got worse after my mom died. But the snake and the tat." Emerson looked down at her arm with a rueful smile. "I'm not against tattoos, mind you. In fact, I'm rather fond of mine. But, I can't explain it. There's something *wrong* with his. And it made the whole experience even more . . . unsettling."

Something tickled the edge of her memories. She'd been so focused on the snake that as she thought back over it, Emerson realized there was more to it all than the actual animal.

What was it?

"What was unsettling?"

Finley's warm smile put her instantly at ease and, in that moment, Emerson suspected the woman was an incredibly good lawyer.

"He controlled the snake in some way."

"Until it looked like he couldn't control it any longer," Drake added. "The snake was after Emerson. I don't think he'd purposely meant to hurt her, which is why I assume her brother lost whatever measure of control he had over it."

"So then it attacked?" Grey pressed them.

"It was aiming for me, but Drake leaped in front of it like some freaking Secret Service Agent."

"That's a rather romantic gesture." Finley's gaze jumped from Drake to Grey. "You're quite a bunch of men."

"It's not romantic. It's—" Emerson stopped herself as Drake's attention washed over her, his interest in her answer palpable. Why was her first reaction always to fight?

"Okay. It is sweet," she conceded, "even if it's the height of stupidity to throw yourself in front of an eight-foot coiled snake."

"Has your brother ever owned snakes?"

Emerson was surprised how Finley's cool reasoning and pointed questions calmed her and helped her think. And each question managed to focus more on what she'd seen back at her own home. "No, never. In fact, he never had that reptile interest a lot of boys go through. He was more of a dog lover, a let's-go-out-in-the-backyard-and-play-ball sort of boy."

"A regular Boy Scout," Drake muttered as he stood, polishing off his second banana. She marveled at his iron-willed strength as he crossed to the Sub-Zero refrigerator. No one would have ever known the man had had venom coursing through his body fifteen minutes before. "Anyone want a beer?"

Emerson gave an absentminded yes as she watched the play of muscles across his broad back. The material of his T-shirt had ripped in long strips where the snake had attacked, and the tanned skin underneath fascinated her as he reached into the fridge for the beers.

As he leaned forward, she saw a gap in the material of his shirt and caught sight of the ink that rode high on his shoulder.

With a rush of awareness, the abstract thoughts she had about her brother solidified and the missing connection between his tattoo and the snake she couldn't quite place came together.

The snake *tattoo* on his shoulders had writhed in matched motion with the live one on the floor.

Magnus fell to the floor in Eris's living room with a heavy thud. He still hadn't figured out this damn porting thing and he sucked ass at it.

He hated being terrible at anything. Which really was a fucking joke since, other than the cold-blooded killer gig, he sucked at everything.

Including playing at Warrior.

What the hell had he been thinking, letting the snake out in his grandmother's home? With his sister just down the hall?

But the *power*.

All that coiled power that lived just under his skin. It called to him, taunting him to play with it. Even now, he felt it writhing across his shoulders, begging to be let free.

Struggling to his feet, he cursed himself a million times over for the lunacy of his actions. But damn if he'd figured out a way to control himself yet.

To control *it* yet.

Eris had explained the snake lived in his aura—whatever the hell that meant. All he knew was that he suddenly had a tattoo that writhed and moved and wanted *out*.

It was like puberty all over again, except instead of a dick that got hard, all he wanted to do was play with the immortal power Eris had bestowed on his body. And like the dick he'd had no clue what to do with when he was thirteen, he was pretty much equally in the dark now.

Eris materialized in the room, a supremely self-satisfied smile covering her face until she caught sight of him. The smile vanished in an instant and her voice was hard when she spoke. "I gave you a very simple set of directions to follow."

He knew where the smile had come from, but opted to keep his own counsel on that one. It was a juicy tidbit that would come in handy sooner or later. "The mobsters you wanted dead have been taken care of. Besides, I needed to come here. I needed to get away from my sister."

Eris nodded as she tossed her purse on the couch. "Does she suspect something?"

You mean when I set a huge snake loose on her and her boyfriend? Keeping his own counsel on that little tidbit as well, he simply opted for, "She's highly intuitive."

Whatever smug bemusement Eris had arrived with was gone by the dark look in her narrowed eyes. "Yes, but does she know?"

"No." The response came out quickly, but even as he thought it through Magnus acknowledged Emerson didn't know. Couldn't know.

He had no doubt his sister suspected something was

going on with him, but she could guess for a million years and she'd never figure out what had happened to him.

Would never guess the power of the choice he'd made.

Or what he'd abandoned to possess it.

"She's quite a powerful woman, from what I understand. And a witch to be reckoned with. You're absolutely sure?" Eris probed once more.

"I can take care of my sister."

"My, my, my." Eris sauntered over to him, the dark storm clouds in her eyes fading as she gave him an appraising look. "Aren't we the confident soldier? Somehow, I find myself questioning this sudden bout of loyalty. You'd turn on your own sister, even as you're chomping at the bit to go after her boyfriend?"

Magnus pulled himself back. Although he hadn't spent all that much time with Eris, it hadn't taken long to learn the games she enjoyed playing.

Twisting words and creating confusion, which quickly led to far darker emotions. She wasn't the goddess of strife and discord for nothing. She'd had millennia to practice and she was damn good at what she did.

"We made a deal from the outset. I will work around my family. Leave that to me."

She nodded, and although the motion appeared as if she were acquiescing, he knew better. She might give the suggestion he'd won the round, but he wasn't deluding himself.

He'd merely staved off the inevitable. He just hoped like hell he'd get better control of his powers before that day arrived.

Before he could dwell on it any further, Eris snapped out orders. "Well, what are you waiting for? The Pisces awaits your attention."

Drake snagged the four longnecks and carried them back to the table. As he laid a bottle in front of Emerson, he immediately caught her pale coloring.

"What's wrong?"

Emerson's lips stood out in sharp relief on her white face. "It was moving."

"What was moving?"

"My brother's tattoo."

"That's impossible." Even as he said the words, Drake knew them for the lie they were.

Tattoos *did* move. He had one to prove it. And so did each and every one of his Warrior brothers.

But if Magnus had a tattoo that moved, he'd have noticed it.

Until he replayed the events in his mind and remembered that he'd only seen the snake and reacted, paying minimal attention to Emerson's brother.

"I know what I saw, Drake. I know it. The tattoo on his skin moved."

"Is your grandmother okay?"

As diversions went, it was anything but subtle. But Grey's words were immediately effective as Emerson's eyes went wide in her face. "Oh my God! I have to go back and check on her."

Drake's grip tightened again. "You're not going over there without me."

"Wait. No. Wait." She shook her head as she reached for the phone in her pocket. "I need to go call her, but I think it's her bridge day with her girlfriends. In fact, I'm almost sure of it."

"Then Quinn and I'll go back and deal with your brother." He added a pointed stare for the ram. "And Grey can begin the business of getting Finley out of here and back to her life."

"You're not dealing with Magnus."

"Well, you're most certainly not." The stubborn set of her chin and the immediate set of a hand on her hip nearly had him smiling, but he held it back.

He nodded toward the phone in her hands. "Go call your grandmother and let me and Grey discuss it."

Although he didn't expect her to accept his direction, clearly the need to see to her grandmother overrode anything else and Emerson left to make her call.

"Somehow I get the feeling you two need to have a discussion." Finley stood from her bar stool. "I saw a very lovely library down the hall that I'd like to go investigate before we leave."

Grey waited until the swinging door to the kitchen had closed behind her before he whirled, his voice a low hiss so Emerson wouldn't overhear. "His tattoo fucking moves?"

"Yep."

"Why didn't you tell me?"

"Shit, Mom, I was a bit busy fighting off a venomous snakebite."

"Okay, I take it back. How in the hell does Emerson's brother have a tattoo that moves?"

"I don't know, Grey. It's a snake. None of Themis's Warriors have snake tattoos. It's not a part of us."

"But the tats are Themis's creation."

"Doesn't mean someone else on Mount Olympus didn't think it was a damn good idea." Drake rubbed the back of his shoulder, and the joined fish that lived under his skin twitched in acknowledgment of his words.

Grey shot a look toward Emerson, but she was still facing the cabinets on the far side of the room, engrossed in her conversation. "And he *used* the snake?"

"That's what I can't get a handle on. I think the snake used him. There is just no way I believe he planned on attacking his own sister."

"My tat can't do that. Either I control it and make it attack something, or it stays where it is."

Drake knew the power in the ram's tattoo—knew the innate strength in all of their marks—and thought back to an earlier time. "Don't you remember the beginning?"

"What beginning?"

"When you first became a Warrior." Without even trying, Drake's memories of those first days and weeks in service to Themis came back in a heavy wash of memories.

The confusion.

The raw power that coursed through his veins.

The never-ending questions that taunted him, suggesting he'd been too hasty in his decision and that she'd change her mind, sending him straight back to Alexander at the first opportunity.

"I sucked ass at it." Grey's smile was rueful as he nodded. "I was clumsy, like I couldn't get my footing."

"Me too. I suspect we all felt that way."

"I didn't understand it then and still don't. I was

strong in my mortal life. Hell, I was a trained assassin for the royal family."

"I was a soldier in Alexander the Great's army, and let me tell you, that fucker took training to a whole new, maniacal level. It didn't mean that suddenly having the body of an immortal, with all the various attributes that went with it, wasn't an adjustment."

"And you think her brother's an immortal."

"I think he's something." Drake shot a look at where Emerson stood across the kitchen. She was still on the phone, but those slim shoulders were more relaxed than they had been and what he could hear of her voice was more evenly modulated. "We need to keep her here."

Grey was the first to speak. "Callie."

Without wasting any time, Drake secured Callie's reluctant help and briefed Quinn. Within minutes, he'd ported them into the kitchen, unwilling to drop straight into the bedroom Magnus had occupied.

"The house feels empty," Quinn noted as he swept through the kitchen.

Drake nodded. "Let's go upstairs."

The Carano brownstone wasn't nearly as wide as theirs—even without the extra square footage that sat on Mount Olympus—and they hauled ass up three flights of stairs in moments.

Drake led the way to the room Magnus had occupied earlier. "He left his things."

"Then by all means"—Quinn's wicked smile flashed in the late-afternoon sun that streamed in the windows—"let's roll the joint."

They worked in companionable silence, Drake taking the duffel that sat on the unmade bed as Quinn searched the walls for some sort of escape. As the bull moved past the window, he let out a low whistle. "That's a thirty-foot drop to the ground, which only reinforces our as-yet-unvoiced concern that he has the ability to port, too."

"Where did he come from? From the few things Emerson's said, it sounds like he's been the family fuckup for a while. I just don't see that making him Warrior material."

Quinn continued his sweep of the perimeter. "It's not like Themis has hit a home run with every man she's turned. Shit, we know that better than anyone. Ajax. Arturo."

Drake couldn't ignore the truth of Quinn's observation. The man's battle the previous spring with a fallen Taurus Warrior had taken a toll on all of them and, despite the passage of time, was still far too fresh for comfort.

No matter how discriminating she tried to be, Themis couldn't counteract simple free will.

"Besides," Quinn added as he opened the room's lone closet door, "this doesn't have Themis's imprint on it. It's too dark."

Drake finished rooting through the T-shirts and a spare pair of jeans in the duffel when his hand hit on something hard. Dragging it out, he turned the small book over in his hands.

"You got something?"

"I'm not sure." Flipping through the pages, his gaze caught on some ancient text. His brain translated the words immediately, the Greek he'd learned as a boy surprisingly clear. Puzzled, he realized it was the story of Eris's triumph with the Judgment of Paris when she used the Golden Apple for the first time. "It's like a diary."

"Of what?"

Drake flipped a few more pages, all more short stories of Eris's triumphs. A peasant uprising in the eighth century in Ireland. A tribe in South America she managed to wipe out in a matter of months. And the particularly nasty mess she made in the French Revolution. "It reads as a series of small stories and triumphs."

"This place is empty. Let's take that with us and see if Callie can figure out what it means."

Drake flipped to the back of the book, an idea taking root. As his eyes roved over the words, he felt a small sliver of fear take hold of his spine. Before he could show it to Quinn, that familiar rush of air filled the room and Magnus landed in front of them.

The port was clumsy, but there was no mistaking the man had done it on his own. The immediate leap to his feet also confirmed his reflexes weren't half-bad. His widened eyes darted around the room. "How the hell'd you get in here?"

"Same way you did." Quinn's laconic voice rumbled from the far side of the room and Magnus whirled on the bull as he realized there was someone else there too.

"What do you want?"

Drake quickly hid the book in his waistband, then moved up into Magnus's face. The tension humming in his system morphed to anger at the speed of light. "Let's start with the fucking snake you let attack your sister."

"Wait. I didn't. It hit you."

He didn't back off, but did see Quinn's stance shift from the corner of his eye. This could turn ugly any moment and they both knew it. "By default. You were aiming for her."

"I'd never hurt her."

"Could have fooled me."

"She's my sister. She just . . ."

Drake refused to back down. "She just what?"

Magnus's voice was low as he clenched his shoulders, the nervous gesture only heightening the tension in the room. "She just got in the way."

Drake knew there was a fourth sense a person honed in battle, the stress of the situation lending itself to a heightened awareness that was very real, even if it couldn't be easily explained.

He could only thank the gods he and Quinn fought so well together.

Without warning, the same snake from earlier leaped off of Magnus's form, striking so fast all Drake had time to do was stumble backward.

Quinn's bull joined the fray immediately, the animal's powerful body keeping Magnus at bay even as its hooves tried to stamp out the snake. Heavy grunts and groans rose up in the small room as the bodies of two large men and two equally large animals crashed onto furniture.

Scrambling to his feet, Drake made a wide circle around the battling forms and, as soon as he had a shot, he took it. With swift footwork, he sidestepped the snake and went in low at Magnus. On a heavy grunt, he pushed the man off balance and sent the snake flailing in the air.

He'd wanted to believe there was some power—some reason for the power—that he'd seen in Magnus earlier, but there was no other explanation. The fact that the snake followed him to the floor meant it operated from within Magnus's aura, not independently of him.

The man had the same set of gifts he and his brothers carried in their own bodies.

Before either of them could get a good grip on him, Magnus vanished once again.

Chapter Eleven

Emerson knew she was being a bitch, but she didn't give a flying fuck. How dare he leave her here?

Like she was some little woman who needed protecting.

She paced Drake's room, the familiar surroundings a vivid reminder of why she was so mad. He knew who she was. Knew what she was capable of. Knew she was strong. He had no right to leave her behind like some child who needed to be watched over.

Especially when it involved her family.

She wouldn't break, damn it. Hell, she had enough power inside of her to blow this place into smithereens. And just like that, Magnus's words curled through her mind like whispers of smoke.

"Don't you want more?"

"Why won't you use it?"

"Don't tell me you're so bound up in all that white witch bullshit you can't see you're entitled to some benefits."

On a hard shake of her head, she sat down on the side of Drake's enormous bed.

What was wrong with her?

She'd never before questioned who and what she was. The purity of her gift and the responsibility that came with its use.

So why now?

She'd been mad before. So mad she'd thought she'd never be happy or bright or fun or normal again.

Why were his words so seductive?

Emerson flopped back onto the bed, the mattress absorbing the hard lines of her body. Despite her best intentions, she felt her body relax at the opportunity to finally sit still and think for a few minutes.

She wanted to be mad at Callie. Had taken a few strips off of her when she'd done the whole block and tackle in the kitchen, but Emerson knew it wasn't the woman's fault. And if the look of rebellion in those dark brown eyes was an indication, Callie wasn't any happier about it than she was.

Her body relaxed another fraction and she instinctively knew Drake had returned. The raging storm that lived in her heart always calmed a little bit when he was near and, despite her anger, this moment was no different.

The light knock announced his arrival just before he stepped through the door. Emerson toyed briefly with the idea of feigning sleep, but discarded it in favor of sitting up and fighting. She caught sight of the still-ripped T-shirt as a new thought took hold.

Maybe she could work off some tension instead.

"You look mad."

She stood and moved a few steps, not fully closing the gap between them. "I'm not talking to you."

"I needed to do it, Emerson. And I couldn't take you back in there."

"For the moment, we're going to ignore the fact that you locked me up in your house to go investigating mine. We're also, for the moment, going to forget that I'm so mad at you I'd like to pour honey over every inch of your body and set a rabid band of fire ants loose on you."

His eyebrows arched, but he didn't stop her.

"And, for the moment, we're also going to forget that you continue to insinuate yourself in my life without asking my permission, which is, frankly, the root of my anger, upset and all-around vindictiveness toward you."

"Em—"

"I said I'm not talking to you."

"Oh." His lips twitched, but he didn't say anything else.

"Take your shirt off."

He did as she asked and Emerson drank him in. The long, lean lines of his body that descended into a narrow torso, capped off by a broad pair of shoulders that would make Atlas weep. He had a swimmer's body, she realized with sudden clarity, the knowledge making perfect sense as she considered his Pisces nature and its connection to how he was.

"Turn around."

The twitch in his full lips turned into a full-on smile. "Isn't this talking?"

"Turn. Around."

He did as she asked, presenting his back to her.

Reveling in the chance to observe him while he was unaware, she continued her inspection of his body. She'd seen his tattoos before, fascinated by the elaborate ink on his skin, but in his silence she could truly look her fill.

Could see the beautiful design that wrapped around his left shoulder before settling on his upper back.

The dark ink swirled over his shoulder into sharp points, with the tribal design surprisingly similar to her own tattoo. From the angle where he stood, she could see the ink as it spread onto his back. As her gaze followed the design, it stopped, giving way to a second tattoo—two fish joined at the tail.

With tentative fingers, she reached out to lightly touch his skin, surprised when the tattoo began to move. Like that feeling when her magic unlocked and began coursing through her veins, the scales of the fish winked an enticing silver as they moved in a slow circle, as if preening under her attention.

The tattoo was relatively small, covering only the upper quadrant of his back over his shoulder blade, but she couldn't fight the sense that there was power there, barely leashed and far greater than it appeared.

How had she never noticed it before?

In all the times they'd been together, she'd looked but never really seen.

Reaching up, she ran her hands along the firm ledge of his shoulders, the warmth of his skin branding her like fire. She felt her own magic rising within her body, coursing through her with a certainty that left her breathless.

She knew who she was and she knew what mattered to her.

With a flick of her wrist, she made their clothing disappear into a heap on the floor. Her gaze descended to take in the firm globes of his ass as need flooded her body, pooling between her thighs.

His body was a marvel. Not a single inch of him wasn't long and lean, hard and *able*. She was half his size and yet when she was with him he was fiercely gentle.

Right now, she wanted the fierce.

Maintaining contact with his shoulders, she slid around him and pressed her breasts to his chest, gratified when his hard erection fit flush against her stomach.

Hard and able was right.

Her arms were still around his neck and he reached up with his hands and skimmed his fingers along the underside of her arms. The light touch was so simple—so elegant, really—and it was her undoing.

He treated her as if she were a precious jewel. When had she come to love it so much? To crave it with a desperate longing she'd never known?

Then she lost the ability to think as his mouth came down over hers and the tables were turned on the huntress. In that moment, Drake brought the fierce.

Drake feasted on her, this small, slender package of conflicting emotions and generous passions.

How had he ever lived without her?

With lips and tongue, he tried to show her what was in his heart. The desperate need he carried for her that wouldn't be sated no matter how many times they were together.

No matter how sweet the touch or how precious the moment, his body always craved the next one with her. *Emerson.*

Her grip on his shoulders grew more urgent as the kiss continued to spin out between them. He caressed his way from the backs of her arms, over her shoulders, until he came around her front and filled both hands with the heavy fullness of her breasts. With a move that tortured them both, he flicked his thumbs over her nipples, satisfied when she arched into his hands.

As her body shifted, her hips rubbed against his erection, sending waves of pleasure coursing through his body. He felt her triumphant smile under his lips and the low rumble of her breath before she caught herself from speaking.

"Nearly caught at your own game, eh?" he couldn't resist teasing her as he squeezed her nipples between thumb and forefinger, gratified as her breath exploded on a gasp with a whispered exclamation of "Bastard" against his lips.

Not to be outdone, her movements faster than a whip, she had her hands between their bodies and wrapped around his cock. With exquisite pressure, her fingers traveled the length in a series of constricting motions that had him seeing stars. Hand over hand, she fisted him until he almost came in her palm.

Any sense of finesse or drawing the moment out vanished in the heat of what built between them. He wanted her with a desperation that bordered on madness and he had to have her.

Staggering to the bed, he wrapped his arms around her and fell backward, absorbing her weight as she sprawled against him. Still gripped in the midst of the heat and need that drove them both, she moved over him, rising onto her knees. Before she could fit him to the wet warmth at her core, he gripped her hips and flipped her aside, straddling her from behind.

She glanced at him over her shoulder—her gray eyes going an opaque blue with passion—before pressing her backside toward him and exposing her glistening folds to his cock.

Drake didn't waste another moment. He fitted himself to the hilt, then reached around to press a long finger against her slick channel, rubbing the sensitive core of her body until she was writhing against him in manic need.

Blind need drove them on as their bodies met again and again, blistering passion consuming them both. Emerson's climax rushed upon her and Drake felt his entire body tightening in answer. On a strangled moan, he buried himself inside her and gave himself up to the mindless needs of his body as it answered hers.

He felt her go limp beneath him, the stiff arch of her back settling as her head fell forward. Another climax gripped his body at her complete acquiescence and he rode the gentler wave, rocking within her tight sheath.

"Emerson?" Drake pressed his lips to the base of her neck, just above her spine as her soft moan of pleasure rose up to greet him.

"I can't feel my arms."

Abstractly he realized she still supported herself and he once again took her weight and pulled her down until she was fitted against him, her small form snug against his chest.

They lay there so long, he almost believed she'd fallen asleep when she finally spoke. "I'm still mad at you."

"I figured you were, but I can't say I'm all that upset by how you express your anger."

Her throaty laughter greeted him, the sound an enchanting blend of feminine knowledge and sexy satisfaction as she shifted up onto an elbow. "It was a far more interesting way to manage our differences of opinion."

Drake ran a finger down her cheek and marveled at how soft her skin was. She was just so damn delicate, yet a core of strength pulsed inside. "A quiet one, too."

The light in her eyes faded. "Did you find my brother?"

"I did."

"Is he all right?"

"I don't know, Emerson. He vanished again."

"What do you mean he vanished? I know my brother has power, just as I do. But we can't disappear from a place and reappear in another."

"I think he's working under a different set of power. Something non-magic based."

"From where? That's just not a power—even a dark one—a witch can possess."

"That's what we're trying to figure out."

She struggled to sit up. "I need to get back over there and see if he comes back. I held off my grandmother and convinced her to stay at her friend's for a few days, but I have to get to the bottom of this."

"Emerson." Drake reached for her shoulders, holding her in place. "Your brother's dangerous. Until we know more, it's not safe for you at home."

"And it is for you?"

"I've got some attributes on my side that you don't."

She stilled, her stare boring into him. "What aren't you telling me? Did something happen? Before he vanished? Something with the snake?"

No matter how badly he wanted to shield her from all of it, she had a right to know. "He attacked Quinn and me. Or more specifically, the snake attacked both of us."

"Oh my God! What happened to him? And what in the name of all that's holy is my brother doing with a snake that goes around attacking people?"

"We have our ideas."

"Well, then, start sharing them, Ace." She swung her legs over the side of the bed and walked to grab her clothes. "I can't believe it's taken you this long to tell me."

Drake dug his fingers into the mattress beneath him. "It wasn't my idea to fuck our way through a fight, Emerson."

"You damn sure enjoyed yourself," she shot back from across the room.

"I didn't notice you offering up any complaints as you shattered in my arms."

"You still could have told me about Magnus."

With a swift kick to the covers, he got off the bed and stormed over to her. "I'm not the one who uses sex to replace anything real between the two of us."

"I don't exactly see you complaining."

"Nor do I see you taking any fucking responsibility for what's between us."

She shoved her legs into a pair of yoga pants, then turned and gave him her back. "I take full responsibility for what's between us. I wanted a ride to work off some tension and I took it. End of story."

"Gods damn it, Emerson!" The woman could infuriate a nun if given half a chance. "What is wrong with you?"

"Everything's wrong with me, Drake. Everything." She whirled around. "Have you seen my life?"

"Don't blame this on what's happening with Magnus. You've been checked out around me for a year. It's got nothing to do with him."

"This has everything to do with him." The beautiful gray-blue of her eyes tugged at Drake as mysteries and painful secrets flashed across them.

"Then explain it to me."

Whatever he saw flashed away, replaced with the same stubborn refusal he'd faced for the past year. "I don't have the things to give that you're so insistent you want. It can't be me. Why can't you understand that?"

"Because I don't believe you. I don't believe you're nearly as unaffected as you say. And I sure as hell don't believe this thing between us is one-sided."

"I hate to disappoint you, but—"

He wouldn't let her finish—refused to let her finish—as he snatched at her and pulled her to him, slamming his mouth to hers. She responded immediately, her low, heavy moan the proof he needed that she wasn't unaffected.

"Why do you push me away?" he whispered against her mouth. "Don't you understand what you do to me? Don't you see?"

"It isn't real, Drake. It can't be real."

At that, he dropped his hold and moved away from her, his hands hanging straight at his sides.

"It's the most real thing I've ever experienced, Emerson."

Rogan walked through the front door of the brownstone, oblivious to the sounds of New York as memories of Las Vegas rode him like a monkey on his back. How had he let his guard down?

And how had the bitch gotten so far beneath his skin?

It would be a fling, he'd promised himself a few years ago when it all started. A couple of consenting immortal adults who knew the score. Knew what went on outside whatever bed they happened to be sharing at the moment.

Yet it hadn't stopped her from going after them with precision and focus.

All the while fucking him blind and brainless.

The text message he'd intercepted burned in his mind's eye. She'd been on that phone throughout the day, no doubt putting his Warrior brothers in jeopardy and mapping out her plans. All while he'd sat blithely unaware, right under her nose.

The smell of dinner and the muted sounds of voices caught his attention and he headed for the kitchen. He'd fill in his brothers and take his lumps; then they'd figure out how to handle this.

Together.

When he paused at the swinging door a few moments later, he was met with the usual chaos that never failed to offer a small measure of comfort, no matter how long he'd been away.

No matter how bad the situation—and they'd all fought through many of them—there would always be this. The easy camaraderie and ready acceptance.

The kitchen was full, with Callie doing her usual food-is-love routine, piling platter after platter on the butcher-block table. Ilsa and Kane were manning an electric wine opener and already had three bottles open on the table while Montana took over pouring duties. Ava was at the stove, Brody behind her, as something sizzled in a large pan in front of her.

Rogan knew the women had brought new life into the brownstone, but this defied description.

They moved around, comfortably in their element, tossing jokes and insults, stopping to give small touches to their husbands or smiles to one another.

As he watched them, it brought into sharp relief what he had with Eris. A relationship he hid in the shadows, unable—and unwilling—to share it with his family.

Before he could pull Quinn aside to take him to the security center, Drake and Emerson arrived at the door. All noise in the kitchen stopped as everyone turned to look at the two of them. The silence had just veered to the far side of awkward when Callie grabbed one of the full wineglasses on the table and handed it to Emerson. "Come on and sit down."

Rogan sensed there were some underlying issues at

play between the Pisces and the witch, but he didn't have time to navigate whatever social drama had unfolded prior to arriving. He moved over to Drake and Quinn and kept his voice low. "You guys have a few minutes?"

Drake glared at the wall of screens in Quinn's security center, the low hum of voices fading into the background as he studied the monitors. Damn, but he couldn't find his center and it pissed him off.

He knew Emerson's routine, and he understood there was something she was running from. He'd been laboring under the assumption that if he had enough patience, he could break through it.

For the first time, he had to wonder if maybe he was wrong. If they really did sit on opposite sides of an uncrossable chasm.

Damn it, she had churned him up today.

"Drake?"

He pulled his attention off the monitors and refocused on the conversation.

"Did you and Quinn find Emerson's brother?"

With a quick recap, Drake filled Rogan in on what had happened next door. "From everything we can tell, it seems like he's one of us."

"He's been made." Rogan's voice was quiet, but his words were unmistakable.

"By whom?" Drake thought about what they'd seen. "He's wearing a snake. It's just not possible. None of us have that mark."

Before Rogan could respond, Drake remembered the diary. "Hang on." He ported to his room and back, the diary in hand when he returned. "We found this in Magnus's things. It belongs to Eris."

Rogan took the diary, flipping through it quickly. "How do you know this is Eris's? And why would Emerson's brother have it?"

"To answer the first part, open to the middle. There's a recap of the Judgment of Paris and her use of the Golden Apple."

Rogan scanned the story, then flipped through several pages.

"You've never seen that book in your work?" Quinn asked.

"No." Their Sagittarius shook his head. "Never."

Rogan's role as their Warrior in charge of rounding up rogue pantheon members meant he'd seen a lot of legendary items. The fact he hadn't seen the diary— didn't even seem to know about it—made Magnus's possession of it that much more curious.

"Did you know Eris was missing her Golden Apple?" Quinn lifted a small pin from the desk and handed to Rogan.

"This is it?" Their archer put the book on the edge of the desk and held the pin up to the light. "This is really it?"

"We're convinced it is."

Rogan turned the pin over in his hands, inspecting it from different angles. "Everything I've ever found on it says the apple was really just that—an apple cast out of gold. Nothing all that suspicious or out of the ordinary, other than the fact that it was made of precious metal. It's what she imbued in it that's got the power."

"Then she may recast the apple as necessary. In this

case, into the shape of a pin worn most recently on the lapel of a mobster." Quinn hit a few keys on one of his keyboards and pointed to the screen. The image of the warehouse where they'd found Finley came up. "It's very real and very dangerous."

Rogan laid the pin on the desk. "It's terribly dangerous. The possessor's every action is one of underlying aggression. But it's subtle and hard to detect. It's why it's so effective."

"But how does it work?" Quinn pushed again. "And why aren't we affected?"

"I don't know." Rogan glanced at it once more, his expression thoughtful. "Maybe it's part of our gifts? It'd be awfully hard to hunt down rogue artifacts and weapons if they fucked with our senses all the time."

"Fair point," Drake had to acknowledge. He'd been able to do lots of things in service to Themis—his dip a few days prior in the drug-infested river a prime example—that he'd never expected.

"But to how it actually works. You know Eris's strength is in her words and her ability to create discord. She does that most often through a cunning ability to put the wrong people together and then let the sparks fly. The apple only enhances that."

"I still don't see how what was basically a beauty contest when Paris was asked to judge the 'fairest of them all' is the same as getting a bunch of mobsters all riled up."

Rogan turned to Quinn, his smile broad. "That's the whole point. It only looked like a beauty contest." When Quinn's eyebrows still shot up in a skeptical arc, Rogan kept going. "You read the story in the diary and you had to have been taught it as a kid. The story goes that she was pissed off she didn't get invited to a wedding, so she cast the apple and said it would be given to whoever was the fairest."

"And Helen of Troy was the one selected," Drake said. He hadn't lived through that shit-storm, as it was before his time, but he'd learned the history as a child.

"Exactly. But it really had nothing to do with a beauty contest. That was only the diversion. The selection of Helen ultimately lead to the Trojan War, which was Eris's real goal all along."

"And the apple did that?"

Rogan shrugged. "The apple in and of itself doesn't matter. It's a conveyance. A device that channels her work, especially since she can't be everywhere at once; nor can she be privy to all the actions of the people she's manipulating."

"It acts as a surrogate for her power." Drake realized with startling clarity just how effective a tool it could be. Like a homing device that amplified the problem, all at the same time.

Quinn pointed back to the image still captured on the screen. "And now she's using the mobsters to do the same thing."

Drake nodded. "Think about it. Eris creates a big fuss with the city's organized crime families to drag focus and attention off of the real score."

"It makes sense. The organized crime escalation and whatever else she's got planned." Rogan picked up the diary again and turned it over. "But what's the Magnus connection? What does Eris have to gain?"

"Go back farther in our history, Rogan." Drake

pointed to the diary. "Flip to the back. It's all there in the last entry, which also happens to be the most recent."

Rogan did as he'd asked and Quinn moved up next to him to read over his shoulder.

"No fucking way," Quinn breathed as Rogan slammed the book closed.

"Magnus is Ophiuchus." Drake nodded. "The serpent bearer. He's the thirteenth sign. He's her new weapon."

Chapter Twelve

Magnus walked through the darkened house, not all that surprised to find it empty. He had no doubt Emerson's bruiser of a boyfriend had already filled her in on what happened earlier and was taking care to keep her away for a few days.

Trudging up the stairs, he focused on the home he'd grown up in. Although the porting was coming easier and easier—his earlier escape was evidence of that—he wanted a few moments to simply revel in the nostalgia of soaking up his childhood home.

He really had been away a long time, and even before he'd left, he'd spent as much time out of the house as possible.

His mother's home.

The brownstone was long and narrow, the square footage of the house found in going up, not sprawling out. He and Emerson had always had rooms on the fourth floor, while the rest of the family had been scattered across the second and third.

Heading for the second floor, he drifted toward his mother's room, the first time he'd been willing to enter it since arriving home. Would it look the same? Or had they changed it, erasing her memory with a new set of curtains and a bedspread?

Whatever he'd imagined, it didn't prepare him for what he found in the room. Or the sucker punch of realizing that while it was different, so much of it was still the same.

The furniture still stood, old and sturdy against the wall. A large armoire that had belonged to his father and a dresser that had been his mother's. He drifted through the room, the snake on his back blessedly immobile for once, allowing him to concentrate.

To finally focus.

Although the furniture was the same, the room had changed. There was a new bedspread, as he'd suspected, and a small crafts table stood in the corner. The pair of glasses and tattered paperback that lay on top gave no doubt the table belonged to his grandmother.

She'd managed to both preserve and renew the space and Magnus found an odd peace in that.

As he turned, he caught sight of several framed photographs on the top of the bureau. Reaching for the first, an image of him and Emerson and Veronica stared back, their Christmas stockings perched on their heads. The memory of that morning rose up to choke him.

After they'd taken the stockings off their heads, he'd taken his and Veronica's and walked around in them, professing himself Bigfoot's distant relative, the Christmas monster, who was going to take all their presents back to his lair.

His sisters had turned on him, combining their collective magic to force all of his presents to hover in the air, out of his reach.

It was at that moment that he'd realized just how much power they could wield and how very little of it he actually possessed himself. He placed the photo back on the dresser as the memory soured in his mind.

His mother had comforted him that day, and so many days afterward.

"My sweet boy," she'd croon in his ear, hugging him tightly. "Your day will come. It's all right."

Until the one day when it wasn't.

Abstract images flew through his mind.

The women his mother got to know after his father died. The ritual he caught her performing with them, their blood pooled on a small altar. And then that day . . . that last day.

He'd followed her to Riverside Park, curious after one of the women she'd gotten to know met her at the back door, a strange gleam riding her gaze.

"Magnus, you need to leave," she pleaded, her eyes wild in her face when she discovered him hiding to watch.

"Mom? What are you doing?"

"Go home. Get inside and lock the door."

"Answer me, Mom. What is this?"

Tears formed and fell rapidly from her eyes as she glanced back toward the circle of women, clad head to toe in black. "They're helping me. They promised to help me."

"Help you do what?"

"Bring him back," she whispered, her lips trembling as a fevered hopefulness filled her gaze.

"Bring who back, Mom?" Even as he asked the question, he knew who she meant.

Knew who she longed to bring back.

"Your father."

"You can't. No one can."

"They can," she whispered fiercely, glancing back over her shoulder. "They know how."

He tried reason once more. "It can't be done."

"You know it can, my sweet boy. You know," she added on a soft whisper, her gaze growing speculative. "You understand it in ways your sisters can't. Don't you?"

"No." He shook his head, but even as he said the words he felt the small stirrings of power flow through his veins.

What if?

It was in that moment—it must have been reflected in his eyes—that she leaped on him, pressing her advantage. "You know it can be done. You know it. Help me. Add your blood. It's his blood that runs in your veins. With your help it will only be stronger. Will only call him back more firmly."

He hesitated, knowing on some level it was wrong. But the drumbeat of power wouldn't go away. He'd show his sisters. He could prove himself with this. Could prove he was as powerful as they were when he brought home their father and made their family whole once more.

Decision made, he followed her back to the circle. His senses heightened painfully as he drew closer, his awareness capturing seemingly everything.

The rustle of a newspaper as it skittered down the promenade.

The night air, snapping and crackling with the sounds that came out only after the sun went down.

The heavy snores of a homeless man who lay on a bench several yards away.

"You bring your son?"

"Aye. He can help us. His blood will be even more potent."

The ritual passed in a blur.

Someone sliced an athame across his palm, drawing his blood and dropping it into the circle already created. The wind whipped around all of them, its howl increasing with each passing moment.

And then the loud, horrific cry as the darkness opened up before them.

Magnus felt it—felt the power in that moment and knew his mother hadn't steered him wrong. In that moment, he knew she'd given him a gift by choosing him.

The darkness pulsed in front of him, dragging at him and drawing him forward. Without care for any consequence, he put one foot in front of the other, unable to resist its hypnotic pull. He felt his mother's hand as she reached for him, but he shook it off, unable to tear his gaze from the dark.

Moving forward, he walked straight through the circle that held the portal in place.

Broke the circle that held the dark magic at bay.

Screams echoed through the night as the results of his actions became clear. The magic barely contained by the circle reached to grab them all.

And it was only when his mother screamed, pulling him away from it and throwing herself into it that the portal closed.

Closed as if it had never been.

It had received its sacrifice.

Magnus shook himself from the memory and

walked swiftly from the room. He flew up the remaining stairs to gather his things, unwilling to spend any longer in the house than he needed to.

Unable to forgive himself for the sacrifice his mother had made for him.

Memories lived here and each and every one of them contributed to the reasons why he'd made his choice and taken what Eris had offered.

He walked into his room, the furniture still askew from their fight earlier. He ignored the lamp that lay broken on the floor and walked toward the duffel that still sat on the unmade bed where he'd left it. He crossed to the dresser and grabbed his toiletry kit to shove into the duffel. As he buried the Dopp kit in the travel bag, he felt his jumbled T-shirts and knew he hadn't left them that way.

Fear skittered though him with the speed of an oncoming train and he turned over the duffel in a mad rush. Even as the clothing fell out in a heap, he knew the one thing he needed—the one thing that had the power to destroy him—was missing.

Emerson took a small sip of her wine as sharp stabs of guilt filled her. She'd been horrible earlier. Really and truly horrible to Drake.

Blaming him for Magnus and using him like he was some sort of human vibrator.

It had to stop. He deserved better than this. Add to it she'd always prided herself on being a decent person and even she knew she was better than this.

What if you just gave in and accepted that you feel something for him?

The taunt from her subconscious was unwelcome and uncomfortable and oh so tempting.

From behind her glass, she watched as Drake looked around at their assembled council of war and quickly brought everyone up to speed on what they'd discovered in Quinn's office. His cadence was succinct and to the point, and he managed to convey a large amount of information to the group with admirable clarity.

Even so, she couldn't put all the pieces together. "I still don't understand something, though. What does Eris have to do with my brother?"

"She turned him."

"Turned him?" Emerson shook her head. "What? Like he's a vampire?"

Quinn took over at that point. "We believe he's been given the same powers that Themis bestowed on all of us."

"Why? Why him?"

"We don't know." Drake reached for her hand. "We don't know why he was chosen, but he's her weapon."

"And this apple?"

"Remember *Snow White*?" Ilsa interjected.

Emerson was skeptical, but reluctantly intrigued. "Fairy tales?"

"The Apple of Discord. It forms the basis of the witch's behavior in *Snow White*. Who's the fairest of them all? The apple that Snow White eats."

The pieces made an odd sort of sense, but it was Ilsa's final explanation that put it all together. "People believe the apple is a fairy tale and it was adapted for the movie."

"It's not a fairy tale," Quinn cautioned. "It's quite

real, in fact. The Apple of Discord has been Eris's favorite weapon since the Trojan War. It—and the Judgment of Paris—is how she started the whole thing."

Apples and Warriors? Emerson knew there were many things in this life people couldn't reason or understand. Hell, she'd spent her life being the subject of that very thing. But it still didn't explain how her brother could be an immortal.

"Even if Magnus is a Warrior like you say, what's the connection with the apple?"

"That's where Grey's lawyer came in." Quinn filled in the gaps. "The apple pin that was on Gavelli's suit jacket is the Apple of Discord."

Emerson finally saw how the various pieces fit. "So you think Eris is using the apple to divert attention off of the real game, which is my brother."

"That's exactly what we think," Quinn added. "Especially since there's no real reason for her to get into the morass of human politics. The mobsters can manage strife and discord quite well on their own. Her stepping in with the added force of her power can only escalate an existing problem."

"Oh, there's a reason." Rogan spoke for the first time. "She's after us."

"Sure she is, Rogan. We've known that since she showed up on my father's boat last fall." Montana rubbed her arms in what Emerson considered a very cold remembrance. "She's the one who held me below deck."

"Yes, but it's more urgent than that. She received a text from Magnus earlier today that specifically mentioned the Pisces."

Whatever leeway she wanted to give her brother, Emerson felt it evaporate with Rogan's words. "Today? You intercepted a text from Eris today?"

"I did." Rogan nodded. "When I was with her earlier in our hotel room."

The kitchen erupted as everyone understood the import of Rogan's words. Questions, shouts and accusations crisscrossed the room in a heated debate of words and emotions. Drake wanted to stay above it—wanted to believe in the sanctity of his friendship with Rogan— but this was too much to believe.

To his credit, Rogan took it all, his stoic features never changing, until Montana's quietly spoken words crumbled his visage. "Why her?"

"I've asked myself that a million times and, believe me, I've tried to leave her alone."

"She's manipulated you in some way," Quinn shot back. "That's her job, Rogan."

"You don't think I've thought of that? Especially since it's my job *not* to be manipulated by members of the pantheon."

"Quinn." Montana laid a hand on his forearm.

"No, Montana." Rogan shook his head. "Let him say what he wants. I take responsibility for all of it. But I don't think she's manipulated me. Not when it comes to this."

Although he didn't want to see it in the same light, Drake couldn't fully fault Rogan for his actions. He knew what it was to need a woman. To need so blindly you kept making a choice over and over.

Even if it wasn't the right one.

He felt her before he saw her, as Emerson slid up beside him and reached for his hand. As their fingers linked, he thought again about what Rogan had unsuccessfully tried to resist.

The alarm sounded off, echoing through the kitchen in great, gonging waves. It broke the clutter of his thoughts as everyone leaped into action, Quinn hollering out details. "It's a breach. Magnus."

Emerson's tight grip on his hand had Drake considering a port out of the kitchen until the fierce whisper hissed in his ear. "You try to get me out of here and I'll cut your balls off. This is about my brother and I'm not leaving and I'm not backing down."

"Don't push me, sweetheart."

An immediate flash of fire rose up in her hand as she lobbed it into the air. "Drake, don't do this to me. Don't make me choose. This is my family we're talking about. I know how to take care of myself." The words were on his lips, nearly spilling out when the harsh set of her eyes turned pleading. "I have to be a part of this."

"I can't let something happen to you."

"I'm tougher than I look, Ace." She squeezed his fingers before leaning in and pressing a hard kiss to his lips. "Have a little faith in me."

Maybe that was what it all came down to, Drake had to admit. He moved into battle position with his family. They all lined up, ready meet the threat as it breached their home.

Together.

Quinn punched in a few keys on one of his endless array of handheld devices. "He's in the foyer. The cameras haven't picked up a snake yet, but we know it's in his aura. The fact it's not out likely means he's developing more control over it, so watch yourselves."

Emerson's grip tightened on his arm at Quinn's words, but other than that, she said nothing.

"On my mark, we move into the dining room and line up. He should be far enough down the east hallway to let us get into position. Keep the wall at your back." Quinn kept his gaze focused on the device. "And . . . now!"

Once they were in position in the dining room, Drake shifted Emerson behind him. "I don't want you trapped, but I don't want you easily exposed either. If you need to, crawl back to the kitchen and hide in the basement, locking the door from the inside."

"I'm not leaving you."

Gods, but she could give Quinn a run for his money when it came to stubborn and pigheaded. Forcing the calm he really didn't feel, Drake pushed every ounce of reason into his voice he could gather up. "I get that, but we don't know what sort of power he's got, Emerson. The snake is a huge variable and possibly a big advantage. I need to know you'll do the right thing. I need to know you'll be safe."

"And damn it, Drake, I need to know you'll be safe. My magic can heal."

He forced bravado into his tone, desperate to get her to leave. "I heal pretty fine all by myself."

That small frame stood still—immovable—as she stared up at him. "You don't know if you'd have healed from the poison of the snakebite." He opened his mouth to protest, but she placed a finger on his lips. "But with my magic, you *did* heal."

He pressed a kiss to her finger. *"Please*, Emerson. Please go."

Drake saw the hesitation—saw the unwillingness to acquiesce—before something changed. An awareness, really, that lit up her eyes with an understanding he'd never seen before. She reached up on her toes and pressed her lips to his cheek, just below his ear. With a whisper, she added, "I'll do it for you, if it comes to that. But trust me that I can make the right judgment if I'm called to."

It was enough. It had to be.

Then there were no more promises or what ifs or maybes as Magnus Carano came down the hallway and into the dining room on a heavy war cry.

Emerson felt the wall pressed to her back as a wall of Warriors stood in a battle phalanx to her front. Aside from their sheer numbers, the set of their bodies and easy familiarity with one another was clearly to their advantage. Ignoring the fact there was a China cabinet on the far side of the room and a table long enough to seat twenty, she could easily envision them on a battlefield.

Her brother materialized in the doorway, and she fought the words forming on her lips. No matter how badly she wanted to drag him aside and demand answers, she needed to let this play out.

"I'm not here for a fight." Magnus's voice quavered slightly and she was reminded of the games they'd played as children. He hated to lose, no matter the game. From Red Rover to Monopoly, that same quaver would alight in his voice the moment he knew he was at a disadvantage. "I want what you stole from me."

Although this was the Warriors' show, she simply couldn't keep quiet. Couldn't lose the opportunity to get some answers. "Why do you want the book, Magnus?"

His dark eyes widened in surprise as he realized she stood behind the line of Warriors. "Em?"

"It's me. And I want to know why you want the book. It looks like a diary of some sort, and since it's written in Greek, it's most certainly not yours."

"It belongs to me."

"Are you sure about that?" Drake interrupted.

"It's mine." That quaver was back. It matched the sudden agitation in his body as he shifted from foot to foot.

"Please answer the question, Magnus. Why do you want it?"

Whatever fear drove him erupted as he screamed, "Give me the goddamn book!"

Although she had a clear view of her brother, Drake blocked her, his shoulders set in a stiff line as he faced Magnus. She reached out a hand and settled it against his lower back, the simple touch and the warmth of his body going a long way toward reassuring her.

When had her brother's life gone so wrong? How had they missed the signs and why couldn't they have done something before it was too late? Before it had gotten to . . . *this*.

"I think you need to leave, Magnus." Even as she said the words, she knew it wouldn't be that simple.

"Give me what I've asked for and I'll go. I'll walk out that door and you'll never see my miserable face again. I'll make it right with Eris and make her leave you alone. Leave you all alone."

The line shifted slightly, the battle-ready tension palpable in the men and women who stood between her and her brother. Despite the tense moments, no one interfered, understanding that she needed to ask the questions.

"Make what right with Eris?"

"Em. You wouldn't understand."

And there it was. The same excuse he'd used their entire lives, varied slightly depending on the occasion.

You wouldn't understand, Em.

You don't know what I'm dealing with, Em.

Get off my back, Em.

"Try me." When he didn't say anything more, she shifted tactics. "What did you mean you'd make things right with Eris?"

Magnus shot a derisive glare at the line of Warriors. "You all think you're so tough. So immune. She's worth a hundred of you. And more powerful, too."

"So what makes you think you have the power to call her off?"

"She'll listen to me on this."

Somehow, she doubted it. But whatever lies Eris had woven around her brother had pretty much eliminated his already questionable judgment.

"Magnus, I can help you. We can help you. These are good people, and we can find a way to make this right."

Drake shifted, reaching for the hand she still had on his back. In that moment, Emerson realized just how true the words she spoke really were.

"And you think I'm delusional. They're a group of vigilantes who go around keeping their own brand of law and order. Hell, this one"—Magnus pointed to

Rogan—"is fucking Eris. You think that makes him a hero? You think that makes all of them heroes?"

"It certainly doesn't make your behavior okay."

"It doesn't make it wrong, either." With that, he leaped, the move far more decisive than his nervous behavior would have indicated.

Magnus hit the end of the line. Kane bore the brunt of the attack, with Ilsa caught in the fray as all three fell to the ground. Emerson watched as a symphony of movement rose up and out of the fray of bodies before Magnus moved back again, balancing on the balls of his feet.

Kane lay in the corner of the room, a large cut on his head pouring with blood as Ilsa hovered over him. Quinn was still on his feet, but he'd taken a few hits as well, as evidenced by the split lip and ripening bruise on his eye.

"You can't take down all these people, Magnus."

"Not by myself. It's a good thing I brought help." The snake she'd been so afraid of seeing again slithered from Magnus's shoulders and fell to the floor next to him. Coiled, it lifted its head and hissed at all of them.

"Ava. Ilsa. Montana. Emerson. In the kitchen," Brody ordered them. "We need more room."

The snake had already anticipated the move and slithered toward the swinging door, blocking any movement. In that moment, it became evident Magnus had a sizable advantage. The reach of the snake would ensure he could manage two ends of the line, and the bunched nature of how they stood there in formation would keep the Warriors' tattoos from full range of motion or freedom.

They were trapped.

Emerson leaned forward and whispered in Drake's ear, "Do you have the diary?"

"Quinn's got it locked in a safe upstairs."

"Good."

"What are you going to do?"

"It seems I'm the only one with an advantage at the moment. Jump in as soon as you have an opening."

Stepping around Drake, she lifted her hand and felt the power well up from her stomach, through her chest cavity and down her arms. Diligently avoiding thinking about the fact that the person who was going to receive the blast was her brother, she let go with a stream of fire directed at the snake.

The heat welled from her fingertips in a rush, the fire a surprisingly potent weapon that grew and expanded in her palm. Emerson tried to make sense of it, even as she kept her focus on the snake.

What was this?

She'd used her gifts before, but never with such precision or strength. Not only was the fire more potent—more focused—it seemed to grow the more she used it, like a building inferno.

She glanced down and saw that her other hand was still linked to Drake.

Was it possible?

Breaking the hold of their fingers, she recognized the loss of power immediately. Felt the change in every cell of her body. The fire was lighter somehow, and it went wild, as if a cross-stream of air lit under it. The steady stream that had held the snake in place wavered, giving the animal a break so it could slither in closer to the Warriors.

Unwilling to waste time trying to figure it out, she reached for Drake again, the connection garnering immediate results. The flame returned, more focused and so hot it edged in blue as the fire coated the snake's body in a steady arc.

Magnus screamed in pain, stumbling away from where he engaged in a fight with Quinn, answering the question of how closely connected he was to the snake.

"Drake. Don't let go of me."

"I have to get in there."

He started to move forward, but she held on to him. "The fire's not as focused when I'm not touching you."

"Quinn, Rogan," Drake ordered, "you take the lead."

The two Warriors ran forward and Emerson kept the stream of fire on the snake as they moved in next to Magnus. The animal had completely stopped moving and lay coiled, its skin charred black. When they had her brother firmly in hand, she pulled back on her magic.

"What the hell was that, Em? How'd you do that?"

"I'm done, Magnus. Start explaining, or I'm going to make sure these lovely people lock you up like a fucking criminal."

"No, seriously. I've never seen you do anything like that. What did you do? Where'd you get magic like that?"

She shrugged, suddenly self-conscious to have it called out. "It's inside of me."

"It's unheard of. Grandma can't do that. Mom couldn't do it, either. How'd you get power like that?"

"It's not power, Magnus. It's magic. It's a gift and it needs to be used as such."

"It's remarkable."

The snake shifted slightly, the charred scales fading into a new, bright pink as Magnus's immortality healed it. They didn't have much time.

"Can Drake and I have a few minutes with my brother? I can bind him if you'd prefer." She winced at the thought, but knew it was the only way to gain their agreement.

Rogan and Quinn hesitated, but it was Drake who supported her. "Please let her have a few minutes."

"Let's go check on Kane." Quinn and Rogan moved through the swinging door to the kitchen, the implied threat of how close they were not lost on anyone.

Shifting her attention back to her healing brother, Emerson created a circle of fire around him, careful to keep the flames away from him as she did so. "Magnus, please let me help you. Whatever you've gotten yourself into, we can get you out of."

Her brother laughed. "Just like that night after the park. You wanted answers that night, too."

Despite the warmth emanating from her body, icy-cold dread coursed through her bloodstream. "What do you mean?"

"Come on. You knew it was me. You had to know."

The tears she'd refused to shed all those years ago welled up now, his acknowledgment as painful as if no time had passed at all. "He was an innocent man, Magnus."

"In the wrong place at the wrong time. I didn't do it on purpose."

"But you did it. You killed him."

"I've had a long time to live with it, and yes." His dark gaze never wavered. "Yes, I did."

The usual urge to rant and rail at him never manifested. Instead, all she felt was an unbearable sadness.

Her brother was lost. Maybe he had been for a very long time, but the truth staring back at her was the final straw.

The snake moved again and she took a few steps back, the flames going higher with her anxiety. "Could you at least put that . . . *thing* . . . away."

Magnus lifted an eyebrow. "Unlike your ring of fire, here, I'm not going to use it on you."

"Like you weren't going to use it on her before?" Drake shot back, his anger from earlier clearly not gone. "You could have killed her with your lack of control."

"It's weakened."

"It lives in your aura," Drake pushed at him. "It's not something separate."

"Look. I just want the diary back. Give it to me and I'll go away. If you believe nothing else, believe that."

"Why'd you take it from her? You had to know Eris would want it back."

"Insurance. And a deep desire to know exactly what I was."

Drake's voice dripped with disdain. "It must have been a big surprise to realize it was in Greek."

"Look, I just took it. I didn't have time to flip through it first."

"Why not just ask her what she did?"

"I needed to know everything."

"So you took a deal with a goddess and didn't know the terms? Bad move, Magnus."

Magnus shot Drake a dark look but didn't back

down from his point. "She made promises. You've been through the experience. Surely you can understand I'd like to know what I'm up against."

"Actually, I can't. But then again, I didn't sell my soul, which is the effective equivalent of what you did with Eris."

"Yeah. And I'm pretty sure there's no getting it back." With that, Magnus evaporated before their eyes.

Chapter Thirteen

Drake took in the chaos of the kitchen as he and Emerson cleared the swinging door. Ilsa held her hand over an ice pack against Kane's head while Montana doctored a cut on Quinn's lip. All in all, they'd escaped relatively unscathed, but the nervous tension of battle hadn't yet evaporated.

"He's gone?" Quinn mumbled around the towel against his mouth.

"The snake regenerated, Magnus made excuses and then he disappeared." Drake tucked Emerson under his arm, the need to hold her a palpable thing inside of him. "What I want to know is how the hell he got in here in the first place."

Quinn threw the towel onto the counter. "I haven't figured that out yet. Best I can tell, he did something to the front door."

"No one walks up and gets into this house, Quinn." Not even Emerson. He'd just given her the codes months ago and only her grandmother'd had them before that.

"I'm working on it," Quinn snapped. "The front door was locked but not fully activated."

"Which meant it was me." All eyes in the room turned on Rogan, a heavy silence accompanying the collective scrutiny. "I was the last one in."

Magnus's taunts when he'd first arrived crystallized in Drake's mind. "Convenient."

"How's that, Fish?" Rogan's green gaze never wavered as they stared each other down.

"You fuck Eris, then show up here and leave our front door unattended."

"You think I left the alarm off on purpose?"

Quinn and Brody moved to the center of the room and placed themselves between him and Rogan, but Drake was beyond caring.

He'd trusted Rogan. Believed in him, just as he believed in all his brothers. And the man's fucking dick had put Emerson in danger. Had put all of them in danger. "What do you want me to think?"

"Drake. That's enough," Emerson hissed at him.

He heard her—heard the subtle undertone in her words to stop—but couldn't back down. Wouldn't back down. "You've got a different explanation than the fact that you've been fucking our enemy?"

Rogan took another step closer. "Since you're fucking the enemy's sister, I don't think you have a lot of room to talk."

"Fuck you!" Drake dived at Rogan. Anger writhed through his system, coiling with the ferocity of the snake that had attacked them. His fist connected with Rogan's cheek on a hard thud, the crack of bone unmistakable.

No one would talk about Emerson that way. The fact it was one of his Warrior brothers made it that much more unacceptable.

"Drake!" Abstractly, he heard Emerson's screams as he landed another punch on Rogan. The archer managed to get one back on him before Quinn and Brody pulled them off each other. Drake felt himself being dragged across the kitchen, but his gaze never wavered off of Rogan.

"I didn't do this, Drake. I didn't purposely let him in."

Quinn's grip was tight where he had him pinned against the wall and Drake shoved at him, desperate to get a few more shots in on Rogan. "Get off me."

"Calm the hell down."

"I'm fine."

Their Taurus wasn't so easily fooled. "I'm not letting go of you until you prove to me you're not going to march straight back over there and pick up where you left off."

"Drake." Emerson laid a hand on his shoulder and he dragged his gaze off Quinn. "Drake. It's okay. Stop this. Please. Just stop."

His shoulders relaxed under Quinn's grip and he felt the bull respond in kind. The moment he had range of motion, he pulled Emerson into his arms.

"It's okay," she whispered against his chest.

He pressed his lips to her hair. "I want to get you out of here. Where do you want to go?"

"Home. Take me home."

"I can't do that."

"Then let's go upstate to my aunt's house. The one I told you about with the cows. It's mine now. And I have the tools there I need to do some work. We need to figure out what the hell's going on."

"Let's go."

Drake had explained they couldn't port since he didn't have a visual of where they were going. Which was how, after the blowup in the kitchen of Warrior Central, she found herself taking the trip upstate in a sweet little Audi sports car she'd had no idea he owned.

They'd cleared the city limits twenty minutes before and his grip on the steering wheel hadn't lessened; nor had his mood lifted above tense and distracted.

With a series of strokes that were borderline covetous, she ran her hands over the dashboard. "If I'd known you had this car, I'd've bugged you to let me drive it months ago."

He glanced over at the comment and she saw his hands relax a bit on the wheel. "What makes you think I'd let you drive it?"

"You're crazy about me, Ace. You can't deny me anything."

"I would have no problem denying you driving privileges in my Roadster."

"Not if I'd employed some creative ways to convince you, involving my lips and tongue and your very persuadable cock."

The car was a sweet driving machine, but even precision steering couldn't keep him from veering slightly off the road at her words. Emerson couldn't hold back

the laughter at his response, the sheer joy of being desired and wanted too wonderful to hold back.

Especially after the fight she'd witnessed.

Drake had defended her against his fellow Warrior.
And while she likely would have been pissed if he
hadn't, the pure violence in his movements had caught
her off guard.

He and Rogan had fought together for millennia
and, despite knowing each other for only a year, he'd
taken her side. Believed in her.

Defended her.

"Why'd you do it?"

The smile she'd managed to draw out with her earlier comments faded in the light of a pair of oncoming
headlights. "No one speaks of you like that."

Tiny flutters swamped her belly, but she couldn't
hold back her point. "His question wasn't entirely out
of line."

"He insulted you and he insulted what's between
us, Emerson. It's that simple."

"You really are a surprise, Drake."

"How so?"

"You're just so . . ." She broke off, trying to figure out
the right word. "Solid. You come off like nothing fazes
you and then you have these moments where this fiery
passion inside just leaps out and swamps you. I don't
know who you are."

"I've told you before, I'm a simple guy. What you
see is what you get. But just because I'm simple doesn't
mean I'm easy."

No, she had to admit, he wasn't easy at all. In fact,

he was downright hard and prickly and difficult when he set his mind to something.

Emerson was suddenly grateful for the darkened interior and the limited amount of lights on the back country roads. There was an intimacy here she didn't normally allow, as if the lack of light and the seat belts that kept them to opposite sides of the car gave a place to comfortably sit back and observe.

To get a sense of what made him tick.

"How do you hold it back? The passion?"

"I watch and wait and I don't feel the need to act on every little thing. But when it matters, I'm not hiding how I feel and I'm not standing down."

"Obviously." A thoughtful pause filled the air before she added, "You and your brothers act pretty decisively and not always in agreement."

"We're all different. Just because we're immortal doesn't make us any less human, with all the foibles and faults that come with it."

"Are you sorry you punched Rogan?"

"No."

"Not even a little bit?"

He turned toward her as much as the drive would allow. "No, Emerson, I'm not sorry. Not in the least. What he said was the deepest insult to you and it won't happen in my presence."

Not for the first time, visions of the knights and Warriors she'd read about all her life in books and stories filled her mind's eye. This old-fashioned streak was something she could get used to.

Maybe, she admitted to herself, she already had.

With that thought came another. "What if he has feelings for her?"

"Rogan? For Eris?" Drake let out a heavy snort, the implacable stubborn streak she associated with his Warrior brothers making its appearance. "Impossible."

"How do you know?"

"Oh, come on. He's getting his rocks off, nothing more."

"The same could be said for us."

"That's not what we're about."

"To you, maybe." Or to me, she added silently to herself. "But you don't know what goes on behind closed doors."

"Last time I checked, you weren't secretly plotting to bring down my family."

"I'll give you that, but I still don't think it's as black and white as you seem to want to make it." The image of Rogan's face as he told them about the alarm on the front door—the sheer agony that rode his cheekbones as he admitted his failure—wasn't made up. "And it's not like he tried to hide his relationship with her or anything."

"He's been hiding it for a long time now."

The "subject closed" sign blinked in bright neon and she knew she wasn't going to get any further this evening. She'd let him process it for a while—would think through it herself—before she brought it up again. "Just think about it."

They spent a few more minutes in silence before he turned toward her. "Why here? This farm?"

"I don't know."

"Don't know or don't want to tell me?"

Emerson thought about it for a moment. They'd come a long way in the last few days. Maybe it was just the inevitability of what had been building between them for the past year, but she found she didn't want to hide her thoughts.

"I like it up here. I feel . . . comfortable here. Like I fit."

"You don't feel that way in the city?"

"I love the city and I love living there, but that's my life. Which means it includes all the shitty moments and the things I don't necessarily want to remember, along with all the things I do love and want to remember. But up here . . ."

She stared out the window at the passing scenery. The traffic-filled streets and well-traveled highways had given way to back roads and long stretches of fields that made it hard to believe Manhattan was less than an hour away.

"I can also access my tools. I'm a decent hand at scrying and I'd like to try to get a handle on Magnus while I'm here. I prefer to do it in the presence of another."

"There are risks?"

She'd never been able to define it, but she'd never quite shaken the fear of getting lost in the images in the mirror. "I just like knowing there's someone watching my back."

"Then I'm your guy." After a moment, he added, "Is there any other reason you picked this place?"

"I have good memories up here. Good memories of my family and good memories of who I am."

"Tell me one of them."

"The summer I was eight." The image filled her mind's eye, so vivid and crisp she could still hear the June bugs as their noise filled the evening sky. "We'd gone to a nearby dairy for ice cream and Magnus, Veronica and I were sitting there licking cones and trying to keep them from dripping."

"What flavor did you get?"

"What?" She broke out of the memory to look at him, bemused by the question. "What flavor did I get?"

"Sure. They say ice cream flavor has a lot to say about a person. I'm a fudge ripple man, myself."

"Mint chocolate chip. I've always liked the color. Wicked-witch green."

His bark of laughter was contagious, and she couldn't hide her own giggles. "Is that some sort of personal statement on your chosen profession?"

"Nah. I'd call it a delicious coincidence."

"Fair enough. So you were eating your very green ice cream. Then what happened?"

"Magnus's chocolate started to drip, and Veronica laughed that he wasn't eating it fast enough. And then she froze a drop from his cone, midair."

"With magic?"

"Yep. She was twelve at the time and hadn't yet developed her loathing for the practice of magic. Instead, she laughed and laughed as this bead of chocolate floated between the bottom of his cone and the ground."

Emerson could still remember the moment. The carefree laughter between all three of them as they sat there on a picnic bench beside the barn. She saw the fireflies that winked in the night air and felt the light summer breeze that floated over her skin.

"Your parents didn't mind you practicing magic where someone might see?"

"There are quite a few practicing witches in this area, so there wasn't the need for such secrecy. And we've always been careful. I didn't fully understand it when I was younger, but my mother did. She encouraged us to practice in safe spaces, as she called them, and know when it wasn't appropriate to let loose with our gifts."

Drake nodded, his voice gentle when he spoke. "It sounds like a nice memory."

"It gets better." She smiled and shifted in her seat so she could look at him more closely. "So there's this drop of chocolate hovering there and we're pointing and laughing at it and, out of nowhere, I got the urge to melt it."

"Your talent manifested itself that early?"

"Yep. I felt the fire come right out of my stomach and course through my body. For the briefest moment I thought I'd eaten too much and was going to be sick, but then it just . . . happened."

"Fire?"

"A small stream of it. More than enough to melt the cold chocolate."

"What did Magnus and Veronica do?"

"They were surprised at first. Veronica hadn't had her abilities for very long and she was still learning the ins and outs. She certainly hadn't had any indication of what she could do at eight."

"But you did."

"Yep. So after we all stared at the chocolate drip on the ground, we got over it and went back to laughing and carrying on. And Veronica and I spent the rest of the time trying to freeze and melt each other's ice cream."

"What about Magnus?"

"He just sat and watched and ate the rest of his cone."

* * *

Magnus could still feel the heat washing over his shoulders as he pouted on the stiff wooden bench. The park had been in his mind's eye as he ported out of the Warriors' house and he'd been sitting there for hours.

He knew his sister had power. He'd always known it. But what she'd wielded tonight?

It was *awesome*.

It was also some scary shit that his little sister could fry things with her fingers.

She'd always been gifted. From a very early age they'd all intuitively understood that Emerson was different. But this? This was off the charts.

How hadn't he realized it before?

Hell, if he'd known she had this much power, maybe he could have avoided his stupid deal with Eris altogether. Emerson could have taught him how to do what she did. He'd be powerful in his own right.

The snake curled over his back, the continued healing ensuring it stayed in constant motion. The unceasing movement was also a reminder of exactly what he'd agreed to when he'd thrown his lot in with Eris.

Although it had seemed like an outrageously good idea at the time, he'd spent the ensuing months trying to remember what he'd hoped to gain. Buyer's remorse? Or just a complete inability to remember why it had seemed like such a good idea at the time?

He knew he'd made an easy mark of himself, hanging with a group of people he had no business knowing. It was always easy to find the drug dealers in a city and the gang that ran Budapest had been no different. He'd found them within days of arriving in the city and had started with a few odd jobs, working his way up.

He'd intended only to drift for a while. Make a bit of money and get his life back in order. More than three years later he'd still been there, managing one of the city's largest networks.

And then everything had changed the night Eris showed up.

Long and lean, she wore a leather halter top that showed off a spectacular pair of breasts and leather pants sculpted to fit her ass.

He'd been hooked, as had the rest of them.

She was mesmerizing and it wasn't just her outrageous body.

They'd gotten in a huge shipment and were divvying it up for selling. Eris had just appeared in the flop where they were hiding, cutting up the stash.

Without anyone realizing why or how, she just took over.

Three months later she'd turned him into *this*.

The air grew heavy without even a hint of a warning, and then she was sitting next to him, her nails digging into his thigh. The overwhelming urge to try and outrun her filled his muscles, but he sat still.

Unmoving.

Which was more than he could say for the fucking snake on his shoulders. Damn it, but the thing just would not stop moving. Endlessly moving, never stopping.

"So, Chuckles. Miss me?"

"I always miss you."

"You've got a funny way of showing it."

He opted to stay silent. Eris knew everything—somewhere deep inside he'd known it all along—and any lies he told to avoid detection would only be revisited back upon him.

"You've had quite a run the last twenty-four hours. Attacking your sister. Stealing my personal property. Invading the Warriors' home."

"I—"

She cut him off with a finger to the lips. "Save it."

Fine. If that's how she wanted to play it, he'd keep his mouth shut and take his lumps.

"Do you know why I picked you? Why you were the one, out of all those fuckwits in Budapest, who I decided to turn?"

He didn't know the answer, but now that he had an opportunity to find out, he was strangely curious. Sitting up taller, he shook his head. "No."

"Because you've got something inside of you, Magnus. Something untapped. You've got potential."

"Is there a reason I feel like Marlon Brando right now? Am I a contender or something?"

The slap cracked across his face before he could even gather himself. "Do you think I have any interest in surrounding myself with inept idiots?"

"Of course not."

"They why do you insist on acting like one?"

"I'm not—"

"Look. I'm not interested in excuses. Nor do I care about what came before. Your sister's boyfriend took something from me. And after you left my diary out in plain sight, he took something else. Now you're going to help me get both of them back."

"You think I don't want to get that diary back? That's why I went over there in the first place."

"Like you could battle a house full of Warriors who have numbers and familiar surroundings on their side."

He rolled his shoulders. "The snake gives me an advantage."

"Yes, it does, but it doesn't give you that big an advantage. You played this one for shit."

"You think I don't know that? You don't think if I could go back and change it, I would?"

"I've invested too much in you to give up yet. So I'm going to give you another chance."

"What do you want me to do?"

Emerson rolled over into a very large, very broad chest and couldn't stop the small sigh that welled up in her throat. Her gaze traveled down over the washboard abs and the morning erection that tented his fitted briefs and felt an answering curl in her belly.

Good Lord, he was magnificent.

On the outside as well as in.

Their conversation the night before replayed in her mind. Her heart gave a little tug as she remembered the sweet expression on his face when he asked her what flavor ice cream she liked. There was a beautiful simplicity about him. Like he knew exactly who he was, no matter what happened to the world around him.

Drake shifted again, throwing an arm over his head, unaware of her scrutiny as he slept. They'd made it to the cabin a little after midnight, dragged themselves into the bedroom and fallen facedown in the sleep of the dead. Based on the angle of the sun streaming in through the window, it had to be almost noon.

She pushed at him slightly as her body hung perilously close to the edge of the bed, but he only grunted, never moving from where he lay sprawled on his back.

Since she made it a policy to never stay through the night, waking up next to him was an entirely new experience. Somehow she'd just never envisioned him as a bed hog.

Or as a furnace.

The covers were kicked down around their feet and she didn't even miss them, he was putting off so much body heat. Of course, waking up next to such a delicious man didn't exactly leave a woman feeling cold and lonely.

Emerson let out a small squeak as Drake opened one lazy eye to stare at her. "I can hear your thoughts."

Feigning a level of disdain she didn't truly feel, she stared down her nose at him. "I'm quite sure that's impossible."

"No, not really." His groggy, sleep-filled voice was extra sexy as he scooted over to give her more room.

"Okay, Mr. Know-it-all, what am I thinking?"

He lifted a heavy arm to count off on his fingers. "I hog the bed, we slept in too late and I've got quite the morning package, which you'd like to unwrap as soon as humanly possible."

"Drake!" She leaped off the bed like a cat who'd been thrown in a tub. "I most certainly did not think those things."

"Did too." His laugh was low and lazy as he grabbed a pillow and stuffed it against the headboard. Propping those impressive arms behind his head, he added, "Come on back and I'll show you just how right you are."

"You're a horny bastard in the morning."

"I'm a horny bastard all the time." His grin turned positively wicked and those genie's eyes flashed with promise. "This morning I'm just a man who knows how to take advantage of opportunity."

Recognizing a losing battle—and the increasing realization that she wanted to climb straight back into bed—she left the room and headed for the small bag Callie had packed for her, which she'd left in the bathroom. After digging out a toothbrush and toothpaste, she hollered back in his direction, "You're right about one thing. It is late."

If he responded, she didn't hear anything over the running water. It was only when she lifted her head to look in the mirror that she realized he stood behind her. "Drake! You scared me."

With one hand he pulled her close, his mouth unerringly covering her toothpaste-stained lips while with the other he flipped on the taps in the shower. "What are you doing?" she mumbled against his mouth, even as she felt her knees going weak at the sensual assault of his lips.

"Multitasking."

"Multi—" The words died out as his tongue swept the seam of her lips, his teeth following with a playful nip.

"I'm saving all that time we don't have," he whispered back before pulling her fully into his arms. "*And* letting you unwrap my package."

Chapter Fourteen

Finley mentally tallied up the number of meetings she'd missed over the last several days and tried not to wince at the image of her career flushing down the toilet. Every day she spent out of the office and away from her cases was another day lost to someone else in the DA's office.

"You doing okay this morning?" Grey padded from her spare bedroom into her kitchen and headed straight for the mug she'd set out next to the coffeepot.

"Fine." She tried to keep the amusement out of her voice but knew she hadn't succeeded when he turned from the pot to give her a look.

"What?"

"I just never expected to see you in sweatpants and a T-shirt."

"I don't sleep in a suit, Finley."

"Could have fooled me."

"Actually, I sleep naked. I just put this on before coming into your kitchen."

The lethal grin and suggestive words hit her somewhere in the vicinity of her panties. She struggled for something to say and then shut her mouth completely, opting for a sip of coffee instead.

Grey took the bar stool opposite her and sat down. "So really. How are you doing today?"

"You mean besides the great colossal mess my job has become?"

"Look, I've told you. We'll get this figured out and you can go back to your life. I talked to Drake last night. He and Emerson are trying a few things to dig deeper into Eris's plans through her brother."

"It's not that simple. Getting back to my life."

"Sure it is."

"No, Grey, it's not." Finley wasn't sure why she was so upset, but the anger she'd held back over the last few days burst forth. She was grateful for his protection, but the heavy-handed routine had to stop.

"Most of us aren't freaking *gods* who can come and go as they please, live in crazy huge mansions and forget about making a living. I'm a grown woman with a life and a career and people who care about me." Which was only a small lie. She had people who wondered about her, but cared?

Worried?

That might be a stretch.

"I make a living."

"No, you have a hobby," she shot back.

"Actually, I do work. I'd never have taken the gig if I was supposed to sit around on my ass."

"And what, exactly, is your gig?"

"We'll get to that. First, I have to say you've asked a surprising lack of questions for a lawyer."

Grey's gaze washed over her, the move a combination of sexy appreciation and an acknowledgment she had an actual brain in her head. Finley couldn't quite shake the warmth that unfurled in her bloodstream that had nothing to with the hot coffee she was currently gulping like a lifeline.

"I learned in law school not to ask questions I don't want the answers to. Besides, I did a fair amount of digging on you before this all started."

"You did?" It was his turn to be amused and she could hear the smile that tinged the edges of his deep voice.

"I did. The complete and absolute lack of information in any and all city systems got me curious, so I started observing."

"And what did you find?"

"A man who puts his waitresses and busboys through college. Pays for day care for their kids so they can work. Ensures they've got transportation when they get off shift at four a.m."

A small sweep of red crept up his neck at her assessment.

Score!

"You're sort of a good guy, Grey Bennett." Finley thought about that soul-searing kiss in his office the night of the warehouse sting.

You're also the most compelling man I've ever met.

"Don't paint me out to be a hero, Finley. You'll only meet with disappointment."

She cocked her head at that, and for the first time

since their little adventure began, she felt like she might have the upper hand. "Oh, I don't know about that. Besides, you're a puzzle and I've never been able to stay away from those."

"If you really want to work through a puzzle, we need to figure out who's running information in the DA's office."

"You're avoiding my questions."

"No, I'm really not," Grey muttered as he got up to grab another cup of coffee. "I just prefer to focus on questions that have actual answers."

"You want me to do what?"

"Fire at me."

Emerson stood beside the pond out behind the farmhouse, squishing in the mud along the banks in a pair of rubber boots as she tried to make him see reason. Drake stood hip deep in the water wearing nothing but a pair of shorts.

"Drake, you may be in the water, but I'll hurt you. You saw what it did to Magnus. He looked really uncomfortable."

"I'm not asking you to napalm me for ten minutes. I just want you to have a go at me."

"But it's going to hurt."

"You said that already. Come on, Emerson, just do it."

"I can't."

"Oh for fuck's sake, woman. Pretend you're mad at me or something."

"I'm telling you, I can't do it."

"Sure you can. Pretend I'm asking you not to leave my bed, darling."

She raised an eyebrow at him, but the barb stuck. "That's not fair."

"Oh. And it's fair of you leave me lonely and unfulfilled each and every night when you sneak home?"

Lonely and unfulfilled?

Seriously?

"That's a lie and you know it."

He clutched at his chest. "My body may be sated, but my heart never will be."

"Asshole."

"I thought I was a horny bastard."

"You're that, too."

"Come on and hit me." He cocked his head. "Or are you afraid?"

"And those would be the magic words, Ace." She pulled on the fire, let it course through her body and fill her up. Extending her hands, she let go with a stream straight at his chest.

He let out a loud grunt, but stood still and took it.

Unlike the day before, when she'd felt like she had a flamethrower at the ends of her hands, the fire was back to its old strength. It was steady but didn't have the same potency. She dropped her arms, pulling back on the power. "You okay?"

"I'm fine."

"You look like you've got a sunburn."

"You can kiss it and make it all better." He sank lower in the water. "Okay. I'm going to let my tat out and I want you to do it again."

She stumbled at that, almost losing her footing. "You can let it out?"

"Sure."

"But it's not an animal."

A small, affronted look flashed across his face as he narrowed his eyes. "Fish are animals."

"I mean it's not a land animal. Like Kane's scorpion or Quinn's bull."

"Which does make it a little less effective in hand-to-hand combat. Lucky for me, I can do also a few tricks with any available water at hand. I'll have you know I'm hell on fish tanks."

The overwhelming feeling of being off-kilter again struck her, along with how good it felt to just stand there and banter with him. Despite all her internal protests about what a bad idea it was for the two of them to couple up, she couldn't ignore one simple fact, no matter how hard she tried.

She enjoyed spending time with him.

"Okay. By all means, release the hounds."

One dark brow arched above that greenish gold, but he didn't say anything, just sank himself chest deep in the water. A light splash sounded as the fish hit the surface of the pond and began swimming around him in a circle.

"You're really doing that?"

"Yep."

"I mean, you're controlling it."

"Pretty much."

She moved in closer, fascinated to see the bright, beautiful scales as the fish swam in a continuous circle around his body. "But that's the interesting part. Magnus couldn't control his."

"It's early in his powers. He probably doesn't know how yet."

"You have to learn it?"

"Well, yeah. It's like any other new thing. You have to take time to get used to it. To adjust and learn what you can do. I still figure out new tricks from time to time."

The fact they were even having this conversation was surreal, but when she focused on what he was actually saying, she had to admit Drake had a valid point. Despite coming in to her powers at an early age, there were still things she learned. Ways to conserve her energy and expand what she was doing. Even the night before, when she'd realized that touching him harnessed her strength, it was a moment of growth with her gift.

"So Magnus is vulnerable right now because he's still figuring it all out?"

Drake nodded, his gaze sparking with awareness as he picked up on her line of questions. "I'd say yes, although he's not to be underestimated. That snake's awfully powerful. And the poison can do some damage. Beheading is the only way to kill an immortal, but poison is nasty in its own right."

"Like Kane," Emerson added, remembering.

"Exactly."

"But if we could get to Magnus soon enough—" She let the thought hang there, unfinished, as images of her brother through the years flew through her mind. Magnus's problems had started long before he was turned into . . . whatever he was. This new development only added to an existing problem.

Her gaze dropped to the fish that still swam in circles around Drake.

Maybe they could get to her brother soon enough. But if they couldn't, they needed to understand the power they had at their disposal.

"Okay. What do you want me to do?"

Drake hesitated briefly, before pointing to his chest. "Try the fire again."

Pulling on the flames, she let the fire stream from her fingers, again aiming for the center of his chest. She nearly dropped her arms when she saw one of the fish leap out of the water and block the fire.

He grinned but waved his fingers in a come-hither motion. "Don't stop."

Focusing again, she pushed more power into the flame, trying to harness it into a tight stream of heat. She saw him wince when she made contact with his chest, then nearly dropped it again when one of the fish leaped up and knocked back the flame.

"How are you doing that?"

"I'm using the power in my aura to push back on the flames."

"But it's not burning you through the fish."

"Nope."

"But it did burn Magnus." She let another stream fly, focusing every thought into it. Another shiny flash of scales, and the flame cut off.

"He hasn't figured out how to protect himself yet."

"You're really doing that."

"I could say the same thing about you." With gentle movements, Drake reached forward and took her hands, pulling her forward. She felt the mud at the bottom of the pond suck at her boots, but still she moved ahead.

Unerringly forward.

When they were close enough, Drake lifted one of her hands and pressed his lips to her palm. "It's inside you. This amazing power."

The underlying awe in his voice touched something inside of her and Emerson felt a tight knot she didn't know she carried untie from the very depths of her soul. His acceptance—and celebration—of who she was mattered.

He mattered.

Waves of sensation coursed through her body, hard and pulsing, as his breath feathered over her palm and down her wrist. "How is it possible?"

He pressed his lips again and added the slightest flick of his tongue. "How's what possible?"

She wanted to ask him how he beat back the fire, but all she could concentrate on was them. On the fire that consumed them both with a magic unlike anything she'd ever felt before.

The hot sun beat down on her back as her nipples beaded in the exquisite sensations brought on by his mouth. Such a simple touch—just his lips on her palm—but . . . *so* amazing . . . so . . . How could he pull such incredible feelings?

"How do you do that?" The words came out on a heavy sigh as she felt her eyelids droop.

"You mean this?" He pulled her closer, lifting her hand so that he brought her fingers to his lips. With aching slowness, he took one into his mouth, drawing heavily with his tongue.

The suction tugged at every part of her, from her

sensitized nipples to the hot warmth at the apex of her thighs.

"Drake?"

He pulled harder with his mouth and used his other hand to pull her flush with his body. The thin material of his shorts couldn't hide his heavy erection, and she felt another answering tug in her core.

"I want you."

They stumbled out of the water and across the yard, a set of fluffy deck chairs on the back porch their destination. Drake had them across the yard in moments, his lips fused to hers. She pulled on his neck, ready to drop into the chair when he stopped her.

"No. Wait." She stood there, puzzled when he dragged the reclining lawn chair off the porch and into the yard.

"What?"

"Lay down." He was already tugging on the thin material of her tank top. The warmth of the rare Indian-summer day bathed their bodies and she reveled in the sun that streamed over her naked skin.

He made equally quick work of her shorts, then gently pushed her back on the thick cushions of the sun-bathing chair. Before she could catch her breath, he was kneeling before her, his hands on her thighs.

"I want to look at you."

"Drake." She wanted to be embarrassed—wanted to shy away from the dark desire that filled his gaze—but all she felt was an answering need. On a nod, she opened for him and nearly had her first orgasm as he looked his fill.

"You are so beautiful."

She wanted to protest, almost did, when he stopped her with a smile. "You're gorgeous, so shut up and enjoy it."

And then there were no more words as his mouth came down on the absolute center of the fire that coursed and pulsed between them. Somewhere in the back of her mind, she thought she might have screamed as his mouth took possession of her body.

With long, wicked strokes of his tongue he drew and drew, pulling her just to the edge of peak before he retreated, forcing her to wait.

Forcing her to need.

"Drake!"

The use of his name drove him harder, the same dragging suction he'd used on her finger now at the very epicenter of her pleasure.

A light breeze coursed over her, adding to the sheer bliss of the moment as it caressed her sensitized nipples. His large palms ran over her thighs as he lifted her legs and pulled them over his shoulders and his mouth . . .

His glorious mouth continued that endless, beautiful, life-affirming assault as he wrung sensation after sensation from her body. The breeze blew again, and as it bathed her already sensitive skin, her body crested, shattering.

She screamed his name and knew it carried lightly on the afternoon wind.

"Tell me again why you think this is a good idea?"

"Since I'm full of them today, you want to tell me why you think it's not a good idea?"

He reveled in the light blush that crept up her neck and wanted to tease her again—wanted to taunt her with the sexy memories that were imprinted on his body—but was drawn back to the road when his Roadster hit the fifth pothole of the drive.

"You said your sister lives up this way, right?"

"Yeah."

"So maybe she knows some things about your brother that you don't. Maybe he's come to see her."

"Drake. Just because she and I aren't close doesn't mean she wouldn't have told me if she'd seen him in the last four years. She knows he's been gone. Besides, we could have just called if all we wanted was the answer to a few questions."

Hesitation was woven through every word she spoke. "You sure that she'd call?"

"Well. Yeah."

"Then humor me and consider this a nice, friendly visit with the family. You can do some catching up and get a read on her body language when you ask her about Magnus."

"It's not a reunion, Drake. We're not those sort of people."

He turned to look at her profile. Her neck was ramrod straight as she stared out the windshield. "Okay, I'll bite. What sort of people are you, then?"

"The fight while we prep the potato salad sort of people, who end up fucking up the day before it even starts with said fight and pouting in the car on the way to the reunion."

"Wow. There's a whole lot of baggage in that one."

"You have no idea."

"It sounds like a far cry from the ice cream."

For a moment, Drake was convinced he'd pushed too hard. The silence stretched out as they bumped over another half mile of potholes when she finally spoke. The usual bravado in her voice was replaced by a quiet tone he'd never heard her use before.

"The ice cream was when we were kids. It all changed a few years later. After my dad got sick."

"When?"

"The Christmas I was fourteen. One day he was there and the next he was just gone."

"What happened to him?"

"Heart attack."

The urge to tell her how sorry he was rose up, but Drake held it back. Some sense told him he needed to let her get through it, start to finish, or he wouldn't get the whole story.

"After he died, things changed."

"Grief does that to people."

"My mother wasn't most people." On a heavy breath, she continued. "She went into this weird period after he died where she convinced herself she could have done something. Could have saved him."

"People often bargain through their grief. If I'd only done that, I could have saved them—that sort of thing."

"No, Drake. She convinced herself she could have saved him with magic."

The image of the night before, fire streaming from Emerson's fingertips, had him turning toward her. "You're a powerful witch. More so than the usual set of talents, I'd wager."

"Yes."

"And your mother? Your grandmother? Also very powerful?"

"It descends through the female side of my family, but my mother married a warlock, so I've got it from both sides."

"Could she have saved him?"

"No." Emerson shook her head. "It doesn't work that way. Unlike you, we're mortal and our bodies are subject to the same things as other humans. Death waits for us all."

"But you said the other day you have a longer-than-average life span."

"Just like other humans, it's the genetic luck of the draw. If you're lucky, it's on the higher end of what's considered long. But the power can't change normal human genetics. My father had a bad heart and when his time was up, he died."

Although he was truly sorry for her loss, from the way she explained things, he puzzled at the outcome. "Why'd your mother have such a hard time with it? Her expectations had to be similar to yours. Mortality, while sad for those left behind, isn't exactly a surprise."

"They were soul mates. Twinned, she often said. Souls placed together at the start of time, destined for all eternity."

When he didn't say anything, Emerson added, "None of us understood it, Drake. I mean, I get the being in love part. In fact, I always took a special sort of pride in the fact that I had parents who loved each other so much. But her reaction? Like she couldn't live another day. It wasn't normal."

"Could magic have had something to do with it?"

"How?" The natural curiosity that was one of her hallmarks had her turning toward him with a subtle tilt of the head.

"Your magic is pure, right?"

"I like to think so."

"But you're a normal human, with normal human emotions."

She nodded again. "Of course."

"So what would keep those emotions from turning? Twisting into something less pure under the proper motivation."

"You think magic turned my mother?"

"Well, think about it. Here's a woman who possessed incredible power. Not as much as you, if I'm understanding correctly, but far more than the average witch. Now she's in a situation where grief is clouding her mind and driving her choices."

"And there's a whole lot of power coursing through her veins."

"It plays for me. Or it at least makes more sense than anything I've ever been able to come up with."

Emerson pointed to an upcoming street and he turned off the road and drove them into a small town. The streets had a quaint, old-fashioned feel to them, suggesting a simpler time.

Which was a misnomer if he'd ever heard one.

He'd lived through "simpler times" and they were anything but easy and uncomplicated.

Conflicted, ruthless and terrifying, perhaps. But simple? No way.

He tore his eyes away from a sign that promised

malted milk shakes. "There's one thing you haven't told me."

"What's that?"

"How'd your mother die?"

"She didn't. Or at least I don't think she did. I don't really know."

"What do you mean?" Drake turned toward her in the narrow confines of the car.

"I mean I don't know. She disappeared a long time ago."

Chapter Fifteen

Veronica's house was the last one on the street. Drake drove down the road slowly, avoiding a few kids out on bikes enjoying their after-school freedom before dinner and homework kicked in.

Drake hadn't said a word since she dropped the little bomb about her mother on him and she couldn't say she blamed him.

God, but they were a fucked-up family.

Her brother wore a snake as both weapon and pet. Her mother was the family pariah, turning on every single thing she'd believed in to abandon them. And her sister had tried desperately to pretend none of it even existed, let alone happened.

There wasn't really a whole lot to say about that.

Gee, Emerson, I'm so sorry. Now I know why you avoid intimacy and anything that smacks of commitment.

The glow from their earlier moments together faded at the sobering thought. On a murmur, she watched the road that stretched out in front of them.

"I haven't been here in a few years."

"Why not? It's not that far from the farmhouse."

"We're not close. And I haven't gotten up this way nearly as much as I'd like to."

"She is your sister."

"What part of 'it's complicated' from all the things we just talked about did you miss?"

She heard the petulance in her voice along with the side helping of guilt. This was her sister and she'd adamantly placed a wall between them because Veronica didn't want the same life she did.

Did that really make her any better than the people who didn't support her beliefs?

Drake pulled into the driveway and she pushed all the thoughts aside as she caught sight of her nephew fiddling with something on the wheel of his bike.

Jackson?

"He's so big," she breathed as she took in the long, lanky kid in front of her.

"That happens."

"But—"

But nothing. She'd missed it. She'd missed his birthdays and Christmases and all the family things that came in between because she'd stubbornly stayed away.

They climbed out of the car and she walked over to him. A broad, metal-filled smile greeted her. "Hey, Aunt Emerson. What's up?"

"Oh, not much. What are you doing?"

"The chain keeps falling off." With the special sort of cocky only a twelve-year-old-boy could pull off, he nodded at Drake. "Who's that? Your boyfriend?"

Since one did not refer to a neighbor-with-benefits in

those sorts of terms to one's nephew and saying no felt like a lie, she simply agreed.

"Yep. He's my boyfriend."

The words felt more than right as they tripped off the tongue. If Drake's raised eyebrows caused a wave of heat to trip up her neck, well . . . that was just the residual effect of what had happened in the backyard earlier.

Jackson stood and held out his hand to Drake and she was again reminded that her little nephew was on his way to adulthood.

"Your mom around?"

"She's in the kitchen helping Emily with fractions. Go on in."

"Oh . . . okay."

Drake reached for her fingers and gave them a squeeze before he pointed at the bike. "I'll stay here and help Jackson, if that's all right."

"Can I see the Roadster first?"

"Be my guest." Drake gestured toward the car as Jackson's eyes lit up like Fourth of July fireworks.

"Sweet!"

Emerson heard the words "inline turbocharger" and couldn't hold back the smile. Drake might be immortal, but his enthusiastic response to Jackson's questions was a funny sort of comfort that he was one hundred percent male.

As she walked to the screened front door, she could see straight down the hallway toward the kitchen, where her sister and niece sat head-to-head at the table. "Hello." She added a soft knock to the door, then opened the screen.

Veronica looked up from the table, a broad welcoming smile in answer. "Em!"

Moving down the hallway toward the kitchen, she was again struck by the evidence of how long she'd been away. The hallway had been updated with a rich, modern red, and a series of practical, cubbylike benches lined the wall, giving the distinct impression of farmhouse chic.

Veronica and Emily both leaped up to hug her as soon as she cleared the doorway to the kitchen. The realization of how big her niece was after two years away struck even harder than seeing Jackson, the small child she remembered replaced by a sweet girl with a long ponytail.

Emerson couldn't stop the tears that burned the backs of her eyes as she hugged them back.

After an elaborate kid ritual involving a lot of shouting about the man out front with the cool car—and Emerson's subsequent introductions of Drake to Emily and Veronica—she found herself alone with her sister in the kitchen.

"I'm so glad you're here." Veronica patted her hand as she set a mug of tea on the table. "It's been too long." Before she could say anything, Veronica added, "On both sides. We need to get into the city more often."

"Grandma comes up here often enough."

"Which is wonderful. But you're not that far away and the kids would love to go into New York to visit their aunt Em."

"I'd like that." As she said the words, she realized just how much she meant them.

"Besides, if the man candy out in my front yard is any indication, I haven't been paying a whole lot of attention on the visits I have made. Good Lord, that man is edible."

A renewed burst of color flooded her cheeks as she was again reminded of her afternoon romp with Drake.

"He's put some very happy color in your cheeks, too." Veronica passed over the sugar. "I'm glad to see it."

"He's special to me."

"That's a bit cryptic."

"It's the best I've been able to come up with."

Veronica nodded and took a sip of her tea. "Would you like him to be more?"

Emerson hesitated, before blurting out the words she'd thought for some time. "You told me once men couldn't handle who we were. What we were. Do you believe that?"

The gray eyes so like her own dropped to stare at the table as Veronica picked at her napkin. "I did think that. Once."

"You don't still think it?"

"No, I don't."

"What changed your mind?"

The picking stopped as Veronica looked up, a proud smile cresting her lips. "Emily's got the gift."

"Really?"

"It's just started to manifest itself, but it's there. I know the signs and—" Veronica broke off. "I just know."

"Does it upset you?"

"That's the funniest part. This thing I've been running from for so long. Now that I see it in my own child, I think it's amazing and wonderful and an incredible accomplishment. I've played around with my own gifts a bit. I'm rusty," she added with a rueful laugh. "But that's what you get for ignoring a part of yourself for more than fifteen years."

"Just like riding a bike?" Emerson couldn't resist the tease.

"Yes, and nearly as enjoyable."

"What does Trevor think?"

"He loves it. In fact . . ." It was Veronica's turn to blush. "He seems to think it's some sort of a turn-on."

"Well, who knew?"

"If I'd known, I would have gotten the stick out of my ass a lot sooner than I did. Isn't it funny?"

"What's funny?"

"That it took my child to make me see reason. To make me realize what a beautiful thing I had." Veronica shook her head. "All those wasted years."

"Ronnie. I have to talk to you about something."

As the nickname left her lips, she realized how easy it was to switch into her old comfort zone. How easy it was to remember the good times.

"While I'm thrilled you're here, I was afraid there might have been a reason. It's not Grandma?"

"No, no. I'd have told you right off. No. It's Magnus."

"What's going on?"

"I don't even know where to start."

On a small sigh, Veronica took her hand. "Why don't you start at the beginning?"

"It's sort of an unbelievable story."

"Since Magnus often makes some rather unbelievable choices, you probably won't surprise me nearly as much as you think."

Drake wasn't sure what he expected, but spending the afternoon with two kids was surprisingly enjoyable. Their attitudes were fresh and interested and they were *fun*.

And if he felt slightly guilty for pumping them for information about their aunt Emerson, well . . . he could live with that.

"We haven't seen her in a while, but Mom's always asking G.G.—that's what we call our great-grandma—about her," Emily told him in an all-knowing voice that sounded way too grown up for what he estimated to be a ten-year-old girl. "G.G. calls her fiercely independent, with a stubborn streak that would make a mule tired."

"She's got a really cool tattoo on her arm," Jackson informed him.

"He's already seen her tattoo, Jackson. You know they're having sex."

Drake nearly choked on the passing breeze as Emily's proclamation mentally smacked him upside the head.

Wha—? How? Before he could sputter his way to a response, Jackson already beat him to the punch. "She is hot. You know. For a grown-up who's related to us."

"Um, maybe you shouldn't be talking about your aunt that way."

Jackson just shrugged. "Whatever."

"She hasn't had a boyfriend in a while, either. I'm glad she found you."

If the sex comment blindsided him, this bit of info

left him poleaxed. Which, he consoled himself, was the reason for his mumbled, "Really?"

"Oh yeah. G.G. says Aunt Emerson needs a strong man who can beat against all her defenses and not get discouraged and still let her be tough. Since most men are pussies, she hasn't found one."

"Emily!" Veronica's shocked exclamation greeted them from the screen door.

Drake had gone toe-to-toe with some of Mount Olympus's most dangerous immortals and he'd never been so glad to be relieved of a situation in his entire life.

"I'm sorry, Drake." Veronica snagged Emily in a head-lock. "Shyness has never been in my children's repertoire."

Emerson strolled up behind her sister, hands propped on her hips. "I think someone's been digging for dirt."

"And my children will happily throw shovelfuls without much provocation." She gave Emily a quick kiss on the head. "Come on in for dinner. My husband will be home soon, and we're ordering in pizza."

The kids' combined shouts confirmed for him this wasn't a normal occurrence. It was the small smile and nod from Emerson that confirmed this wasn't only a good idea but a welcome one.

And who was he to argue with pizza?

After-dinner drinks with Veronica and her husband, Trevor, was one of those rarest of experiences: time spent with people where he could just be himself.

He and his brothers and all the immortals who spent time on earth filled a lot of those hours avoiding detection. The fact that he not only didn't have to hide who he was—but could openly talk to them about his life and his abilities—was a rare treat.

They'd even accepted his explanation of Themis and Zeus and their agreement that laid the groundwork for the creation of the Warriors.

"So let me get this straight." Trevor lifted the half-drunk bottle of very nice Cabernet and refilled glasses all around. "You think my brother-in-law is some sort of Warrior?"

"That's exactly what we think." Emerson lifted her wine. "It appears he has the same set of skills Drake has."

"Minus the good nature and desire to help people," Veronica confirmed just before her mouth widened in a large *O* of realization. "Oh my God! What about Grandma?"

"She's at her friend Eve's house for a few days as we get this figured out."

Drake anticipated the protest before Veronica even got the words out. "And we've got surveillance on the house. If she decides to come home early, she'll be intercepted and taken back to my home."

"Do think he'd hurt her?" Veronica reached for Trevor's hand.

An image of the snake leaping out to strike Emerson sent a renewed wave of anger coursing through his system. "I don't think he'd intentionally harm your grandmother. The problem we're fighting is that he can't control the beast yet."

"And you can control yours?" Trevor's question was without censure.

"It's hard at first—awkward, really—but the gift

lives in your aura. *You* control it. Magnus doesn't seem to have developed that skill yet." Drake caught Emerson's raised eyebrow as he omitted the part about just how out of control Magnus was with the snake.

Veronica didn't miss the exchange, a skill he wasn't sure if he should chalk up to intuition or a talent honed over more than a decade of motherhood. One thing was for certain—she wasn't going to remain in the dark. "What happened?"

"Nothing happened," Emerson shot back.

Veronica might have been a pushover with the pizza dinner, but her impressive drill sergeant routine at bedtime with her children had been inspired. With the same tenacity, she stared down her younger sister. "Spill it."

"How does she do that?" Emerson asked her brother-in-law as disgust rode her lips in a thin line.

"The woman is magic." Trevor laughed with a small shrug. "In more ways than one."

"Fine. I never could keep a secret from you anyway. Magnus's snake tried to go after me, but Drake stepped in and absorbed the attack."

"Oh my God, Emerson! Drake?" Veronica's attention ping-ponged between the two of them.

"I don't think he meant it, though," Emerson quickly defended her brother.

"Em. Come on." Trevor hadn't let go of his wife's hand. "He sounds dangerous. And based on some of his choices in the past, isn't it possible this is the natural next step?"

"Did it seem intentional?" Veronica probed, the whispering notes of hope in her voice obvious.

Drake was curious to see the byplay between Veronica and Trevor. The subtle touches and private glances. The easy comfort they shared, even in the midst of difficult news.

In all the years he'd been alive, he'd never had that level of comfort with a woman. Had never wanted it.

Until Emerson.

"The snake attack seemed more like lack of control as opposed to deliberate action. But"—Drake saw Emerson's encouraging nod before continuing—"he did act deliberately when he got into my home and attacked my family."

"It just keeps getting worse. Did my brother hurt anyone?"

"Everyone healed. We're sort of wired that way," Drake added with a smile.

Veronica didn't return the smile; nor did her direct stare waver. "That wasn't my question, Drake."

"Magnus did some damage before he left. And the snake in his aura adds some serious muscle based on its length. He gets a pretty wide range of motion. And"—she hesitated before coming out with it—"it appears that the snake's venom, if it gets that close, has an effect on Drake and, presumably, any immortal."

"What are we going to do?"

"We?" Emerson leaned forward. "Ronnie. We'll deal with this."

"Not without me you're not. He's my brother, too."

"This isn't your fight."

The heat in the room rose so fast Drake was surprised he didn't get singed as Veronica volleyed back to Emerson. "The hell it isn't. I've got the gift, too, little sister. You're not the only one."

"A gift you've refused for, like, twenty years. You're out of practice."

"I've been practicing. And it hasn't been twenty years. I'm not quite that old."

"Damn close. Look, Ronnie, you're not equipped for this." As if to prove her point, Emerson conjured up a small fire in her palm. "Can you do this?"

"Fire's never been my gift and you know it. I have other skills. Other talents."

"Then think about something else. You're a mother."

Drake caught Trevor's raised eyebrows as the two of them exchanged a knowing glance. If Drake wasn't mistaken, a very large battle line had just been drawn.

"What the hell is that supposed to mean—I'm a mother?"

Emerson didn't miss the instant fire that leaped to light in her sister's eyes, or the distinct change in her voice. What had been a brewing disagreement had morphed with lightning speed into an out-and-out fight. "You've got your children to think of."

"What sort of example would I be to them if I didn't act on the things I believed in?"

"Possibly a dead one, if Magnus can't control himself and what he's become. How good will you be to them then, Ronnie? What kind of example will you be to them then?"

"So it's okay for you to ride in like the fucking cavalry? Last time I checked, you were as mortal as I am."

"You can't just swoop in and do this. You gave up

your gift, and now you want to change your mind when it's convenient."

The comment hit its mark. Emerson saw it the moment the words were out of her mouth—words she couldn't snatch back, no matter how much she wanted to.

The room got so quiet Emerson heard her heart pounding in her ears. And while the sudden, glassy sheen of tears in Veronica's eyes went straight to her heart, she couldn't quite muster up the proper amount of regret.

Her sister had made her choice. Had denied what she was. And in doing so had denied everything Emerson held dear.

Everything she believed in.

Everything she was.

"So it's back to that?"

"I guess it is," she said, quiet regret forcing the words to stick in her throat.

Chapter Sixteen

"You were awfully hard on her."
Drake knew the comment would elicit a fight and was oddly surprised by how much he looked forward to one. Although he knew a good portion of why he cared for her was tied to her stubborn tenacity and tough-yet-vulnerable shell, he wasn't going to stay silent on what he'd observed.

Emerson and her stubborn pride and her immediate willingness to push people away.

People she loved.

"Nice going, Ace. You waited until we pulled into the driveway to drop that little bomb."

"Yes, I waited. I look someone in the eye when I dress them down."

One eyebrow quirked over the gray storm clouds gathering in her eyes. "Is that what you're doing?"

"I'm about to." He got out of the car and slammed the door, then walked around to open hers. As expected, she beat him to the punch and was halfway to the porch before he caught up to her.

Her fingers shook as she shoved the key in the lock on the front door and he closed his hand over hers. "Why were you so hard on her?"

Shoulders slumping, she leaned her head against the door. "Because I can't let it go." Before he could say anything, she whirled on him. "Because I can't let it go, Drake! She gave it up and now I'm supposed to sit back and let her put herself in danger? With our brother, no less?"

He refused to back off. Instead, he stood there and stared down at her. That small pixie frame quivered with anger and hurt and so many years of self-reliance she'd forgotten what it was to share herself with anyone.

And he'd allowed it to go on for long enough.

"Veronica's decisions aren't yours. And denying her the freedom to choose doesn't make you a saint. She's the one who's lost out all these years."

"I'm not a saint, Drake."

"You sure? Because you have awfully high expectations for everyone."

"I have a set of standards. There's a difference."

"Standards of your own making."

She turned back to fiddle with the lock, but he didn't miss the fact she needed to unclench those small fists before reaching for the key. "What the hell's wrong with that?"

"Nothing, except you seem to think what you want is what everyone else wants. You take no one's thoughts into the mix, save your own."

"You know, this conversation is veering awfully

close to a discussion about us. And here I thought you were berating me about my sister."

"Same symptoms, same problem."

"I hardly think what's between my sister and me can be compared to what's between us."

"Oh, I don't know. Take the sex out of the mix and it looks like the same fucking problem from where I stand. Lack of communication and an unwillingness to acknowledge the other person has any feelings or role in the relationship."

She finally got the door unlocked and marched through the door. "You and I don't have a relationship, Drake. We screw around on a regular basis. I believe the term is 'friend with benefits.'"

Her words hit him so hard Drake was surprised he didn't actually stagger.

Was that truly the way she saw what was between them?

Memories of their afternoon outside filled his mind's eye. The easy laughter and comfortable camaraderie between them. Yes, the sex was spectacular, but it wasn't all that was between them. In fact, the reason it *was* so amazing was because there was so much more they shared.

"Well, that proves my point right there. I thought we did have a relationship. I guess I was mistaken."

Without waiting for a response, he headed toward the spare room he'd seen earlier on a tour of the farmhouse. He'd sleep alone tonight.

Eris stared at her phone for what felt like the nine hundredth time in the last hour. Probably because she *had* looked at it that many times.

Tossing the phone back on the counter, she turned to pace her small kitchen again.

Damn Rogan. She'd texted him hours ago and nothing. Complete and utter radio silence. They'd just been together in Vegas, so it was lunacy to want to meet up so soon. But once he caught wind of what she was planning with Magnus, she'd likely not see him for a while.

A loud pounding echoed from her front door, and she padded down the hall, glad there would be some reprieve from her maudlin thoughts. And was shocked as hell when the object of them was standing on the other side of the door.

"What are you doing here?"

"We need to talk." Rogan barged in without waiting for a formal invitation.

"You got my text message?"

His gaze shot to where her phone lay on the counter. "I'm not here to fuck around, and you know it."

"Then why are you here?"

Rogan turned on her, the vivid green of his eyes a hard emerald. "You were the one who turned Magnus."

The diary. Of course.

Although she'd known the truth would inevitably come out, she had forbidden Magnus to talk of it or the deal they'd made. She'd reveal what she'd done at the proper time.

So why was it so hard to ever envision a proper time as she stood there staring at Rogan? Like a drunk who couldn't keep her eyes off a bottle of vodka, she couldn't stop looking at him.

Those immense shoulders covered in a black T-shirt. The jeans that molded to slender hips and powerful thighs. And those stunning green eyes.

They were eyes that told a story in vivid, living color.

"Why did you do it?"

"What makes you so sure it was me?" As bluffs went, it sucked. But she wasn't willing to admit defeat quite yet.

"It wasn't all that hard to figure out. Enyo's not nearly that creative. Or that smart."

She preened under the words, even as she knew they weren't meant as a compliment. She'd spent her life in the shadow of her sister. The great goddess of war, revered by all.

Very few saw the crazy-ass bitch who bounced from project to project like a maniacal rabbit.

So Rogan was right. She'd seen an opportunity and taken it. Themis wasn't the only one who could create Warriors. And thank the gods humans were so easy to rile up.

She'd seen report after report about the "Thirteenth Sign," and known she had her answer.

Ophiuchus was real, his place in the heavens secure. But the world had forgotten about him as that nice, round number of twelve took root in the public's conscience.

Twelve equal houses with twelve equal signs.

Themis and her balance.

Funny enough, for all her talk of balance, the goddess had been surprisingly forgetful in leaving the serpent bearer out.

So Eris had made a Warrior to her specifications.

She'd tried before, to varying degrees of success. But Magnus was different.

He was *real*. Not simply a physical embodiment of her powers. As projects go, Magnus wasn't all bad. He was eager to please and seemingly had no regrets about his choice. It was the inherent connection to the Warriors through his sister that was the bad luck.

Rogan began to pace, running his fingers across the counter as he measured his words. "Look, Eris. Whatever you've done, I can help you. Magnus isn't fully turned. He's not fully empowered yet. Let me make it right."

Her gaze never left his broad back as he moved, the elegant lines of his shoulders shifting as he reached to play with her cell where it lay on the counter. No matter how much time they spent together, she was fascinated by the hard strength of his body. "There's nothing to make right."

"Damn it, Eris. Turn him back."

"There's no turning him back!"

The words seemed to freeze in time, full of all the unspoken truths between them, and Rogan froze along with them.

"No, there is no turning back. There's only moving forward." Rogan turned from the counter and headed for the door.

"Where are you going?"

"You've made your choice and I've made mine."

She followed him to the door. "What do you mean?"

"We're over."

"Rogan." She heard the edge of desperation that

tinged her voice and tried to pull it back. Drawing on the nerves of steel she was known for, she modulated her voice, dragging it down a few notches. "We both knew exactly what this was when it started. Exactly who the other was. And we agreed to keep all of that separate."

"You changed that when you came after my family."

"I didn't—" She broke off, knowing his comment wasn't true but wasn't entirely untrue. She'd done her homework and she'd learned months ago that Magnus's sister was involved with the Warriors.

"So you did purposely come after my family?"

"It's a bad coincidence Magnus is related to a woman dating your friend. That's all. That's all this is."

"If your goal wasn't my family, then what was it?"

They didn't share this. Didn't open up about this part of their lives. "Rogan, you know the agreement. That's off-limits. What we each do is off-limits."

He whirled on her, grabbing her just below the shoulders and dragging her forward, the green of his eyes clouded with anger and . . . guilt? "Not when it involves my family."

Gods damn it, how could she make him understand?

She placed her hands on his shoulders, tentatively stroking the soft cotton of his shirt. "Do you know the inherent power that lives in your skin? I need that. I can use that."

"You can't just take it."

"Why not? You and your brothers aren't totally aboveboard. And you're not the only ones entitled to it. Neither is Themis."

A completely irresponsible tug dragged at her belly as his hands slammed onto his hips, his biceps tightening underneath that stretch of black.

"You can't just go making up Warriors, Eris. Adding to the pantheon. It's not done."

"It was fine for Themis and Zeus. Why should they be the ones to make the rules?"

"My brothers and I are the good guys."

She couldn't hold back the laughter at that one. "You can't be serious."

"As a heart attack."

"Oh, come on. Look in the fucking mirror, Rogan. You think because you're the good guys it means you can make the rules? Hello, Captain Vigilante."

"We don't kill for sport."

She wasn't a killer by nature. A pot stirrer, yes, and a goddess who reveled in creating chaos. But a killer? Only when someone got in her way. "And that's what you think I am? What I do?"

"I think you bend the truth to gain your own ends. I think you've been doing that so long, you don't even know what the truth is any longer."

She dropped her hands and stepped back. "Oh hell, Rogan. If that's the definition, do any of us know the truth any longer?"

"What's that supposed to mean?"

"It means we've all been fighting this battle forever and the endgame never changes. The outcome never changes."

The harsh set of his shoulders relaxed slightly. "Do you really feel that way?"

"Don't you?"

"Then give it up."

Eris had watched discord and discontentment grow for the endlessly long millennia of her life and she'd become quite adept at knowing when a conversation turned for the worse.

By her own estimation, this one just went off the rails.

"You want me to give up who I am? Give up my very identity?"

"Give it up for something better."

"It's who I am."

"No, it's who you choose to be. There's a difference."

Pain ripped through her with razor-sharp talons. When had his opinion come to mean so much? And now that she was faced with the realization that it wasn't a very positive one, the urge to strike back—swiftly—reared up in response.

"Speaking of choices, you've conveniently forgotten you and your brothers have my apple. It belongs to me and I'm entitled to get it back."

"It's dangerous."

"It's mine."

"You can't have it back."

"Who the hell made you judge and jury?"

She'd never harbored the same sort of grudge against any of the Warriors that her sister did. Sure, they got in the way of her plans, but they weren't enemies, per se.

They simply worked at cross-purposes.

But this?

She'd get what belonged to her and she'd continue with her plans. And Rogan Black wasn't going to stand in the way.

She no longer had time for distractions.

Emerson stepped into the ceremonial circle and closed it behind her, anxious for the calming, soothing effects her magic brought her. She'd learned long ago that the power that lived within her skin had the beneficial side effect of calming her nerves and helping her find her center.

The grass was cold under her naked bottom, but she ignored it, absorbing the inherent power that lived latent in the earth. She allowed the evening breeze to float over her bare skin, coating her with its whispered secrets.

She knew she wouldn't be out here long. The fall night had shed the warmth from the day, giving proof that winter was well on its way.

A few prayers wended their way through her mind, but she ignored them and instead focused farther inward. Into the core of herself and the secrets that lived in her heart.

Drake had accused her of unreasonable expectations and a harsh set of rules. Maybe that was true, but what else could she be?

What else could she expect of others?

She'd known what she was from the earliest age. Had reveled in that gift and hoped to use it for good. For the betterment of others.

So how was she supposed to respond to those who didn't feel the same? To those who actively shunned their gifts and told her that she had to be different.

That she wasn't good enough just as she was.

Wind whistled through the night sky and she abstractly felt the cold as she replayed the time at Veronica's in her mind.

The instant warmth and acceptance. The reminder that they'd had something special once. A bond.

Sisterhood.

She'd had a long time to get over Veronica's choices. To make herself into what she was. To hone the gifts she'd been given.

But Veronica hadn't. What if she did go head-to-head with Magnus and lost?

"It's awfully cold out here."

Her eyes snapped open to see Drake holding a blanket.

"Come on. Get up and let me wrap you up in here." She held up a hand, but before she could say anything, he added, "I know you're inside a ceremonial circle. I won't breach it. But I'd like you to dissolve it and come out."

A small kernel of warmth pierced her heart as she nodded at his words.

He respected what she was doing. Respected the protection she'd created around herself.

With quick motions, she stood and dissolved the circle, offering her thanks to the goddess. Moving into the blanket Drake held up, she wrapped it tightly around her shoulders. "Thanks."

"Why are you out here?"

"I couldn't sleep."

"I probably have something to do with that."

"A little bit, yes, but not all of it." She shrugged, the

blanket brushing the tops of her feet at the movement. "You were right to say something." She padded over to the lawn chairs they'd sat on earlier, the vivid slash of memory taking her breath away as she thought about his hands on her.

His mouth.

The power in his body and the power that rose up between them when they made love.

He was right to say something. More than that, he was entitled.

When he was settled in the chair, she turned toward him, pulled her knees up to snuggle further under the blanket. "It's more than judgment."

"Tell me about it."

"What if she can't do it? What if she walks into a fight and can't pull the trigger?" At the questions in his gaze, she added, "Metaphorically. Magnus is our brother. And despite all the things he may have done, nothing will change that. What if she can't take him down when it's necessary? And what if he takes her first?"

"The same could happen to you."

The moonlight played off the green and gold of his eyes as their gazes met, and she saw the fear behind his words. Felt it in the quiet way he reached for her hand where it gripped the wooden arm of the chair.

"You think I don't know that? He's my brother, Drake. No matter what he's done, I can't change that simple, immutable fact. What if I can't do it when the moment's right? What if I'm put to that test?"

When he reached up and cupped her cheek, she leaned into his warmth. "Can I really do what it takes?"

Chapter Seventeen

Drake followed Emerson into the house, the anger that had ridden them both when they'd arrived home from her sister's nowhere in evidence. Instead, all he felt was a desperate need that coursed in time with the throb of his pulse.

Something had changed. Evolved, really.

He felt it in the gentle cadence of Emerson's words and the softening of her gaze as she looked at him. Reaching for his hand, her words were quiet in the dark. "Come upstairs with me."

He offered no response other than to take her hand and follow her.

They'd slept in the master bedroom the night before, but Drake looked on it with fresh eyes as they walked through the door. A large four-poster bed dominated the room, but instead of the expected old quilt to cover it, a heavy satin duvet lay across the top in a deep, rich purple. The color was a match for the bed and the room—rustic charm meets contemporary chic.

Oddly, the combination reminded him of Emerson.

She managed to straddle two universes—the magical history and power that coursed through her bloodstream and the contemporary world in which she lived. It was a heady combination.

The blanket she'd wrapped herself in outside floated to the floor and his little goddess stood naked in the moonlight. "Drake," she whispered as she moved into the circle of his arms, "I want you."

He wanted to question her—wanted to ask if the change he felt in her was real. If something *had* evolved between them and grown deeper. But he held back and focused on the moment, unwilling to risk ruining it for what the future held.

"I want you, too." He leaned down and cupped her face in his hands, pressing his lips to hers. "Always."

Her fingers were light at his waist and made quick work of the jeans he'd hastily thrown on to go look for her. Her small hands ran the thick material down his body, stopping to linger on his backside with a sexy squeeze. The side of her breast brushed against his arousal, and the simple touch had him shuddering.

How could she do this to him? How was it even possible?

No matter how many times they were together, it was always like this.

Desperately needy and infinitely sweet.

She continued her unerring course to the floor, her fingers running languorously over his thighs, then his calves, until his jeans pooled on the floor. Before he could reach for her, her clever fingers were back at his waist, dragging his T-shirt up and over his head.

"Now, that's *much* better." Her smile gleamed in the moonlight as his shirt landed with a soft thud a few feet away. "Nothing like an even playing field."

"I can't argue with you there." He bent his head to take her mouth, arousal heavy in the air between them. Her hands ran over his chest, across his pectoral muscles and up over his shoulders as the kiss spun out between them.

She was so tiny, the top of her head coming only to the upper part of his chest. Not for the first time, he wondered how a woman so small and so very delicate could make every inch of his large body ache.

Yet it did.

He burned for her—body and soul. It lived and breathed within him, a desperate, driving thing that consumed him from the inside out. Life without her was unimaginable.

And yet he knew—just as she did—that what they had was fundamentally fleeting. Their time would pass. This age would turn into the next.

No matter how fervently he wished it, she couldn't see the next one with him.

Emerson wondered at the sadness that telegraphed to her from Drake's large form.

Had she done something?

Dragging her lips from his, she placed both hands on his cheeks. "What is it?"

"Nothing." With a slight shake of his head, he offered her a smile that didn't quite reach the green of his eyes. "It's nothing."

She nearly stopped right there to force the issue, but

something held her back. No matter when they'd ever been together—in bed or out—he'd always been so strong. So completely in charge.

But the look on his face reminded her of that night so long ago.

The first night she'd seen him when she was a teenager, his head pressed to the door as his shoulders sagged, seemingly against the weight of the world. He'd captivated her in that moment, the contrast of outward strength with such a deep, inward struggle. She'd thought it long gone. But looking at him now— *sensing* it, really—she saw the familiar.

Saw the man she'd fallen in love with so many, many moons ago.

"Love me, Drake. Please."

The words had the desired effect as whatever weight dragged on him evaporated. Before she could sense his intent, he had her up in his arms and moving them toward the bed. He followed her down onto the mattress, covering her with his large form.

She reveled in these moments, no matter how many times she told herself he was a drug she needed to quit cold turkey. Reveled in the feel of that large body covering her—*consuming* her. She felt small and protected and so very, very feminine.

When she was in his arms, she didn't feel like she had to do everything on her own.

Didn't have to *be* everything on her own.

When she was in his arms, she could be bare, both literally and figuratively.

Human.

Vulnerable.

When she was in his arms, the words she'd carried in her head her entire life—that no man could accept the power inside of her—quieted and faded away.

Drake shifted, moving down her body until his mouth was flush with her breast. The hard, urgent tug of need unfurled in her stomach as he ran his tongue over her nipple before dragging the tip fully into his mouth.

Oh God, he made her burn.

She clenched her fingers in the silk of the duvet as his mouth created the most wondrous sensations inside of her. While his tongue and lips teased one breast, he mimicked the motions with his fingers on her other. He plucked at the other nipple, groaning against her skin as the tip went hard in his hands.

Her own moan drifted into the air between them, soft and needy as he played her body like a virtuoso.

With lightning-quick movements, that hand shifted and moved unerringly to the apex of her thighs. Another moan welled up in her throat, heavier this time, as his fingers delved into her core in long, determined strokes. He had her to peak in moments, the greedy orgasm consuming her body in blazing waves of heat.

Before she could even catch her breath, he'd shifted and buried himself inside of her. "I need you." His voice was ragged in her ear as he began to move. "Now."

"Yes." One word, dragged from her lips on another moan as her body clenched around him. "Oh yes."

If there were any more words, Emerson couldn't say. All she was—the entire world—coalesced in that moment.

In the two of them.

As the pleasure built inside her once more, their bodies pounding together in mindless need, she felt him stiffen on a heavy moan. "Emerson!"

His name fell from her lips as, together, they rode the moment.

And together, she realized, they shut out the rest of the world that desperately sought to push its way in.

"What do you need me to do?" Drake stared at the framed mirror Emerson had placed on the table earlier, abstractly aware of her bustling around in the kitchen.

"I need you to make sure I stay put and that I come out of the vision."

"But you'll be here."

She moved over to the table with a teakettle and poured steaming water into a plain white mug. "Physically here, yes. But the vision will take me somewhere else."

Drake was caught up short at her description. "Your soul?"

Emerson glanced briefly at the mirror before resting that grayish gaze on him. "Yes."

"Are you sure you should do this? Maybe we should call your sister."

"Come on. This is the only way."

Drake nodded, even as his discomfort rose by the second.

"I'm going to drink this and will need about five minutes for it to take effect."

"And the drink?" He nodded toward the mug.

"It'll help the visions come easier and make them more expansive. I'm not trying to spy on Magnus at this very moment, but I want to reach out and find the high points."

"And you call my gifts unique."

Emerson smiled at that. "They are."

"Last time I checked, I couldn't conjure up memories out of mirrors, so you've got one up on me there."

She took a large sip and simply smiled at him over the rim of the mug. So much had happened over the last several days. So many moments that drew them closer, even as he lived in growing fear of something happening to her.

After a few minutes, she nodded. "I'm ready to begin."

He stood with her as she leaned over the mirror and reached for her hand, hoping for quick answers to their questions. And as their fingers linked, Drake vowed to help her deal with whatever she discovered.

Emerson was conscious of Drake's anxiety as she allowed her mind to reach out through the mirror. The tisane she'd brewed had gone a long way toward calming her nerves, but nothing could stop the adrenaline that pumped in her veins at the opportunity to finally get some answers.

Reaching out, she probed the air through the mirror, searching for the whispers that would show her to her brother. She'd always found it easier to focus on family members, and as she caught on Magnus's essence, she wondered why she hadn't thought of this sooner.

Images flashed before her, some familiar as she saw

him in their kitchen, then in their backyard as he waited for her to come home.

She couldn't get a bead on his thoughts, but she got a sense for his feelings.

Impatience. Indecision. Fear?

Taking a calming breath, she refocused herself, trying to go more deeply into the secrets the mirror offered. Now that she had a bead on Magnus's essence, she probed with a combination of her magic and her mind, allowing her senses to reach out.

And stumbled into a memory that had the flight instinct rearing up within every part of her being, both physical and spiritual. Tamping down on the urge, Emerson forced herself to look.

Magnus faced a woman—long, lean and leather-clad—who wove tales of power and what she could turn him into. She watched as his eyes filled with greed at the promised offerings—strength, power, domination.

She saw Magnus extend his hand to the woman, clasping her smaller, outstretched one as he took what she offered. Saw as the clothes were ripped from his body and his slender form expanded and grew into the hard-planed Warrior she'd seen most recently.

And finally, Emerson saw the tattoo that rose in dark ink over his shoulders, the snake that coiled and wrapped itself around him.

Although she couldn't hear the words he and the woman spoke, the memory emblazoned itself on her, its contents as clear as if they'd happened to her.

When she finally pulled herself from the vision, Emerson was forced to acknowledge the truth.

Her brother was lost.

* * *

The car ride back to the city was a quiet one, both of them full of the emotional overload of the last few days. Drake risked a sideways stare at Emerson as they drove down the West Side Highway. Dark circles colored the thin skin beneath her eyes and her small frame grew increasingly tense the closer they got to Manhattan.

"Do you know what I've been thinking about?"

Her quiet words pulled him from his thoughts as they turned down their street. "Your sister?"

"No. Finley. What must she think of all this?"

Drake considered Grey's lawyer and what the last several days must have been like for her. From her capture in the warehouse to all that she'd been exposed to since, it had to have taken its toll. "Grey hasn't exactly been forthcoming with her."

"She's in this whether he likes it or not. He's trying to protect her, but he does her no good keeping her ignorant."

"No," Drake agreed on a small sigh. "He doesn't."

She cocked her head, the inquisitive motion a combination of sexy and sweet. "You're not nearly as bullheaded as the others."

"That's not what you usually say."

"Okay, when it comes to us you're incredibly stubborn. But put that aside for a moment. How do you manage it?"

"Manage what?"

"You lead quietly. It never ceases to amaze me. Even when you're marching in like the alpha dog on parade, you do it in a way that's not insulting to anyone else. Least of all me."

"I never stopped to think about it."

"No, you probably don't. You just do it." She hesitated for a moment, and Drake got the distinct impression she was weighing her words. "You're a good man, Drake. You may even be the best man I've ever met. That's why once this is over, we need to stop seeing each other."

The words smacked with the force of an oncoming semi, but somehow he kept his hands steady as he bypassed their homes, heading one more block east to the parking garage where he stored his car.

"Interesting decision. Care to tell me what's prompted it? Especially after last night?"

"Last night made it all clear. You deserve better. Better than me and what I can give you. What I'm willing to give you."

"Why are you so convinced you know—to use your term—'better'?"

"You do it often enough to me."

"Yes, but I'm right."

"There you go again. This weird power play that makes you think there can be more between us. Well, there can't. I finally understand that now."

"Give me three reasons."

"My fucked-up brother, your insistence that I'm some sort of dream woman and immortality." She rattled them off with a speed that suggested she'd spent more than a few moments thinking about them. "In no particular order."

"You're *my* dream woman and I'm not changing my mind about that." Drake pulled into the parking garage and saw an attendant waiting for them. He jumped out to gather their bags from the trunk, his mind whirling with Emerson.

How to convince her? How to break through that freakishly stubborn skull of hers and make her see what he knew in his heart to be true?

She felt the same things he did. He hadn't ever really doubted it, but last night had proved it.

They *fit*, gods damn it. Perfectly.

Distracted, he didn't even realize the mistake as he made it. A few moments . . . just a simple twist of fate.

As he handed the attendant a tip, the bag on his arm slipped, jarring his hand. Their fingers brushed slightly, and that's when Drake felt the rush of static electricity up his arm.

"Emerson, get down!"

Whirling, Drake slammed the bags at the Destroyer, using the momentum to force the man against the car while he got his hands free.

Sparks shot off the side of the car as the Destroyer's body made contact with the metal and Drake wasted no time. Leaping on the guy, he immediately went for the throat, seeking the quickest way to end him. He didn't care who had sent him and he wasn't looking for answers.

He wanted the threat removed.

The Destroyer generated a fireball, and Drake felt the liquid fire of it as it brushed his arm before veering off wildly and petering out. As another wave of electricity flashed, going even wider than the first, Drake saw Emerson from the corner of his eye. "Get away from this," he ordered through gritted teeth.

"Remember yesterday?"

Before he could answer, her small hand gripped the waistband of his jeans and her fingers made contact with his body. A wave of fire shot from her fingertips, coating the Destroyer's face in a steady blaze.

He barely felt the fire as it burned above where his hands struggled to grip the flailing body. The fire gave him the momentum he needed, throwing in an added distraction to the Destroyer as Drake worked to get the handhold on the neck he needed.

"A little higher or you'll hit the car," he grunted as the Destroyer threw all his weight against the frame of the Roadster, trying to dislodge his grip.

"Seriously?" Emerson shouted in his ear. "That's your worry right now?" But she did as he asked, lifting the stream a few notches higher.

It gave them the last bit of power they needed, and as Drake's grip tightened firmly on the Destroyer's neck, he gave a swift, hard twist.

The results were immediate. He dropped his hands, reaching for Emerson's forearm to still her. "Enough. He's gone."

"Oh my God, Drake." Emerson released her hold on his jeans to wrap her arms around him. "He knew we'd be here."

"Yeah, he did."

Drake knew it was useless to tell her to get in the car and drive. While it had sustained some damage to the frame, she could have used the Roadster to get out of there. But he knew it was a futile request.

"Which means we need to figure out what happened to the real attendant." He snatched his phone and made a quick call to Quinn, giving him the details of where they were. He'd have the added benefit of getting the bull to wipe the security system once he was here as well.

Drake's gaze alighted on a CLOSED. LOT'S FULL sign and grabbed it, dragging it to the entrance. It had been quiet since they arrived. It was late enough in the morning that there would be few people looking for their cars, but he wasn't taking any chances.

Keeping Emerson firmly behind him, he held her hand as they walked toward the small office in the back of the garage. The door locked from the outside, but Drake got a firm visual of the small, cubicle-sized space through a gated hole on the door. "Stand here and don't move."

With a quick port, he was inside the room and then opened the door outward. Emerson's eyes widened as she saw the evidence of what lay behind him. Pushing past him, she kneeled down beside two bodies, one still in uniform and the other stripped to a T-shirt and underwear.

"They've each got a pulse, but they're both out cold." She lifted her hands from the stripped guy's neck, running her fingers toward his heart, and stopped when she got to the midpoint on his chest. "Look there. I thought it was dirt at first, but these are burn marks." With a quick shift on her heels to focus on the other guy, she found matched markings on his shirt.

Drake recognized the marks immediately. "They both took a serious level of voltage to knock them out like this."

"Will they be okay?"

"If they're still breathing, that's a good sign." Although he didn't want to leave her, she could pull the door closed behind her and be safely locked inside the small office. "I want you to stay here and call Callie. She'll know what to do."

"They need doctors."

"We can't put anyone else in danger until we figure out if anything else is in the garage. Callie will know what to do in the meantime."

"Yes, I will." Callie materialized behind them, along with Quinn. Emerson stood to give her room as she knelt between the two men.

"Keep them sedated and out if you can without it hurting them. We need a few more minutes," Drake instructed before turning to Quinn and updating him on what had happened since they pulled into the garage.

"Let's go."

"I'm going, too."

"You're staying here with Callie."

The mulish frown was immediate and Drake reached for her arms. "Emerson, I need you to wait for me."

"You've seen how we fight, Drake. It makes us stronger."

"And we can't go spreading fire inside a garage full of cars and leaked gas and oil on the floor." He pressed his lips to her forehead. "Please wait with Callie."

He saw the moment his words registered, her gaze alighting on a small row of auto equipment against the wall. "I see your point."

"This won't take long."

A heavy thud echoed behind them, followed by a scratchy, raspy noise he couldn't place. As Drake turned, he was greeted by Magnus and the very large snake that coiled around his feet. The rub of its scales on the concrete floor of the garage produced the sandpaper sound.

"No. It won't take long at all."

Pain stabbed her in harsh, terrifying bursts at the sight of her brother and what he'd become.

A monster.

He had the same gifts as Drake and his Warrior brothers—but not. The talent may be the same but the manifestation in Magnus was just twisted and wrong.

"Em, get out of here." Magnus tilted his head toward the exit of the garage. "Go home and wait for me there."

"I can't. You can't do this, Magnus. Stop. Please stop. We can get you help."

"I don't need help."

What could she say? How could she make him see reason? "Of course you do. This isn't you, Magnus. It's not who you're meant to be."

"Get out of here, Em!"

The fears she'd harbored about her sister reared up and slammed her like a storm on the sea. She'd questioned Veronica's ability to act in a crisis, but could she do what had to be done? Could she look at Magnus as something other than her brother and acknowledge what he'd become? What she'd *seen* him become with her own eyes.

"There's a way out of this, Magnus. There has to be."

"My life, my choices. They don't concern you. I just need you to get out of the way."

"Of course it concerns me. You concern me!"

The snake stilled as her words echoed off the concrete of the garage.

"You're my brother."

"And you're my sister. I don't want to hurt you. So go. Please."

The last word—the "please"—tore through her along with the raw, painful memories of all that had come before. His desperate need for them to understand him and accept him never went away. Never faded.

But the things he wanted them to accept . . . to understand.

It was madness.

All his adult life, Magnus was always asking for their understanding of things that he had no place doing in the first place. Her, her grandmother, even Veronica. He wanted them to accept his actions and disregard what those same actions said about him as a person.

"Oh, Magnus. I've watched you make one bad choice after another. Do you have any idea how that makes me feel? How that makes Grandma feel?"

"They're my choices."

"We're your family."

"You wouldn't understand. You *can't* understand."

"Then help me. Help me understand how any of this possibly makes sense." Her gaze dropped to the snake, surprised when it not only fully stilled, but seemed almost catatonic.

"After Mom—"

When he broke off, she pushed back, unwilling to

hold back the anger and the frustration and the horrible, awful fear any longer. "What about Mom?"

"There you go." He waved a hand. "I can see it, Em."

"See what?"

"The fucking judgment. It screams off you in mind-numbing waves. I can hear the words in your head."

"There are no words in my head."

"Bullshit! They've always been there. Pounding with a verdict I couldn't defend myself against if I tried."

"I don't judge you, Magnus. I'm trying to understand you."

"You'll never understand me. And you'll never understand what I've become. You're too pure."

She shook her head as a nauseous kernel of fear slipped into her belly. "Pure?"

"You're a white witch. You believe in the raw beauty of your power and you won't take from the dark."

"I'm no different than many others."

"But it's not what you come from!" The words ripped from him, the outburst even more immense for the fact that the snake remained perfectly still.

The fear roiled faster now, hard, choking waves of it in her stomach that rose up toward her throat. When she finally got herself under control and could speak, her voice was an agonized whisper in the quiet garage. "What do you mean?"

"I was there! I helped Mom in a black magic ritual."

"You couldn't have."

"She wanted me there. The witches helping her told

her if she used my blood, she'd be stronger. The magic would be stronger to bring him back."

"Magnus, no." She shook her head, trying to puzzle through his words. To make sense of her mother's actions. "No."

How could her mother do something like that? Was her grief for their father that strong?

Or was his loss simply the catalyst to spring free what had always been there?

"Yes, Em. It's true. But she changed in the end. The woman—the one who'd told her it would bring Dad back. That woman turned on her. Tried to use me, instead." Magnus's voice exploded on a loud rush—part shout, part sob. "She saved me. Pushed me from the circle and took the punishment instead."

"And that's why you changed? Why you became so different?" She hesitated, her emotions ricocheting as she imagined the ritual gone bad. On a deep breath, Emerson pushed for all of it. "And the man in the park? Did you kill him?"

"He was there, Em. The night . . ." Magnus broke off. "He saw. He knew."

Dark, oily waves of grief swirled through her, dragging on the very fibers of her soul. "So you did kill him. And now you've traded your soul to possess another kind of magic? Another sort of darkness? Did you learn nothing from Mom's sacrifice?"

The anger—the mind-numbing, soul-searing anger—tore through her from the very top of her head to the tip of her toes. It rose up with a unique power all its own, and for the first time in her life, she sensed the truly dangerous edges of her magic.

"She died in vain if this is what you've become!"

The air around her grew heavy, and Emerson abstractly realized it wasn't caused by her.

On a rush, a woman materialized before them, her stance aligned with Magnus.

"Isn't this cozy?"

Eris.

Drake tamped down on the urge to leap forward and drag Emerson into a port and get her out of there. Much as he wanted to protect her, even he knew she had to see this to fruition. They all did.

Life had certain inevitabilities a person learned over thousands of years of living and the one that sat at the top of the list was that you couldn't outrun your fate.

No matter who you had on your side or how hard you tried.

As he kept his gaze firmly pinned on the pixie-sized woman who had captured his heart with her tough talk that hid cotton-candy-sweet emotions, he knew he was facing his own fate.

He'd known it, of course. But as they stood there with so many unanswered questions hanging in the balance, it was all crystal clear.

He was in love with Emerson Carano.

Emerson moved to stand next to him and placed her hand in his. The simple gesture was obvious and immediate—they'd combine their power to take down the threat.

Just as they'd practiced.

"You ready?" He turned to look at her. Tension rode her features, evident in every part of her body from the widened set of her feet to the stiff set of her shoulders to the steely grip she had on his fingers.

"Yep."

"Isn't this sweet?" Eris crooned as she placed a hand on Magnus's arm to keep him still. "What do you have there, Drake? She looks like one of Charlie's Angels. The spiky hair and tats add a unique touch." Eris put her free hand on a hip. "Surprisingly feminine and just a little bit wicked."

"She's worth a million of you and you know it."

"Too, too sweet." Eris smiled, her grin wolfish. "I think someone's in love."

"Or pissed off," Emerson suggested, her tone casual.

Drake felt the heavy squeeze of his hand before all hell broke loose.

Fire streamed from Emerson in a hard arc, focused dead center on Eris's chest. The swift, immediate action had the desired effect. The goddess dropped to her feet, momentarily shocked by the speed of the assault. Before she could even breathe, Emerson shifted tactics and focused on the woman's midsection, careful to keep the flames high enough to avoid any possible oil slicks on the ground. It wasn't foolproof, but she was conscious of what she was doing.

Consciously trying to keep them all safe.

Quinn's breathless "what the hell" was followed by his war cry. Emerson stopped the flame as the bull leaped on Eris, her high-pitched screams echoing off the heavy walls of the garage.

As Quinn moved, Emerson shifted her focus to her brother, bathing the coiled snake in golden streams of fire. Magnus let out a harsh scream of his own but moved out of the line of fire, having already learned his lesson from the other day. That movement was all Drake needed. With a quick squeeze of his own, he whispered to Emerson, "Please stay back with Callie."

And then he leaped.

Chapter Eighteen

Magnus struggled against his hold, but Drake refused to let him up. The snake was damaged from the burns, but was quickly regaining its strength. Drake could feel the snap of its head as it dived for his ankles. Its venom and fangs weren't functional as the snake regenerated itself from the fiery assault, but it clearly wasn't going to be left out of the fight.

Marshaling his own tattoo, Drake let his senses reach out. Lifting off his body, the conjoined fish went to work, seeking any life-giving water in the vicinity. As the tattoo aided him, Drake refocused on his quarry. He pounded on Magnus, grunting when the asshole got a good, heavy box in over his ears, and still, he maintained the connection as his aura sought the water.

His senses roved over the garage, seeking the source he knew was somewhere. He landed another punch on Magnus, this time to the stomach, before a wave of pain shot up his left leg as the snake's fangs sank into his calf.

No poison followed the bite, and he was about to shake it off when he felt the fangs retract and the weight of the snake shift away. Heat licked close and he realized Emerson had moved up and was firing on the animal yet again.

Their lack of touch meant her fire went wider, not as focused as what she could create when they were together. It was that mistake that nearly cost them all.

As her stream of heat went wild on the snake, one of the residual pools of oil that abounded all along the garage floor caught fire.

"Emerson! Get away!"

The barrier of heat knocked her back, throwing her against the external wall of the small office where the unconscious attendants still lay. Drake caught her movements from the edge of his vision. The urge to go to her was strong, but when she waved a hand to indicate she was okay, he again focused on his task.

Where is the water?

The flash of fire had momentarily distracted Magnus, but the man had regained his feet. Drake rose to meet him, the heavy fist that plowed into his midsection a clear signal Magnus had gotten his second wind.

With an answering fist of his own, Drake resumed his search of the garage and . . .

There!

Through the open door of the office he sensed the water. A row of large jugs, the type that were used on top of a cooler, drew his attention. Without wasting any more time, he pulled on the water there, dragging it toward them and the still-burning fire.

Drawing on every drop he could reach, Drake pulled

at the water, willing it to cover the floor first, before marshaling what was left of it to aid in the fight.

Quinn continued to grunt next to him as he engaged in battle with Eris. The fight was completely physical, and whatever reserve he and his brothers might normally have about hurting a woman wasn't in evidence as the bull and the goddess went toe-to-toe.

"What have you done to my sister?" Magnus grunted as he whirled away from the torrent of water that pummeled his midsection. As the force pushed Magnus back, Drake shifted his focus and forced a wave at Eris.

"Nice one, Drake." Quinn exhaled as the wall of water tripped up Eris in her four-inch heels.

"I've done nothing to your sister except love her and accept her just as she is." The available water supply was waning and Drake knew it was time to end this. "She's made every glorious inch of herself all on her own."

Magnus wiped at the blood that pooled in the corner of his mouth. "Her abilities are amazing. Even for my family, they're unheard of. My mother couldn't even do that."

"She's gifted." Drake lunged the moment he saw an opening. Magnus's midsection was exposed and the snake was recoiling on the floor. With heavy movements, Drake slammed his booted foot on the snake's head while he rammed his shoulder into Magnus.

The well-timed movement had the desired effect, knocking Emerson's brother backward while using the snake tethered to his body to hold him in place.

Although none of their tattoos could technically be

ripped from their bodies, the sheer force of the battle had the snake dissolving back into Magnus's aura, relieving him of one of his battle strengths.

Unwilling to give Magnus time to figure out how to work around it, Drake continued his assault, his movements determined as he pressed Magnus on across the floor, until a concrete wall stopped his backward movement.

"She's worth so much more than you," he gritted as he caught Magnus's neck in a tight grip. "And yet you cause her endless pain. You throw her love back in her face."

"You know nothing," Magnus grunted back, the cords of his neck sticking out with the effort of his struggle.

"She would have helped you. Done whatever she could. Yet you shame her with what you've become."

"I'm just. Like. You." The grip on his neck had the words coming out in whispered fits.

"You're nothing like me."

Drake felt the tide of battle shift as the fight moved in his favor. The urge to simply destroy him was a living, breathing thing inside of him, yet Drake knew it wasn't an option.

His duty was to rid the world of threats, but this was the brother of the woman he loved.

Could he do that to her? Or live with himself if he did?

Themis.

He'd capture Magnus and call on Themis. Gain her aid to turn him back to whatever pathetic waste he was before.

"Drake. Please." The small hand on his forearm

stopped him. Pulled him back from the internal debate on what to do with the man. "Please. You can't hurt him."

"Em," Magnus gasped out. "Make him. See reason. He's going to kill me."

Her gray eyes swirled with misery and an odd sort of acceptance, as if her entire life had led to this moment. "Is there any other way?"

"There is."

The complete and utter focus on Magnus had him forgetting Quinn's battle a few feet away. The loud shout tore his attention away for a fraction of a second, but it was all Eris needed.

A white-hot burst of light crashed over all of them with the force of a tornado. Drake lost his grip on Magnus as Emerson went flying back to land in a heap near the small office.

"You will not take what is mine." Eris's voice echoed off the concrete of the garage as her hand tightened on Magnus's shoulder.

Before any of them could move in to stop her, the goddess and her charge disappeared into a port.

The back porch had always offered an odd sort of comfort and this moment was no different, Drake thought as he held Emerson in his arms. It signified home as well as the end of a battle.

He'd never known which he appreciated more, but the moment of arrival always brought out a quick instant of reflection.

"Let's get her inside." Callie shifted from foot to foot as Quinn fiddled with the security system.

Emerson had taken quite a hit off of Eris's fireball

and Drake was unwilling to put her through a port until Callie thoroughly checked her out. Add to it he hadn't had breakfast and was fairly drained from the fight and the possibility of a bumpy ride wasn't out of the question. She'd remained lucid, but limp in his arms for the block and a half walk back to the brownstone.

"We're almost there, baby," Drake crooned against her temple as he headed for the deep couches and warm atmosphere of the library.

"Where do you think she took my brother?" Emerson's voice was quiet, but her eyes were more than clear as she looked up at him.

He laid her gently on the couch, the mix of fear and pain that rode her features an arrow to his heart. Kneeling down next to her, he linked his fingers with hers. "I don't know."

"Were you going to kill him?" The words were even quieter than the last and they held a world of meaning.

"I wanted to get him to Themis. To see if she can fix him."

"You weren't going to kill him?"

"Only if he touched you."

"He's my brother, Drake. My family." She struggled to sit up, but he gently held her still. "He wouldn't do that."

"I don't think he wants to, but he may not be able to help himself."

"He can't be saved? Is that what you're trying to tell me?"

"Emerson, you have my word that I'll try to get an audience with Themis to get him help."

"And if that doesn't work?"

"We won't know unless we try."

Her eyes narrowed and he knew she wouldn't be put off. "But if it doesn't work. And he comes back."

"You come first."

Finley stared at the file on her computer, nausea churning in her gut. Why had she come here?

Why hadn't she listened to Grey?

She'd fought him about coming to work, claiming she needed routine. Needed to be a part of things until he'd finally agreed.

And now she knew exactly what she was a part of: a corrupt office with a colleague who was in way over her head.

Her gaze skimmed over the window next to her before settling on the clock. It was well into the afternoon and she hadn't eaten yet.

Maybe she wouldn't come back.

She shot a quick text to the security detail Quinn had assigned her and Matthew texted back he'd meet her in front of the building. The man had made no secret of his dislike of waiting that far away from her, but even Grey had agreed she didn't need to tip anyone in the DA's office off by running around with her new accessory in tow.

Committing the file to a thumb drive, she shook her head, surprised and saddened by the discovery all over again.

Melanie Claridge.

It had been Melanie all along, even after Finley'd dismissed her possible involvement several times.

They'd started in the DA's office at the same time,

both fresh out of law school and eager to make their mark on the city's legal system. Where had Melanie gone so wrong?

Quinn had run the information remotely and sent it to her, the results as clear as water. The woman had a series of case files saved to the personal drive of her computer that she'd not worked on. On their own, none were incriminating. But when looked at in aggregate, it had been immediately evident she'd focused on researching the Gavelli crime family.

From there, Quinn had quickly dug through the layers of her files, including sorting through all the personal e-mails she'd sent from her work machine. If you put aside the stupidity of that one, the rest of what she'd done had been surprisingly crafty. Not to mention deeply disappointing.

And all for a man, Finley thought with no small layer of disgust.

Melanie had taken up with Gavelli's eldest son. Franco Gavelli Jr. was next in line to run the family business and had built up an impressive set of scores all on his own. He ran the family's drug trade and had evidently put his MBA to good use, streamlining their money laundering into a new art form.

Finley grabbed her purse and took the stairs the two floors to the lobby. She saw Matthew through the revolving front door and felt an odd sense of relief at his presence. Breezing through the doors, she took a deep breath and concentrated on putting one foot in front of the other.

She'd get some food and fresh air, and then she'd figure out what to do.

No, correct that, she thought. She'd work with Grey and Quinn and the others and *they'd* figure out what to do.

She had backup now. People she trusted.

The sounds of the city surrounded her as she headed down the block toward the deli she loved. Jerry, the lovable bear behind the counter, would make her a tuna fish on wheat and she might even treat herself to a black and white cookie. Or maybe a Rice Krispies Treat.

That'd work, something gooey and sinful.

She turned toward Matthew to see what he wanted, but a heavy sound caught her attention before she could get the words out.

The large man was on the ground. Before she could go to him, she was blocked by a tall, slender woman.

"Ms. McCrae, I'm going to need you to come with me."

Before she could even process the instinct to run, the woman had her forearm in a tight grip and the world vanished.

The tangy burn of fear lit up her taste buds, but Emerson forced herself to ask one more question. "You'd kill my brother?"

Those genie's eyes, so often full of mystery or humor or knowledge, held only cold, harsh truth. "If he hurts you, I will destroy him."

There was a time she'd believed Magnus wouldn't hurt her, but that time was long past.

Her vision had cleared and she saw him for what he was.

Magnus couldn't control who he was—he never

could. And now that he had these . . . skills, the problem had only grown.

"And that woman who was with him, Eris?" When he nodded, she continued. "She's the woman in my vision from the mirror. The one who made him. What could she possibly want with my brother?"

"That's what we need to figure out. It's also what I'm hoping Themis can help us with."

Emerson lay silently, the events of the last hour playing through her mind in vivid detail. All these long years she'd worried that Magnus was lost to them and she hadn't really known. Hadn't understood just how lost he really was.

And her mother. Lost, too, just like Magnus.

Somewhere deep inside she desperately tried to conjure some feeling—some emotion—about her mother's betrayal.

And couldn't find a damn thing when she counterbalanced it with the fact that her mother had made the right decision in the end.

She'd saved Magnus.

And he'd thrown away that gift.

An odd thought replaced it and she shifted to Drake. "When were you turned?"

Drake had stood to pace the room and her question stopped him as he stood staring at a row of books on one of the many shelves. "What?"

"When you became a Warrior. With Themis. When did it happen?" Oddly enough, she'd never thought to ask the question before. Now that she had, how he answered was strangely important to her.

Was his turning different from her brother's? Were

there reasons a person selected this life that weren't so dark and power hungry?

"I was turned in the fourth century BC."

The mere idea of it was mind-boggling. "That means you're—"

"Old," Drake answered for her, a wry smile springing to his lips. "I'm ancient."

The idea of it was astounding. Especially when the face that gazed back at her—a face that had become as important as her next breath—looked as if it were no older than thirty-five. "Wow."

"I was a soldier in Alexander the Great's army."

"No way!" She sat up at that, unwilling to simply lie there despite the bruises that throbbed under her skin. "You can't be serious."

"It's true."

The same thoughts that had haunted her for years— how he seemed like a hero of old—weren't all that far off the mark. "So you really were a Greek warrior?"

"We preferred to be called Macedonians, but yes. We're Greeks. I'm Greek by birth."

"And your parents? Your family?"

"I came from a very wealthy family at the time. My father was in great favor with Alexander's father."

Emerson's mind whirled with the possibilities. "Your father was friends with Philip of Macedonia?"

"You know your history."

"I love that stuff. Battles and power and the expansion of humanity in a never-ending set of conquests."

"Bloodthirsty." Drake took the seat next to her.

"Just fascinated." Another thought grabbed her as

her mind whirled with what she knew of Alexander the Great. "He was taught by Aristotle."

"So was I."

"Holy shit." The words came out on a rush of breathless wonder she was helpless to hold back. "No wonder you're so calm in the face of battle. You trained at the side of the world's greatest general and were taught at the knee of the world's greatest philosopher."

"I was about ten years older than Alexander, so I fought with him as part of his army for only a couple of years."

"What happened?"

"While in service to his father, I'd heard tales of a woman who made immortal Warriors. Something about the story enthralled me and wouldn't let me go. I sought her out."

"Themis, you mean?"

"For years and years, I searched for her, hoping she'd find favor with me."

While Drake's story fascinated her, she couldn't stop the small kernel of unease that unfurled at his telling. It was strangely akin to what she'd felt when Magnus pushed at her, telling her to take advantage of her powers. "What did you want with her?"

"I'd long grown tired of war. I'm good at it, but I can't say I like it all that much. I'd also seen all the backstabbing and machinations that were a part of court life."

"Philip was assassinated, yes?"

"That was the beginning of the end for me. I saw the allegiances my father made. Hell, I knew the pressure that was on me to continue as a leader in Alexander's army. I just wanted some sort of escape from all of it."

"By becoming a different sort of Warrior?"

"Exactly. Although Themis was honest with me and let me make my own choice, in the end there was a bit of simply trading one set of problems for another."

Emerson sighed, thoughts of her own personal choices through the years swamping her. "The human existence. We always think the grass is greener."

"And it's always just a new patch of grass. Different from the one we had, but not fundamentally altered in makeup or definition."

She stopped at that, thinking about the changes he'd brought into her life. She'd fought it—fought it with everything inside of her—but her life *wasn't* the same any longer.

She hadn't simply traded one patch of grass for another.

"Did you have a family of your own?"

"At the point of Philip's death, I was betrothed to a daughter of a high-ranking official."

Emerson couldn't have stopped the hard clench of jealousy that rose up in her stomach if she'd tried. Forcing a layer of calm into her voice she didn't feel, she pressed for more of the story. "Why didn't you marry her?"

"We were waiting for her to be of age—which was part of the appeal, I realized later. I'd wanted out for a long time. I just hadn't been able to put a name to it or understand how I'd go about it. Her age was a handy excuse to avoid marriage as I worked through it."

"You were in the army, too. I can't imagine she was

all that excited about having a husband who was never home."

"Which was the other handy excuse that allowed me to drag my feet as long as I did." Drake shrugged. "Not that it would have mattered. Political matches have very little to do with even liking each other, and being apart is actually more ideal that not."

"Was she beautiful?" The words were out before she could stop them.

"I can't say I really know. Athene was a child—I'd only ever seen her a handful of times."

"So you didn't love her?"

The twin sparks of mystery and fun lit up his eyes, replacing the harder emotions she'd seen there earlier. "No, I didn't love her." His smile fell as he paused. "I shamed my family because I refused to go through with it. The last time I spoke to my father was the day I told him I wouldn't marry and left to march with Alexander's army into Persia."

"You never saw him again?"

"Once. On the day of his burial, I snuck into the house to gaze upon him for the last time."

"Times like that—the times you're from. They could make a person hard and unyielding. But you're not either. Why is that?"

Drake shrugged, his words soft and strangely tempting as he lowered his face toward hers. "You tell me."

"I think you fight it. I think you fight the hard. Fight to be the person you want to be on the inside. The person who doesn't want to war. Who doesn't want to fight. Who doesn't want to be with someone you don't love."

His lips rested against hers, so light she barely felt them, even as everything she was centered itself in that moment. "How do you know me so well?"

Before she could respond, a loud bellow echoed outside the hallway as Quinn appeared in the room. Drake leaped up, his battle-ready stance the evidence he was truly a Warrior at heart.

"She's gone."

"Who's gone?" Drake moved toward the door, his focus on the bull and whatever had him so riled.

"Finley. I just got word from my man I've got posted with her. They were attacked on the street and she's been taken."

"Fuck. We need to find Grey."

As if conjured, the Aries materialized in the library. His shirttails hung from beneath his coat and his hair stuck up in sharp spikes.

"Eris has her."

Chapter Nineteen

Grey had never really understood the term "out of your mind" until that singular moment when Eris's note had arrived at Equinox. Short, terse and unsigned, the message was easy to decipher.

> *Counselor McCrae's been a model prisoner, but I know I'll tire of her quickly. Kindly bring my apple and my diary if you hope to see her alive.*

"How the hell could you let this happen to her?" He heard the accusation in his own voice but refused to hold it back as he railed at his Warrior brothers moments after receiving the note. "I listened to you. I trusted you that your security detail would be enough. Well, it wasn't fucking enough, Quinn."

He'd be damned if he'd play the whole we're-a-brotherhood-and-no-one-gets-mad-at-the-fuckup routine.

Because someone *had* fucked up.

Royally.

"Drake and Emerson needed our help." Quinn's voice was quiet but the authority—and responsibility—was unmistakable.

"So you just left your man on her—your mortal man—with no backup? You might as well have put her in the middle of fucking Times Square with a target on her head."

While responsible, the bull also wasn't taking his shit. "What the hell else was I supposed to do? She's not our prisoner, Grey, and she's not yours. She's a grown woman with a life. The fish needed us."

"Finley needed you. She needed our protection."

And even that hadn't been enough.

"She *had* our protection. Now it's up to us to get her back."

The urge to port away was strong, but Grey knew he needed to stay and work through their game plan. Knew that he needed to calm down and focus.

Focus through the mind-numbing fear of what awaited her in her real life, where monsters plotted and lurked to hurt her. So instead of telling her how he felt and how concerned he was, he'd hidden himself away. He'd refused to give her any part of himself or any sense that he was in this with her.

And now Eris had her.

"Look. She can't have had her for long," Emerson reasoned from where she had her elbow in a bowl of ice on the table. "The attack at the garage just happened a little over an hour ago. She was under surveillance before you came to us. Right, Quinn?"

Quinn nodded. "Absolutely."

"Why weren't *you* watching her, Grey?" Callie's voice was rapier sharp and—as always—right on the money.

"I've been scouring the streets trying to find the people in her office responsible for setting her up."

"No, you were hiding." Callie's gaze never broke as she dropped the next bomb. "And if you'd give Quinn half a chance, he could also fill you in on the information he found."

"What the fuck?" He refused to hold back the anger, the adrenaline and the frustration that his family hadn't thought to loop him in. "You don't tell me?"

"You. Weren't. Here," Quinn shot back, his anger telegraphed in the set of his shoulders and the distinctly forward-leaning posture he'd adopted.

Grey knew that pose. It was the one that said he'd just waved a red flag at their bull.

"You could have let me know."

"Or maybe you could have responded to the call and the text I sent you."

Grey threw his hands up, torn between the underlying acknowledgment they were right and the ruthless fear that continued to press on him as he struggled to understand where she could have been taken.

"Look. It hasn't been that long. Add to that we know a lot more than Eris thinks we do and we'll find her." Quinn moved up and Grey felt the acknowledging slap on his back. "We'll find her, Grey."

Although it was a far cry from comforting, his brothers did have his back. Grey knew that, no matter how mad he was. "How? Eris could have her anywhere."

"And if she wants us to bring her her goodies, she's going to need to let us know where she is."

"She won't bring Finley to the meet."

"We won't deal, Grey. If she doesn't bring Finley, she gets nothing." Grey looked down where Quinn laid a hand on his forearm. "We're going to get your woman back."

"She's not my woman."

"Could have fooled me."

Finley stared down at the fire-engine-red polish on her toenails and realized she needed a pedicure.

Which was an absurd thought, really, since the fact that she was a kidnapping victim for the second time in less than a week meant an hour in a salon chair should be the least of her worries.

No matter how many times she told herself that, her gaze continued to travel over each nail, looking for imperfections. The small chip in her second toe on her right foot kept drawing her attention, even as she resisted the urge to peel off more polish.

If she was going to die today, she'd like her feet to look as nice as possible.

Die today.

It was not only possible, it was highly probable. All because she thought she knew better.

Why had she gone into the office?

Her frustration whispered to her as she ran the pad of one finger over her second toe. Like that chip in the polish, she had a fundamental flaw.

She *always* thought she knew better. Always thought she was right.

And look where the hell it had gotten her.

Abstractly, she wondered if Grey knew she was gone. Would he really care?

When they were together, he acted like he had an interest in her. She certainly hadn't made that kiss up all on her own. But all the kissing in the world couldn't change the fact he saw her as a chore. A chore he thought he could maneuver.

A chore he assumed he knew better how to handle.

Which really didn't make them all that different, she realized with a small laugh.

Take out the immortality and the ability to fly through space at the summoning of your will and they were all too alike.

Two stubborn idiots who thought they knew better and who were damn sure they weren't going to share what they really thought with the other.

God, she was a prize.

All the brains in the world and the ability to reason through things like a lawyer and it hadn't done her a lick of good. And now she had a chipped toenail, was likely to die and was never going to kiss Grey Bennett again.

She wasn't quite sure which upset her the most.

The guy she'd seen earlier—the one who looked like he'd been smashed through a blender—opened the door and walked into her room. Although he looked moderately better than earlier, there was a distinct hunch to his broad shoulders that she found eerie. Like he was hiding something.

"What do you want?"

"Eris wanted me to check on you."

"I'm locked in a windowless room. What the hell was she expecting? A tap dance routine?"

The endless string of women-in-danger movies she watched on Sunday afternoons had prepared her for a slap or a scream or some form of retaliation, but the guy simply held his ground across from her, an odd, speculative stare on his face.

"You've taken up with the Warriors, too?"

She battled between saying nothing and using his overture to get some information. The same innate curiosity that had called her to the legal profession reared up and she knew there was no way she could keep her questions to herself.

It was inevitable.

Like the way she loved Grey or the fact that she *would* peel at that polish on her toe.

Loved Grey?

The knowledge had her stumbling over her next breath, but she held herself steady as she took air in and out in slow, easy gulps.

She couldn't love Grey. It simply wasn't possible. Smart, successful women didn't fall for bad boys, no matter how well pressed or expensive the suits they clothed themselves in or quality of the wine they drank.

But she had. Oh God, she'd fallen for Grey.

"Are you going to answer me?"

She pulled her attention back from her wildly flinging thoughts. "Answer what?"

"You're just like my sister, taking up with one of the Warriors."

"Why do you care?

And why was he so chatty? Although she realistically knew Lifetime Movies of the Week weren't necessarily a stand-in for real life—hell, she'd read enough case files to know that for certain—she also wasn't expecting a casual conversation about her whereabouts for the past week.

"Curiosity."

"Well, take it elsewhere."

He didn't move from his spot, his breath steady and even. "You're the bargaining chip. You know that, don't you?"

Adrenaline ricocheted through her body, and Finley felt the recoil as it kicked through her stomach on a return trip. How to play this? Brazen and bold hadn't really worked on Gavelli and his men in the warehouse, but playing dumb didn't seem like an effective tactic, either.

On a silent prayer, she tried brazen and bold once more. "Forget me. What about you? Why have you done this to your sister?"

The quiet, almost subdued demeanor he'd walked in with morphed in the blink of an eye. What replaced it had her taking several steps back as he stalked across the room, his movements surprisingly sinuous for such a large man.

"You know nothing about me and my sister."

Finley stayed on her guard, but there was no way she was keeping her mouth shut. She'd seen the haunted look in Emerson's eyes and with startling clarity realized she was looking at the man who'd put it there. "I know that you've nearly destroyed her with whatever it is you've become."

"I'm fulfilling my destiny."

"Is that Eris's sales pitch before she turns you into a freak?"

"And that fuckwad my sister has taken up with isn't? Don't delude yourself. I'm as powerful as they are."

"With a side of psycho to boot."

Magnus didn't move, his posture so still she almost wished he had leaped at her to shut her up. Instead, a sudden, distinctive feeling washed over her as his dark gaze bored into hers, and she took a few steps backward.

Prey.

He kept her in his sights, his dark eyes almost hypnotic as they stared at her, unblinking. As that gaze continued to bore into her like a drill, a large snake unfurled off his back.

Where it came from, Finley had no idea, but she took a few more steps back. The frenzied urge to move quickly nearly overtook her, but she kept her pace even— measured—as she sought to put space between them.

It wasn't until her shoulders hit the heavy concrete blocks that made up the walls of her prison that she finally allowed herself to scream.

"I'm not staying here, Drake. Don't even think about it."

Drake tossed a casual glance at Emerson as he paced around his room, opening drawers and dragging out a variety of weapons. He'd considered and discarded several as he crisscrossed the floor with determined steps. "You can't go."

"You can't keep me here."

"Emerson, you've been hurt. I can't see you get hurt even more." The image of her lying against the far wall of the parking garage wouldn't leave his mind's eye, no matter how many times he looked at her—no matter how many times he touched her to reassure himself she was okay. "I can't worry about something happening to you again."

"This is my brother we're talking about. You know he's a part of this with Finley."

"So is Eris, which means you need to leave this to me. My Warrior brothers and I will take care of this."

"It involves me, Drake."

"Emerson, you're a liability if I spend the entire time worried about you."

She slipped off the bed, the frustrated anger that had simmered under her words for the duration of their conversation shifting into something far more confrontational.

Something far more lethal.

"Let me tell you something, Ace. You use that condescending tone with me one more time and I'm going to hurt you."

"It's not condescension; it's the truth. I won't let you go back into that. I nearly got you killed earlier. I'm not going to knowingly take you into another situation like what we faced in the garage."

"You don't have a choice."

Whatever sedate abilities she believed he carried were nowhere in evidence as fear and frustration rocketed through him in equal measure. "Fuck if I don't."

He was across the room in a heartbeat, dragging her into his arms, desperate to make her see reason as he pulled her close. "I can't lose you."

"I'm in this."

"No, you're not. *I'm* in this. Grey's in this. Even Magnus is in this. You're not."

The large ceremonial sword he'd taken off the wall, then rested against a large armoire after deciding it lacked the degree of subtlety he was looking for, shuddered against the wood of the chest before drifting toward them. Drake watched it move, almost mesmerized by the floating steel, until he registered its intent. As the sword moved across the room, it picked up speed until it raced for his throat in a heavy, sweeping arc.

With a tight grip, Drake ported them across the room, the sound of the sword clattering to the floor greeting his ears as he and Emerson landed. "What the—?"

Had she really done this?

The fire had been one thing—expected, almost—but *this*?

Before he could tighten his grip on her—before he could even stutter out a few questions—Emerson was out of his arms and crossing the room, her hands outstretched. The tip of the sword hit the floor a few times before it was again airborne and headed for her hand.

Drake heard the self-satisfaction in her voice before she turned with a matched smile. "Now do you believe me?"

"How did you do that?"

"Remember the drop of ice cream?"

Ice cream? "The one from when you were a kid?"

"Yep."

"What does that have to do with this?"

"Same principle."

Pride and wonder mixed with raw fear made an awfully strange combination, but that was the exact brew that boiled in his system as he crossed the room toward

her. "Same principle, my ass. This is a forty-pound ceremonial sword. It's nothing like a drop of ice cream."

"Actually, magically speaking, it is."

"I thought you couldn't do inanimate objects?"

"I'm not *doing* anything. I'm moving it and using its
physicality to my advantage. There's no spell on the
actual object."

"But you just moved it across the room."

"Right. I moved it through space. I can't put an actual spell on the sword. On any inanimate object." As if
to prove her point, she extended it to him by the hilt.
"Go ahead. Hold it."

When he took it from her, he almost expected it to
light up with some sort of electric shock, but the sword
felt just as it had when he'd removed it from the wall.
Like a heavy, lethal piece of metal. "It doesn't feel any
different."

"And it won't. It isn't different."

"You just tossed it across the room."

"Which would be no different than if you had held
it in your hand and ran it across the room. I didn't do
anything to it."

"How did you do it?"

"Magic."

Drake shook his head, trying to make some sense
out of this new development. "You've been holding
out on me."

"Not really."

"Yes, really." Drake searched her wide eyes and innocent cupid's-bow mouth, but other than a very stubborn hand cocked against her hip, she didn't offer up
any further protest. "I knew you had skills. Power. But

this . . ." He turned the sword over in his hand once more. "This is just not possible."

"You can throw your body into the space-time continuum at will. I can move things. Do you really want to talk to me about possible?"

"This doesn't change my mind."

"It has to."

"I can't put you in that sort of danger."

Her small hands folded over his where he held the sword. "Don't you get it? Don't you get how much more powerful I am when we're together? What we can do when we're joined, just like those fish on your back?"

As if her words conjured their response, the tattoo on his back leaped in seeming agreement. Unwilling to acquiesce, he sought some other argument to change her mind.

To make her see reason.

"It doesn't change the fact you're mortal."

She pried his fingers off the hilt, taking the sword. With her free hand, she linked their fingers. "Watch this."

A small painting sat above his dresser on the far side of the room. The image depicted the twelve signs of the zodiac in a circle, with lines crisscrossing between the twelve, evenly demarcated signs. The lines all came to a point in the middle of the circle, at the exact center point of the painting.

As her fingers tightened on his, Emerson lifted her other hand and let go of the sword. Rather than fall to the floor, the weapon sprang from her hand and flew toward the painting.

Drake watched in awe as the tip hit dead center.

Chapter Twenty

Emerson marveled at the raw power that coursed through her veins as she looked at the sword embedded in the wall across the room.

She'd done that.

She knew she had power. She'd honed it over the many lonely years of her life, to both celebrate her gift and to stave off boredom. But she'd never shown it off to another.

And she'd certainly never before been willing to show off her magic—or display the full dimension of her power—for the man she loved.

It was exhilarating.

"You look awfully proud of yourself."

"I am. And I'm also trying to figure out what took me so long."

Drake turned toward her, the delight in his gaze only reinforcing her satisfaction at finally showing her true self.

"I've been hiding this from you and now you

know. And you seem to still want to drag my clothes off."

"I think you're amazing. Always." The evident pride that sparkled in the flecks of gold in his green eyes morphed into something even more seductive. "And I always want to drag your clothes off, too."

"Well, you can't right now. We've got a job to do. I presume Quinn's already got a council of war going downstairs and we should be a part of it."

Drake crossed the room to yank the sword from the plaster, his smile falling. "None of this changes how I feel."

"About my clothes?" She tossed the joke back at him, knowing full well what he meant.

"It doesn't change how I feel about you going with us. It also doesn't change the fact that while you wield a very powerful magic, you'd still have to use that power on your brother."

Drake's words stopped her, as her memories of the fight in the garage ran through her in a cold shiver. She'd turned her fire on Magnus twice now. Had taken her magic and not only used it against another, but used it against a loved one.

What did that make her? A betrayer of her gift or a betrayer of her family?

Or both?

"It doesn't change how I feel, either. I'm in this and I want you to accept it." When he turned to argue, she added, "I *need* you to accept this."

Drake settled the sword back against the armoire, his movements gentle for such a large man. Her gaze drank in the broad stretch of his back and the raw physicality of his form.

He was a Warrior.

And when he turned back to face her, the responsibility of that calling was etched across every inch of him.

"Do you know why I never married that woman? The one I was betrothed to?"

That familiar spurt of jealousy at the knowledge he'd been engaged to someone was quickly tamped out by curiosity. "No."

"I didn't love her."

Emerson had thought about his story—hadn't been able to stop thinking about it since they'd sat in the library—and she'd come to her own conclusions. "From what you said she was a child when you met. You'd have come to love her. Would have come to love the family you made with her."

A small smile ghosted his lips as Drake nodded. "You sound suspiciously like my father. But he was wrong, and so are you."

"Drake, come on. You lived in a time when people didn't marry for love."

He never moved from his spot across the room, but his words held a strange, enthralling power she was helpless to ignore. "Another one of my father's arguments. He claimed I had a duty to uphold. A duty to my family and to my country."

"And you felt differently?"

"I did, even though I couldn't put a name to it."

"What was that?" The question rose to her lips on a breathless whisper. "Why did you feel differently?"

"I wanted love."

"Everyone wants love, Drake. It's part of our human existence."

"Do you think so?"

Emerson heard the question beneath the question. "Don't you?"

"I think many people want what's convenient. Or they want the idea of love, but they're not really interested in the sacrifices that come with it."

"Maybe people aren't brave?"

"Or maybe they don't realize what it takes. What's required of them to love another."

"And you think you know?"

"I always thought I did, but now I don't know. I want to support you, Emerson. I want to believe in you and give you the freedom to be who you are. Because you're the woman I love. You're the woman I knew was out there."

With slow steps, he crossed the room. She felt that large, powerful body wrap itself around her as he took her in his arms. Felt him shudder as her arms went around his neck.

"But the gods help me if I'm brave enough to let you be who you are."

Finley curled on the small couch in the windowless room, unable to stop the shivers that racked her body. What had she done? And why hadn't she listened to Grey?

His heavy-handed tactics had chaffed more than she wanted to admit, but he had protected her. Had worked to keep her safe. But the stubborn, willful heart that beat in her chest had finally made a decision that would be her end.

Her hubris was her doom.

Although Magnus had held the snake at bay, using it only to taunt and frighten her, she saw in his eyes what he was capable of.

She'd first thought it was malice, but after a long hour spent shivering in mind-numbing terror, she acknowledged what it really was that lived in his dark eyes.

Fear.

She'd lived her entire adult life around criminals and she'd learned early on that fear was a far more dangerous emotion than malice or greed or even out-and-out evil. It was what turned a good man bad and decimated his soul.

Magnus Carano lived in a constant state of dread from the woman who'd made him and of what he'd become.

And she'd come blithely calling at the devil's door.

On a deep breath, Finley wrapped her arms around herself and willed the shivers to subside. She tried fervently to resurrect the spirit she knew she'd buried somewhere inside at the sight of that horrible snake.

On a heavy breath, she willed her nerves to calm as she fought to think rationally about her situation.

In . . . out . . .

What did she know?

Although it felt like she'd been in this room forever, she knew the reality was that she'd only been here a few hours. She'd simply run out for a late lunch—the corner deli a block from her office—when she was grabbed by the mystery woman. She'd even brought the security detail Quinn had assigned to her along.

But it hadn't mattered.

Halfway down the block, her hand had grabbed her arm. Before she could even struggle, her body had been thrown into that disorienting sensation Grey called a port. Then she'd been shoved into this room and the door had slammed behind her.

In . . . out . . .

What else did she know?

She'd already surmised they were holding her in some sort of basement and also suspected they were still in the city because she could swear she heard the heavy throb of traffic at regular intervals.

In . . . out . . .

Where could they have taken her?

The door banged open and Finley leaped to a sitting position, the heavy exhalation of breath catching in her throat. A small cry echoed across the cavernous room as a small, petite body fell through the door before it was slammed closed once again.

Melanie?

Finley raced to the woman only to have her scrabble away as she came close. "Don't touch me!"

"Melanie." When the woman just shook her head, Finley raised her voice. "Melanie! It's me."

The blond head stopped its wild shaking as her gaze focused. "Finley?"

"Yes."

"Why? How?" Melanie lifted her head farther as hope bloomed on the pale pink of her cheeks. "What are you doing here?"

White-hot anger sharpened into a narrow point as Finley moved toward the still-huddled woman. "You mean you really don't know?"

"Know what?"

Feelings she hadn't even realized she'd repressed came barreling out. The shivers that had consumed her only moments before shifted on a rush of adrenaline. She clenched her hands into tight fists to try and stop them from reaching for Melanie. "You've been setting me up for weeks."

That slight wash of pink in her cheeks vanished. "But I haven't."

"Cut the bullshit, Melanie. I know about the files on your computer and your relationship with Gavelli." The woman's eyes went wide with surprise, but Finley pressed on. "I know all about it."

"But you can't know. He told me you'd never know."

"Who? Your mobster boyfriend?"

"Franco told me it was all for the greater good and that he just wanted a chance to explain. That you were out to get him for something he didn't do and that he had evidence that proved he wasn't guilty."

"Guilty for what?"

"He said you were trying to frame him for those murders up in the Bronx last January."

What?

The urge to simply throw up her hands was strong, but Finley waited. Something in the woman's voice—in her broken gaze—held her back. "Why would I do that? Why would you think I'd done that?"

"He had evidence. E-mails."

Finley ran the history of the case through her mind,

unable to make a connection with the Gavellis. "Those murders had nothing to do with a mob hit. I never even pursued that angle because the police had already gathered quite a bit of evidence that suggested it was a gang retaliation."

"But Franco had evidence."

"And you believed him?"

The shoulders that had looked broken when she'd arrived bent even further under the weight of her misjudgment. "Oh my God. Finley. Oh God, I'm so sorry. I didn't know. I . . ." A heavy sob shook her. "I love him."

Finley wanted to rant and rage.

Wanted to tell the woman what an idiotic sap she'd been, but playing judge and jury didn't rest all that well on shoulders that only moments before had shook with the knowledge of her own stupid decisions.

"Love, Mel? Really?"

Large tears welled in Melanie's eyes and spilled over. "I'm the worst cliché. But I swear he was telling the truth."

"What would possibly make you believe him?"

The woman's slender shoulders crumpled and the blue of her eyes shined with a sudden clarity. "I don't know, Finley. I really don't know."

Finley moved forward and dragged the woman into her arms. "Come on. There's a bed over here you can sit down on."

They crossed the room and, as she held Melanie's shaking body close, she couldn't help but wonder what would come next.

* * *

Drake kept his gaze focused on the big-screen TV that Quinn had hooked up to the security center for their briefing. They'd descended into the Batcave, as Ilsa had dubbed it, in the basement of the brownstone rather than all crowd their way into Quinn's office.

While the leather couches were more comfortable than hard rolling chairs, all the comforts in the world couldn't calm the roiling nerves that filled the room.

"Where did Eris get a warehouse, Quinn?" Grey argued with the bull as Quinn pointed out the only entry point on the building he believed housed Finley. "She's got to be somewhere else."

"It's Gavelli's warehouse and it's the first place I looked." Quinn tapped the flat screen. "Luckily, I still had the feed set up from the other night and on a hunch I looked at it. Finley's there."

Grey wasn't calmed by Quinn's reasoning. "You've got no video of the surrounding blocks."

Drake inserted himself into the conversation. Although Quinn had been in Grey's spot not all that long ago, it was obvious his patience was fried. "And if Eris ported her in—which is likely—there won't be any."

"Wait a minute." Quinn tapped at a few keys. "I can pull up the city's cameras. She had to have been taken near work."

"Which I should never have let her go back to," Grey muttered.

"Son of a bitch," Quinn breathed on a heavy groan, ignoring Grey's words. "There she is."

They all stood and moved closer to the screen as Finley's form came into view. They could see Quinn's man walking behind her, attacked from behind just off camera as Eris got her.

The port began instantaneously, the two women evaporating from view. Emerson let out a choked cry as the image of her brother stepping over the guard and porting away filled the screen next.

"Oh my God, he can really do it." She gripped Drake's hand, shaking her head all the while. "I believed it. I knew he did it, but I didn't actually see it happen. Magnus can port on his own, not tethered to Eris."

"Emerson. Come on. Sit down; it's a lot to take in."

Despite the subtle pressure on her arm to sit back down on the couch, she stood firm. "No, Drake. I can handle it."

Grey pointed to the screen once again. "Rewind it, Quinn. I want to see it again."

"She has to know we're going to put up a fight," Quinn murmured as he stared at the screen.

"And she's using Finley to keep us in line." Grey's gaze snapped to him.

"Finley's handy. It's the fight she wants." Rogan stood at the doorway.

Grey moved immediately for the archer, but Drake and Quinn were up and after him before he could make contact.

"Fuck you both!" Grey struggled against their hold. "He's not welcome here."

Drake pushed back, refusing to relent on his grip as Grey continued to fight them. "He knows her better than any of us."

"He's a gods damn traitor."

"He's your brother," Drake bit out, the power of those words slamming him swiftly in the gut.

Brother.

The knowledge of what that meant—of what they'd shared through the years—dragged at his conscience. He'd turned on Rogan, too. Had been quick to blame him for an error in judgment any of them could have made.

"He put her in danger. He put us all in danger," Grey spat out as he continued to push against the tight hold.

"I never meant to cause this. Never." Rogan's words were clear and unwavering. He stood at the door, his hands at his sides, ready to take whatever they dished at him.

Moving forward, he walked up to Grey all the while keeping his hands at his sides. "She's a hot fuck, Grey. I put us all at risk for that and I'm sorry. I'm so sorry."

Grey's tense form slackened as Rogan's words sank in.

"But I can help you get Finley back. I went to see Eris and I put a tracking device on her."

"You what?" Quinn moved forward.

"Grab your equipment. It's one of the new ones you gave me a few months back. I put it on her phone."

Quinn reached for the ever-present handheld device he carried and started tapping on the screen.

Rogan turned to address all of them, but his gaze never left Grey's. "You have my word. I will hunt that bitch to the ends of the earth, but first I'll help you get Finley back."

"Love doesn't simply evaporate, Rogan." Emerson's words filled the silence that had descended between all of them. "I now know that better than anyone. Magnus is my brother and I love him. I can't change that, regardless of the fact I know what needs to be done."

Rogan shifted his gaze from Grey's to rest on the small pixie with the iron will. "This isn't the same. I don't love Eris." When she simply raised an eyebrow, he added, "Will you do what must be done, Emerson?"

"Absolutely."

"As will I."

As Drake stared at the men he loved like brothers and the woman who was the only love he'd ever known, he fought the rising dread.

They were his family.

What if he lost them?

And then it didn't matter when Rogan stretched out his hand and Grey took it, dragging him close for a brief embrace. Their archer's voice was low and meant for Grey's hearing, but none of them missed his words in the quiet room. "With everything that I am, you have my word. We will bring Finley home."

Chapter Twenty-one

Drake paced the observatory, his gaze going repeatedly to Emerson's back fence where it had all started. Had he really stood here only a few nights ago and watched Emerson in the backyard?

So much had changed.

Between the two of them.

Between all of them.

"You look like you lost your best friend." Ilsa's voice carried on the summer's breeze. "Or like a sad sack of shit. Take your pick."

"Refreshing, as always."

She walked over to join him, the sly smile that usually rode her features notably absent. "What are you doing up here all by yourself?"

"Thinking. Preparing." He sighed, not sure where the sudden impulse for honesty came from, but going with it all the same. "Trying to figure out ways I can trick Emerson and leave her behind."

"She's going to be fine, you know." Long auburn locks streamed about Ilsa's face in the breeze.

"You can't possibly know that."

"I can believe it to be true."

Drake had always been willing to listen to that sixth sense—the one that told him his heart knew something long before his head did.

But this time . . . he just couldn't take the risk.

"Believing it won't make it so."

"She's your soul mate, Drake. She's in this. A part of this to the very end."

"Don't you understand? That's the very reason I can't let her go in there. She's a mortal, Ilsa."

"A mortal with a shitload of firepower behind her."

"She's still a mortal. I saw her today. In that garage after the fight with Eris. She was crumpled in the corner against the wall and my heart broke."

She reached out a hand to stop him, but he shrugged her off, turning to pace. "It fucking broke in two! I can't keep her safe."

"Kane can't keep me safe. Brody can't keep Ava safe. You have to trust."

"It has nothing to do with trust. You can't be broken like that. Neither can Ava and neither can Montana. It's not the same and you know it."

"None of us can conjure fire with our hands, either. She's got a gift, Drake, and it's hers to use as she sees fit. You can't stop her from doing that." Ilsa was quiet for a moment. "You have no right to stop her, either."

When had it all gotten so complicated? And why did every reasonable word out of Ilsa's mouth only reinforce his sense of dread?

"Even if I could find some way of agreeing with you, it's her brother. Do you understand the pain of that?

She has to take her gift and use it against him. She talks a tough game, Ilsa, but I've seen what it does to her. No one should have to make that choice."

"But again, Drake, it's her choice to make. Yes, it's her brother who breaks her in two. But because it's her brother, she has to see this through to the very end."

Before he could protest any further, Ilsa had her hands on his shoulders and turned him toward her. Her small hands cupped his face and her gaze bored into him with millennia of wisdom behind it.

"I've been where she is, Drake. I know what it is to need to see something through. To finish it. I couldn't be the woman Kane loves if I hadn't seen to my demons."

Her gaze softened as her mouth turned up into a smile. "She's the woman you love for a reason. And she loves you, too. Don't do something that will change that love and make her resent you."

"How'd you get so damn smart?"

"Natural talent." Her smile broadened before her hand snaked down to slap him on the ass. "And I also had a lot of years of fucking up before I figured it out."

"Oh, is that the secret? Fake it until you make it?"

"Nah, it just feels like it at the time." In another one of her lightning-quick changes, she linked her arm with his and pulled him toward the staircase, her sky-high heels clacking the entire way.

"So what is it, then? This mysterious secret you claim to know."

"Ah, sugar, you already know it, too. I know you do. Love's the answer. The rest of it is sort of meaningless if you don't have that."

Drake followed her down the staircase, her words echoing with every footstep he took.

Love *was* the answer.

Which was why his insides were liquid, thinking of what he'd do if he lost it.

Emerson stood in the weight room, using the last hour to practice. She'd already carb loaded on roughly half a pizza and was trying desperately to work off the case of nerves—and moderate indigestion—that had attacked her as she contemplated what she was about to do.

What she might be called to do.

With total focus, she lifted a hand weight off the floor with her mind and tossed it at the far wall. The ten pounder flew straight and true, landing with a thud against the heavy padding that coated the concrete.

Her line of reasoning to Drake hadn't been false bravado. She wasn't willing to back down. This was her family and her fight and she needed to see it through.

It didn't mean she wasn't sick with worry she'd have to make an irreversible decision.

"That's quite a trick."

Grey stood inside the doorway, clad head to toe in black. It was the first time she'd seen him in anything other than a suit and the contrast was startling. The suave, debonair businessman had been replaced by a gym rat in sweats.

"Thanks."

Grateful for the audience, she used the distraction to her advantage and focused on another weight. Keeping her gaze on Grey, she reached out with her gift, mentally focusing on the weight bench. She felt the ten pounds in her mind, then thrust it toward the far wall.

The thud on the floor indicated she'd missed her target by several feet.

"You never looked at it."

"Which is why I shorted the target," she muttered on a wave of disgust, before walking over to grab the weight.

"He doesn't want you to go."

"I know."

"I don't blame him. I'd feel better if you stayed here, too."

The weight felt extra heavy in her palm, as if she held his censure along with ten pounds of metal. "I can't do that."

"Doesn't mean I can't ask."

"I know."

Emerson mentally reached out for the weight again while she allowed her gaze to roam around the room. The dumbbell lifted in her mind before launching across the room.

Another thud indicated it hit the floor and missed the target.

"Damn it."

Between two misses and Grey's oppressive stare, Emerson whirled on him. "What do you want?"

"I want to talk some sense into you. He loves you, you know."

"Yeah. I know." Emerson tried to reach out with her mind, but nothing would take root there around Grey's words. On a small sigh, she abandoned her attempt on the weight and turned toward the Aries. "I love him, too."

"So why can't you put his mind at ease and stay here?"

"Because then I wouldn't be true to myself."

"Does that really matter? Isn't it supposed to be about putting the other person first?"

"Not when it comes at the expense of who you are."

Grey shook his head, and in that moment Emerson knew the long, endless years of being alone finally made sense.

They'd made her who she was. The person ready to be in a relationship. The person ready to give herself to another.

The person ready to face her own demons and defeat them.

She wasn't her mother, unable to live her life without a man. And she wasn't her brother, unable to face any of the challenges life holds. And while Veronica had come a long way, even she had ignored the harsh reality of facing who she was.

Emerson knew exactly who she was.

And it's why she knew that when this was all over, she'd embrace what she and Drake shared. Embrace what it brought to her life and would no longer try to put a box around it.

Or a definition.

She loved him and that was enough.

"Would you please sit still?" Eris tamped down on her rising discomfort as she and Magnus sat in the small office. She'd sent a missive more than ten minutes ago and hadn't heard one word back from the Warriors on her proposed drop point.

Magnus had damn near paced a hole in the floor, walking back and forth with that freakish snake following behind him. "And can't you control the snake yet?"

"No."

That was strange, too, she had to admit. Themis's Warriors all knew how to control their tattoos.

So what was Magnus's problem? She'd turned him more than six months ago and it was almost like he was regressing.

Despite his hangdog face and rather constant bitching, he was a fine specimen. His large body screamed Warrior of old, and he was fairly quick-footed in the midst of battle. Add to it he had a family history of magical abilities and you'd think the guy would be damn near bulletproof. But nothing seemed to work all that well.

It was like he hadn't quite gelled all the way.

The snake sure as shit wasn't cooperating and she'd yet to see any evidence of magical abilities.

"I don't have a good feeling about this. Why are we keeping Finley again? And now that other woman from her office?"

"They're insurance."

Her phone buzzed with an incoming text and she glanced down at the screen.

Ah, right on time. Humans actually *were* good for something.

WE'RE HERE.

She moved to the back of the warehouse to let the Gavellis in with their quarry. Magnus's heavy footfalls sounded behind her as she walked through the open space. "Where are you going?"

"I'm meeting our latest delivery."

"Another one?"

She threw the heavy lock back and pushed the door open. The gasp behind her was audible as Franco Gavelli and his father pushed through the door in their designer suits, their charge between them.

Hippolyta Carano stared at them from the other side of the door. Her old frame was hunched and her short gray hair stuck up in disarray. Although Eris had known she wasn't young, she looked considerably older than the photo Magnus carried in his wallet.

The woman's dark eyes went wide as they alighted on her grandson. "Magnus!"

"Oh my God. Grandmother."

Disorientation overtook Emerson the moment they moved alongside the warehouse. An odd sense of the familiar, sort of like a magical déjà vu. She and Drake already held hands, but she reached with her free one, dragging at his sleeve. "Drake. Something's wrong."

"It's all wrong."

"No, I mean beyond the fact we're hunting my brother down like a criminal. Something is *wrong*. I feel it."

Drake pulled her up short so that their backs hit the outside wall of the building and motioned the rest of them over.

"What's the problem, Fish?" Quinn's voice was all business as he moved up beside them.

"Something's not right," Emerson whispered again, unsure of any other way to define the unease. "It's something magical. I can feel it, but I can't explain what's different."

"Have you ever felt it before?"

Emerson wasn't sure why it mattered so much, but the immediate acceptance was enough to calm her nerves. Reaching out with her senses, she tried to get a bead on what was wreaking havoc with her instincts.

Like the moments with the weights, she allowed her magic to leave her body, weaving into the night air.

Searching . . . seeking . . . *breathing*.

She broke off the search and squeezed Drake's hand in frustration. "Nothing. I know it's there, but like something you can't quite see from the corner of your eye, I can't get to it. Can't focus on it."

"Should we go back?" Kane's low voice floated over them. "Regroup?"

"We don't have time," Grey muttered, already moving out of their stopped formation to move ahead.

"Are you okay to keep moving?" Drake's gaze reassured, even as she continued to fight the tendrils of unease that swirled around her.

"Yes. Let's keep going. I just want this over with."

"All right." Quinn extended his hands and pointed to opposite ends of the block. "As we planned it."

They broke off into formation, each knowing their part in the battle plans they'd prepared back at the brownstone. Rogan was already headed to the opposite end of the building while Montana stayed close to Quinn as he moved on in front of them.

Grey was the only one too far out in front.

Too exposed.

Again, Emerson couldn't fight the feeling that something was wrong, but knew by the determined set of Grey's shoulders he wouldn't listen. "He's putting himself in danger," she whispered to Drake.

"I think he welcomes it. In fact, I think he'd be thrilled if he could draw Eris out on his own. He blames himself for this."

"It's not entirely his fault."

"He could have handled it differently."

Emerson kept moving, but that pervasive sense of the familiar wouldn't subside. Another hit of déjà vu crowded her mind and she nearly stumbled from the intense wave of sensation.

"Emerson!" Drake's whisper was heavy in her ear even while he sounded very far away. Yet another attack of sensation bore down on her, as if willing her to figure it out.

Willing her to remember.

Familiar. The sensations were familiar and warm and oh so recognizable. Magic curled around her senses, tugging at her in heavy, syrupy waves.

"Drake?" The streetlights wavered at the edge of her vision as her mind rushed to figure out what was so familiar, yet so alien, all at the same time.

Time. There wasn't any more time.

She put one foot in front of the other as she clung to Drake's arm.

"Emerson!" Again, his voice sounded from far away, echoing through her mind from a great distance.

Once more, she forced her senses outward, seeking the power that came with knowledge and understanding.

Familiar. Warm. Home.

On a wave of dizziness, she barely held back the cry that sprang to her lips.

"Gram!"

Chapter Twenty-two

Drake raced after Emerson as she tugged out of his grip and took off for the end of the block. The warehouse loomed alongside them with a dark, creeping menace as he caught her and dragged her up in his arms. "Emerson!"

Agonized cries fell from her lips as she clawed at his arms. "She's got my grandmother."

"Shhhh. We'll get her," he crooned in her ear as he tried to soothe her. "We'll get her, but you have to calm down."

"My family, Drake," she cried while the agony poured off of her in waves. "She's got my family. She ruined my brother and now she has my grandmother."

"Emerson, I need you to calm down and trust me. You can't help them like this."

The words had their desired effect. Her struggles stilled as she quieted in his arms. With renewed focus, she turned pleading eyes on him. "We need to port in there and you have to port her out. Just get her out of there as fast as you can. Then you can come back for me."

Her words pulled at something deep inside of him and in that moment all the reasons he loved Emerson coalesced into one. She loved selflessly and with her whole heart.

And she had all of his.

She had stolen it from the first moment he'd laid eyes on her, his soul somehow recognizing her before his heart even caught up.

Pressing his lips to her ear, he kept his voice low yet urgent. "We need to take this slow. Eris wants the apple and the diary, and she's not going to make any rash moves until she has them."

"Is that your professional opinion"—Eris materialized behind them on the sidewalk—"or wishful thinking, Drake?"

"Where the fuck is she?" Emerson shot back as she turned to face Eris.

"Keep a tight leash on her, Drake," Eris sneered. "I'd hate to see her make any rash decisions."

Emerson's grip tightened on his arm, telegraphing her intention. Drake shot her a brief glance to let her know he was in complete accord and, with an ease that defied how little time they'd worked together, Emerson let go with a stream of flame as the two of them marched toward the goddess.

The leather that covered Eris from head to toe crackled under the flames and she screamed. But she quickly moved out of the way, porting out of range.

"Where'd she go?" Emerson whispered as they turned in a complete circle.

Quinn hollered for them from the end of the block before launching into his own port, but in his gut Drake knew it was wasted effort.

When Eris reappeared in front of them she had Hippolyta in her arms.

Grey prowled through the warehouse on quiet feet. He heard the screams outside and could only depend on the knowledge that his brothers would do everything they could to fight the battle as far away from Finley as possible.

He scanned the length of the warehouse as he moved, trying to find a door or stairwell of some sort. There was no evidence of anyone in the large, cavernous space as he worked his way along the wall.

Had they been duped?

Was Eris keeping Finley somewhere else entirely?

The faintest echo of voices reached his ears and Grey stilled, crouching low with his back to the wall behind a row of old, rusty cabinets. Footsteps pounded closer as the voices rose and Grey immediately recognized the leader of the Gavelli crime family as he walked the length of the room.

He was no longer the young buck who ruled New York with an iron fist. The years of running a dark and evil empire had taken their toll. His body had grown paunchy and dark circles rimmed his eyes.

The image was in stark contrast to his son.

Franco.

Grey didn't need to see the silk suit and Italian loafers to make the son. Long and lean, Franco Gavelli walked the floor like he owned the place. The son was clearly primed to take over the family business. The faint outline of a gun was visible through the fit of his suit and his confident gait suggested a man who believed he owned his world and everything in it.

Magnus followed them, his movements awkward. Grey wondered briefly at the stiff posture until he realized Emerson's brother was doing everything in his power to hide the tattoo that refused to stay shrouded within his aura.

"Where is she?"

"The basement." Magnus pointed toward a door at the far side of the warehouse, about twenty yards from where Grey hid.

"We brought the old lady, so we're walking out with the lawyer. That's the deal," Franco intoned.

"Yeah, that's the deal," Magnus agreed as he reached for the door.

Grey clenched his fists as he tried to decide how to play this. The addition of the mobsters was a variable he hadn't planned on. Finley wasn't insurance at all—she was a bargaining chip. The mobsters' payment for their part in this little drama.

And that was what made Eris so dangerous. They should have counted on the fact she hadn't been using the humans for fun.

That she'd had a purpose for them all along. Rile up the mobsters, then keep them happy with a prize of their own. He and his brothers had thought them to simply be a diversion while she groomed Magnus for bigger things. None of them had calculated just how big a distraction they could actually be.

A low whistle sounded from behind him. Grey

turned to see Rogan's face in the window. After Grey's quick nod, the Sagittarius ported in beside him.

"Where is she?"

"Downstairs. With Gavelli, his son and Magnus."

Rogan extended his hand, his mouth a grim slash. "Let's go even up the odds."

"Gram!" Emerson cried at the sight of her grandmother wrapped in Eris's arms. The woman who had always seemed so strong—so invincible—looked small and frail with Eris's arm around her neck.

"We can make this easy or we can make it hard." Eris smiled broadly as she kept a close grip on Hippolyta. "I don't kill old ladies and really have no interest in starting now. That said, I want what belongs to me."

"Emerson." Her grandmother's gaze never wavered. "What is this about?"

The calm, cool strength went a long way toward alleviating the panic rocketing through her system and Emerson focused on that familiar, steady brown gaze. "It's about Magnus, Gram."

"Actually, it's not." Eris tightened her grip once more. "It's about my belongings."

"Which is about Magnus," Drake shot back, "as well as every other deviant thing you've done since the dawn of time."

"What do you have to do with my grandson?" Hippolyta asked again as she twisted to look at Eris.

"You have no idea." Eris smiled to herself at the little joke. "Your grandson's been a most accommodating subject. A puzzling one, but incredibly helpful and compliant. You should be quite proud of him."

Emerson thought about the Xiphos strapped to Drake's leg. Could she do it? Did she have enough power to remove it and stealthily bring it around to Eris's neck?

Before she could contemplate it any further, Eris shouted for Quinn, who had stopped several yards back, keeping watch as things unfolded. "Get over here, Quinn. Where I can see you."

Eris's gaze alighted on Montana, where the woman had moved up next to Drake. "And if it isn't my old friend Montana. Things sure have changed for you, sweetie. Enjoying your new life?"

"No thanks to you."

"Oh, I don't know. If I hadn't kept you locked up for so long, Arturo might have gotten to you before your ascension and then where would you be?" Emerson saw Montana blink at that and wasn't surprised when Eris purred her next comment. "I'm really not all bad."

"Then let my grandmother go."

"Give me my things and I'm out of here."

The image of Rogan's face as he confessed his relationship with Eris resurrected itself in her mind's eye. Just as she'd told Drake several days ago, she couldn't shake the idea the Sagittarius had fallen in love with the goddess.

And if he had fallen in love with her, could she be all bad?

"If you're as serious as you say, turn my brother back. In exchange for the apple."

"Magnus made his choice."

"Likely without full knowledge of what he'd become," Emerson shot back.

"He's a grown man, Emerson. He doesn't need your interference. He never has."

Emerson looked at all of them. Montana to Drake's left and Quinn on her right. Her grandmother's proud stance as she fought to stand upright under the pressure of Eris's hold. And then her gaze caught on something that flashed in Quinn's back pocket under the streetlights and she realized he'd shoved a knife back there.

Could she really do it?

As her gaze flickered back over her grandmother, she saw it. The brief nod that said Hippolyta knew exactly what she was thinking.

And approved.

Offering up a quick prayer to the goddess, Emerson held tight to Drake's arm and allowed her magic to flow out through her senses. The knife lifted from Quinn's pocket and, with a speed born of sheer desperation, she flung it into the night.

Magnus turned at the scream from outside the warehouse just as he opened the door for Franco and his father. "They're down there." Without waiting for a response, Magnus vanished and Grey knew they had to let him go.

His brothers would deal with Magnus.

Grey and Rogan moved up to the entrance and peered down the narrow stairs. They saw a second door open at the bottom and Franco and his father stepped through it. Grey's stomach turned over as he heard a voice echo back up the cavernous space until he realized it wasn't Finley's. "Franco! You came."

With a sideways glance, he nodded at his brother and Rogan nodded back. There was just enough space to see the floor of the basement and, by silent agreement, they'd port in one after the other. Grey unstrapped his Xiphos from his leg, the well-worn hilt a comfort in his hand.

He went first, the air gathering speed around him before launching him down into the basement. The moment he regained his feet he leaped on Franco with a fierce war cry and knocked the gun from the man's hand, his Xiphos clattering to the floor in the process. Rogan's matched cry echoed mere moments later as he arrived in the same spot, then faced off with Gavelli Sr.

Grey braced for an attack as Franco immediately reacted to the threat. He reveled in the fight, slamming his fists into Franco's midsection with a satisfying thud as he beat the man slowly across the room.

The fierce need for retribution burned within him as he continued pummeling the future crime boss. Franco gave as good as he got, but Grey had the momentum. His hands reached for Franco's neck, the move so instinctive after long years of fighting Destroyers, he barely registered the man turning blue as he gripped the neck that corded in a desperate attempt to get air.

His hands tightened further and it was Finley's scream that stopped him.

"Grey! No! You'll kill him."

Her voice still vibrated in his ears as he realized what he was doing. In his fury to punish the one who'd held Finley, he'd missed the real threat. As he loosened his grip slightly, three gunshots filled the air.

*   *   *

Eris screamed as the knife hit her shoulder. Although it was a wound she'd easily shake off, it did enough damage to have her loosening her grip on Hippolyta.

The older woman didn't waste time. She dropped to her knees, slipping from Eris's grip, before crawling toward them. Drake called out orders as he moved forward to intercept the woman. "Montana, take her home."

Quinn's wife ported Hippolyta away immediately, the quick rush of air the only evidence they'd even been standing there. On another set of orders, he hollered over his shoulder toward Emerson, "Stay back. She's mine."

Words he hadn't thought in years echoed through his mind. Alexander's battle cry.

No mercy.

The knife still stuck out of Eris's shoulder and with a thick pop she pulled it free. Blood poured from the wound, but it evaporated before it even hit the sidewalk. She and Drake circled each other. Impatient with the dance, Drake leaped, the satisfaction of knocking her off her feet short-lived as Emerson's scream took his breath away.

He looked up from where he had Eris pinned to the ground, and saw where they'd miscalculated.

Magnus stood behind his sister. The snake that rode his shoulders had wrapped itself around her, from just underneath her breasts to the top of her knees.

Grey crawled toward Finley, his gaze never leaving the expanding pool of blood on her chest. The moment he reached her, he pulled her into his arms and cradled her as gently as he could manage.

The blond woman he'd heard earlier calling to

Franco clutched the gun, her hands as steady as if she were holding a church hymnal. She now had it pointed at Rogan's head. "It's such a shame about your girlfriend."

"Who the fuck are you?" Grey ground out, his mind whirling with what to do. Although there wasn't much he and his brothers couldn't survive, a kill shot to the head was pretty effective. Their speed of regeneration simply couldn't beat the clock on keeping the brain alive.

His gaze ricocheted between Rogan and the ever-expanding patch of red on Finley's chest.

"Don't think about leaving, sweetheart. Or my finger just might slip on this trigger. One. More. Time." As his brain slowly reengaged, Grey realized he knew the woman. She was a colleague of Finley's and he'd seen her at Equinox on several occasions.

"You set her up."

"Of course I did. And she was buying it all the way until you fucked it up. I'm rather proud of my quivering, whimpering impression right here in this very cell. It was a personal best."

"She wasn't buying nearly as much as you thought."

"No." The blonde shook her head. "She'd bought it all. Our dear little Finley isn't nearly as smart as she'd like everyone to think. Especially since her panties started getting wet over you. She's been groomed to be the best, but even she didn't see what was right in front of her nose."

The woman pressed the barrel of the gun harder against Rogan's temple as she focused her attention on Grey. "I saw the way you two looked at each other. And as soon as I saw what was going on, I told Franco we had our gal. Someone with access inside the DA's office and inside your world."

Grey saw the archer grimace as the barrel bored into his skull and he struggled to make sense out of it.

Was Eris behind this? Or was it all done at the hands of these mortals?

"So why shoot her?"

A mulish expression settled on the woman's lips. "Franco comes first."

Gods, they were fucking nuts. He'd observed it at his club over and over—the webs humans entangled themselves in—and he'd always ignored it. But now?

Now it was personal.

The need to take care of Finley overwhelmed him, but Grey kept his gaze on the mortals. "What did you have to gain by all this?"

Cold laughter met the question, but it was Gavelli Sr. who finally spoke. "You think your woo-woo shit is all a secret? You think no one knows there's a band of immortals running around the city? Why should you get all the fun? We're just getting in on the action."

Grey refused to answer—refused to confirm what the man obviously knew—but he didn't miss the look Rogan shot him across the way. A good old-fashioned "What the fuck?" mixed with "How the hell did we miss this one?"

"You think you're so clever," Melanie added. "You think power's meant only for you? We're going to take over the city."

"Melanie." Franco Jr. laid a hand on her arm, the

first moment of restraint Grey had seen since they got down there. Gavelli Jr. was working his way to the top and it was clear he saw the writing on the wall.

It was equally clear he knew how to keep his own counsel.

Finley gasped and opened her eyes, dragging his attention off all of it. Her blue gaze was filled with pain, the reality of it stabbing him with a million needles of regret.

"You?"

He smiled gently down at her, remembering their exchange not even a week before in what felt like another time. "Yeah. It's me."

On a heavy gasp, her head fell back.

The moan that left his lips was feral, like a wounded animal as he clutched Finley's body against his own. Great, heaving gasps filled his chest as he tried to make sense of what had happened.

Tried to make sense of the fact that the woman so vibrant—so full of life—lay lifeless in his arms.

Across the room, Rogan wasted no time. As soon as the blonde's focus shifted to Finley, he moved, knocking the gun from her hands.

"Go, Grey! Get the fuck out of here!"

Grey wasted no time. He was mindless with grief, but he knew where he had to go.

The only place he could go for help.

Emerson felt the snake tighten around her midsection and strained for breath. She thought through every bit of magic she knew, but the speed with which the snake moved, coupled with her inability to use her hands, had her ruling out everything she thought of.

"Step away from Eris," Magnus hollered over her shoulder. "Porting distance away."

Emerson saw Drake's nod as he and Quinn moved away from the goddess.

The snake tightened another fraction of an inch, and she discarded another magical idea as a small memory assailed her.

She recalled their father as he lay on his deathbed.

She and Magnus were the only ones in his hospital room, her mother and sister having gone off to find coffee. Magnus was sitting in a chair, watching a football game, and she was perched on the edge of the bed, holding his hand.

"Are you afraid, Daddy?"

Tubes and machines surrounded him and his voice was hoarse when he spoke. "No, sweetheart, I'm not afraid."

Tears welled in her eyes, but she fought not to let them fall. "But this isn't supposed to happen. You were fine. A few days ago, you were fine."

He reached up and pressed a hand to her cheek, his thumb sweeping across the first tear that fell. "You play the hand you're dealt, baby doll. And you live life to the fullest. That's all you can do. That's all any of us can ever do."

Magnus looked over from the TV, his sullen face full of tears and the anger only youth can truly summon. "How can you be so calm? How can you accept this?"

The hoarse, sickly tone vanished and for a moment, the strong, true voice of her father rang out through the room. "Because I've been loved."

The snake tightened again, the pure power in its muscled strength a shock as it pulled her from the memory.

"Magnus. Please," she couldn't stop herself from crying out.

"It's not me, Em. I can't control it any longer. Maybe I never could."

"But you can control it. I know you can."

"I'm not like you, Em. I *can't*."

Her breaths became more shallow as the lack of air began to take effect. "You were loved, Magnus. Please don't ever forget that. By me. By Mom and Dad and Ronnie and Gram. By all of us. You do have a choice. And you *are* loved."

His voice was low in her ear, so only she could hear. "You play the hand you've been dealt."

"You do remember."

For one brief moment, Magnus rested his forehead against the side of her head.

And then he vanished as if he'd never been.

She fell to her knees, gasping for breath as sweet, sweet air filled her lungs. She didn't need to hear Quinn's shout or feel the safe haven of Drake's arms to know Eris had quickly followed her brother, the promise of retribution on her lips.

Bring it on, Emerson thought with no small measure of satisfaction.

"I'm sorry," Drake mumbled against her ear. "I'm so sorry. I wasn't there for you."

She shifted to press her lips against his. "You are there for me. You've always been there for me. I just didn't realize it."

"I'm always going to be there for you. Until the day neither of us is here any longer."

She pressed her hand against his chest, stilling his movements. "What are you talking about?"

"Choice, my love. I'm going to talk to Themis. I don't want to be an immortal any longer. She made me this way. I've no doubt she can unmake me when the time is right."

"But, Drake, you can't do this. You can't leave your brothers. Or the work that you all do."

"I've got a long time to figure it out. To work with Themis to determine how to fulfill my promises to her."

"But your immortality?"

"Isn't the only gift I give to Themis. We'll figure it out. Together. And when the time is right, we'll both know. I won't walk through this world without you, Emerson. So someday we'll make the decision that ensures I won't have to. This is the right choice for me." He pressed another kiss to her lips and lingered longer this time. "For us."

As Emerson wrapped her arms around his neck, she thought about what he was willing to sacrifice for her. What she'd almost never even given a chance.

"I love you."

"And I love you. Now let's get out of here and go find your grandmother. I've suddenly got a powerful desire to get her blessing on something."

"Before you do, can I borrow your phone?"

Drake kept one hand firmly on her shoulder as he dug into his pocket for his phone with his other hand. "Who are you calling?"

"My sister. I need to apologize. And I want to tell her our good news."

She dialed quickly, suddenly anxious to fix what she'd so carelessly broken. And even more eager to share her news with someone who mattered.

Deeply.

Emerson heard her sister's "hello," then let out a loud, squeaking giggle as Drake's mouth descended on hers.

It was a long moment before Emerson could sputter out, "Ronnie! I've got some news."

"No, Ronnie." Drake leaned in toward the mouth-piece. "*We've* got some news."

Epilogue

Grey fell to the floor of Themis's home with Finley still wrapped in his arms. The goddess stood in front of her Mirror of Truth as tears fell freely from her face.

"You have to help me."

She shook her head, as that long fall of red hair ran down her back. "I cannot."

"You must. You have to help her. You have to make it right."

Themis crossed to him, her gaze never wavering. "She is gone, Grey."

"She can't be. She cannot. There has to be a way."

As the blue gaze stared back at him in silent understanding, Grey knew he must offer something. Knew he had to offer her the balance that would make it right.

With swift movements, he crossed the room and placed Finley's lifeless form on the couch. He pressed his finger to her still lips before crossing back to kneel at Themis's feet.

"Goddess, I offer you my promise of balance. I'll do whatever you ask of me. Just tell me what I can do to make this right."

"Nothing will make it right, my Warrior."

He refused to accept her words—refused to accept such a bright, vibrant light would be diminished. "She acts on your behalf, bringing justice for her fellow humans. Surely you can find favor with her for that alone."

"It isn't done, Grey. Her fate has been sealed."

Anger filled him as Grey stood to his full height, refusing to accept the words of the woman he'd followed with complete devotion for millennia. As he stared into the depths of her eyes, a memory slammed through him with enough force to have him stumbling back. "You knew. You sent me into that warehouse because you knew she'd be there."

Themis's gaze remained steady. Unwavering. "She needed protection."

"You had me save her only to take her from me?"

"She wasn't meant to go that way. Wasn't meant to be caught in the middle."

"It wasn't your call to intervene."

"Would you rather she'd died that night instead of this one?"

"I don't want her to die at all!" The words dragged from his lips, each one an agony.

"It's her time."

Grey glanced back to Finley's still form. "No. No, it's not. She was caught in something bigger than herself and she doesn't deserve this."

"Fate takes what it needs."

"Then take it from me to compensate."

"It isn't done." Although her words were harsh, the compassion in her aqua gaze gave Grey the small measure of hope he needed to make her see reason.

"I will give up everything that I am. I will change my own fate. Just tell me what I must do to bring her back."

ARIES/PISCES STAR CHART

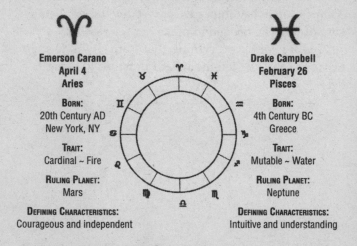

Emerson Carano
April 4
Aries

BORN:
20th Century AD
New York, NY

TRAIT:
Cardinal ~ Fire

RULING PLANET:
Mars

DEFINING CHARACTERISTICS:
Courageous and independent

Drake Campbell
February 26
Pisces

BORN:
4th Century BC
Greece

TRAIT:
Mutable ~ Water

RULING PLANET:
Neptune

DEFINING CHARACTERISTICS:
Intuitive and understanding

The immediate attraction between an Aries and a Pisces is the stuff of legend. Exhilarating and maddening—all at the same time—these lovers wield a passion for the ages.

The fiery Aries woman incites her Pisces man to poetic heights, but his dreamy sensitivity will confuse her until she understands it hides an inner core of strength and deep sincerity.

Pisces is a man of refined tastes, and he seeks a woman who can stimulate him in all facets of life. His ability to maintain his masculinity yet tap into his deeper emotions ensures his partner always knows where she stands . . . and that she is loved.

Although Emerson and Drake forged their love in the fires of passion, the success of their relationship will be based on their understanding of each other. Their ability to give each other emotional support and a deeply rooted sense of belonging will bind one to the other with a forever love.

GLOSSARY

Ages of Man—the stages of human existence, as identified by the Greek writer Hesiod. Most often associated with metals, the Ages—Gold, Silver, Bronze, Heroic and Iron—reflect the increasing toil and drudgery humans live in. The world only thinks the ages are myth. . . .

Apple of Discord—a powerful weapon owned by Eris, the goddess of Discord. The apple was used to incite the Trojan War and Eris maintains it as one of her most prized tools. The apple itself is small and innocuous and can be reformed and reshaped to her needs. It's latest iteration is as a lapel pin.

Cardinal—a sign *quality*, Cardinal signs (Aries, Cancer, Libra, Capricorn) mark the start of each season. Those born under Cardinal signs are considered dynamic and, like each season, forceful in their beginnings. Cardinal Warriors are equally dynamic, forcing change with their impatient natures and independent spirits.

Deimos—the son of Ares and Aphrodite, he is the god of dread. He is the brother of Phobos.

Destroyer—a soulless creature created by Enyo from an emotionally damaged human. They take on the appearance of men, but their bodies are nothing by husks, filled with a superconductive life force. They can be slowed and hurt, but quickly recover. The only way to kill a Destroyer is by removing his head. Each Destroyer Enyo creates takes some of her power, an innate balance agreed to during the creation of the Great Agreement.

Element—just as all signs are Cardinal, Fixed or Mutable, each sign also possesses an elemental quality of Fire, Earth, Air or Water. Each Warrior has an elemental nature to his sign, allowing for additional powers for those who have learned to develop them. These elemental qualities exist beyond those granted to all Warriors—immortality, the ability to port, rapid healing and above-average strength—and have begun to express themselves as the Warriors have grown more comfortable in their abilities and better understand the full range of their skills.

Enyo—the Goddess of War, Enyo is the daughter of Zeus and Hera. Equipped with the ability to create anarchy and death wherever she goes, Zeus offered Enyo up to Themis for their Great Agreement. Before Zeus allowed Themis to create the Sons of the Zodiac, she had to agree to a counterbalance to the Warriors' power. Enyo provides the balance, at constant war with Themis's Warriors. For each battle Enyo wins, her power grows. As such, for each she loses, her power is diminished.

Equinox—a nightclub owned by Grey Bennett, Aries Warrior. Each Warrior has a role within the whole and Grey's is to keep an eye on the underbelly of New York for Enyo's likely crop of new Destroyers. What none of the Warriors know is that Grey carries a secret— one that will lead him to his destiny or to his doom . . .

Eris—sister of Enyo, Eris is the goddess of Discord. She wields power far more subtly than her sister, focusing on the underlying chaos that causes problems in lieu of overt action. Eris's days of wreaking havoc are peppered throughout history and it is Eris who was responsible for the start of the Trojan War.

Fixed—a sign *quality*, Fixed signs (Taurus, Leo, Scorpio, Aquarius) mark the middle of each season. Those born under Fixed signs are considered quite stubborn and persistent. Fixed Warriors are equally stubborn and persistent, unwilling to yield to their enemies.

Great Agreement—an agreement entered into during the Iron Age (the Fifth Age of Man) by Zeus and Themis. Fearful that her beloved humans had no protection from the trials of life, Themis entered into an agreement with Zeus that created the Sons of the Zodiac. The Sons of the Zodiac are Warriors modeled after the circular perfection of the heavens and each Warrior carries the immutable qualities of his sign. Under the Great Agreement, the immortal Warriors will battle

Zeus's daughter Enyo, the Goddess of War, for the ultimate protection, quality and survival of humanity.

Hera—wife of Zeus and mother of Enyo.

Iron Age—the Fifth Age of Man, generally thought to be about ten thousand years ago, when humans toiled in abject misery. Brothers fight brothers, children turn against their fathers and anarchy is the rule of the land. During this age the gods have forsaken humanity. It is during this time that Themis—desperate to alter the course of human existence—goes to Zeus and enters into the Great Agreement. During this age, the Sons of the Zodiac are created.

Mutable—a sign *quality*, Mutable signs (Gemini, Virgo, Sagittarius, Pisces) mark the end of each season. Those born under Mutable signs are the most comfortable with change, making them easily adaptable and resourceful. Mutable Warriors are the first to see the big picture, able to adapt and shift their battle plans at a moment's notice. Their ability to see issues from multiple angles make them strong Warriors and a comfort to have watching your back.

Ophiuchus—known as the "Thirteenth Sign," Ophiuchus is portrayed as the serpent bearer. Presuming the zodiac is tied to the specific placement of constellations and not divided into twelve equal divisions, the proponents of the Thirteenth Sign more closely follow the path of the heavens. It is this disparity that gives Eris the opportunity she needs to create her own warrior . . .

Phobos—the son of Ares and Aphrodite, he is the god of fear. He is the brother of Deimos.

Port—shortened form of teleport. The Warriors and Destroyers both have the ability to move through space and time at will. Porting will diminish power.

Sons of the Zodiac—created by Themis, the Goddess of Justice, upon her Great Agreement with Zeus. The Great Agreement stipulates for a race of Warriors—156 in total—that will have the traits of their Zodiac sign. Tasked to protect humanity, they are at war with Enyo. A Warrior is immortal, although he may be killed with a death blow to the neck. Removal of a Warrior's head is the only way to kill him. The Warriors' strength may be reduced from extended time in battle, multiple ports and little food. A Warrior's strength will be replaced with food, sleep or sexual orgasm. Each Warrior has a tattoo of added protection that lives within his aura.

Themis—one of the twelve Titans, Themis is the goddess of Justice. Disheartened that her beloved humans toiled in misery and abject drudgery, she petitioned Zeus to allow her to intercede. With Zeus she entered into the Great Agreement, which provided for the creation of the Sons of the Zodiac, 156 Warriors embodied with the traits of their sign. Originally she envisioned twelve of twelve—but upon reaching her agreement with Zeus gained an additional twelve Warriors so Gemini might have his twin. Themis's Warriors live across the globe, battling Enyo and keeping humanity safe.

Titans—the original twelve children born of Uranus (Father Sky) and Gaia (Earth). Themis is one of the Titans, as is Cronus, Zeus's father.

Warrior's Tattoo—the Warrior's Tattoo is inked on his body, generally on his upper shoulder blade (right or left). The tattoo lives within the Warrior's aura and, when the Warrior is in danger the tattoo will expand as an additional form of protection. The tattoo is never separate; rather, it provides additional protection through the Warrior's life force.

Xiphos—an ancient Greek weapon, the Xiphos is a double-edged blade less than a foot in length. The Warriors each carry one strapped on their calves. Although a Warrior may deliver a death blow to a Destroyer's neck when in close range, the Xiphos provides them with an additional tool in battle. Although a Warrior may use any Xiphos—or any weapon—when necessary, each Warrior was granted a Xiphos at his turning. Although nothing more than metal, many Warriors find a personal connection with their Xiphos through many years of battle.

Zeus—the king of the gods and ruler over Mount Olympus. Zeus is married to Hera. Zeus's first wife was Themis, the Goddess of Justice and one of the Titans. Zeus entered the Great Agreement with Themis that resulted in the protectors for humanity—the Sons of the Zodiac.

Read on for a special preview of the next contemporary romance in Addison Fox's heartwarming Alaskan Nights series,

COME FLY WITH ME

Coming in November 2012 from
Signet Eclipse

Grier stared out her window at the bright lights of Anchorage as the plane did a hard bank to the right. After miles of darkness, the lights were a welcoming beacon.

She was home.

Or at least what passed for home for another month. Six weeks, tops.

That had been Walker's latest estimate of how much longer it would take to clear up Jonas Winston's last will and testament.

He'd been kind enough to give her an out the week before, suggesting she could stay in New York and allow him to handle the majority of the proceedings, with her presence only necessary once everything was finalized, but she'd refused.

It was bad enough her half sister, Kate, had been the recipient of their father's love and affection for the first twenty-six years of her life. She'd be damned if she'd let the woman have easy access to Jonas's things while Grier sat four thousand miles away waiting for news.

The funny thing was, she acknowledged to herself as she reached beneath her seat for her tote, it wasn't even Jonas's possessions she really cared about. She had a home; she certainly didn't need his.

What she did need were answers.

And some small piece of him she could keep.

Sloan smiled a groggy half grin from across the aisle. "You ready?"

"As I'll ever be."

Walker helped her collect her suitcase from the overhead, and as if time were moving in fast-forward, before she could blink she was filing out the plane's side door.

The jet bridge was a short walk but her gaze caught on one of the many tourism posters framed along the corrugated walls: INDIGO TRAVEL AND TRANSPORT.

Mick's company.

As if to simply reinforce the connection, the photo showed Mick and his partner, Jack, bookending the front propeller of one of their planes, broad smiles on their faces. Each sported shoulders like a football player, but where Jack had the heavier build of a grizzly bear, Mick was long and rangy.

Not for the first time, Grier tried to understand exactly what it was that made the men up here quite so appealing. She'd assumed the men of Alaska would be hale and hearty. She hadn't counted on them being quite so lovable.

A couple of women behind her giggled and Grier tuned into their conversation, pulling her attention from the poster as she continued moving down the jet bridge.

"Rachel said the men up here were good-looking."

"She didn't say they looked like Greek gods." Another giggle floated up. "I think we need to kick off our visit by supporting the local economy."

"Indigo Travel and Transport," her friend replied and Grier didn't miss the light slap of a high five.

Sloan turned from where she walked a few paces ahead and reached for her hand.

"Come on," she whispered on a tight squeeze. "It'll be fine."

Grier took comfort in the warmth her friend always seemed to know how to share with such simple, effortless ease.

And then the jet bridge ended and Grier suddenly realized she had a far bigger problem than misplaced jealousy over giggling singletons.

Mick O'Shaughnessy was waiting for her.

Mick fought the wave of nerves that dive-bombed his stomach as he waited for Grier to come out of the door to gate seven. He'd played the conversation in his head about fifty different ways since walking into the airport an hour ago and hadn't settled on anything.

"Hi." Yeah, real smooth opener.

"Good to see you." What was he, a talk show host?

"Happy New Year." If he were Dick Fucking Clark.

And then there were no words save one as Grier walked through the door with Sloan and Walker.

Wow.

Mick lifted his hand in a wave to catch her attention and the rest of the airport faded away.

How had this happened?

He loved women. He loved their perspective and the way their take on the world around them was just . . . different than his. And unlike a lot of men he knew, he loved their company in bed and out.

But Grier Thompson was different.

She was . . . so much *more*, somehow. More interesting. More enticing.

"Hi."

"Hi." He leaned down before he could stop himself and pressed a quick kiss to her cheek. The light scent of her filled his nose and the nerves flooding his stomach shifted into something a great deal more interesting.

Hunger.

Walker slapped him on the shoulder and reached for his hand, the moment shattered in the wake of his friend's exuberance. Mick didn't miss the frustration that crossed Sloan's gorgeous cheekbones, and it was that slight acknowledgment that had him smiling and slapping Walker on the back as they embraced.

Damn, but he'd missed his friend. Even if he was about as subtle as a freight train.

He reached for Sloan next, not surprised to hear the lightly whispered "Sorry" as she hugged him.

"Good flight?"

A round of murmured "yes's" and they were off.

Mick reached for the handle of Grier's suitcase and pointed toward the herd of people heading down the corridor. "Baggage claim's that way."

"This is all I have."

Mick glanced down at the small roll-aboard in his grip and the large bag that sat on top of it. "But you were gone over a week."

"I packed light."

"Oh."

The first smile he'd seen lit up her face. "You were expecting six pieces of matching Louis Vuitton?"

He couldn't hold back the grin, the last vestiges of nerves fading in the bright light of her smile. "Maybe only four."

Grier's smile brightened even further as something suspiciously like mischief alighted in the depths of her gray gaze. "Ask Sloan how many bags she brought."

Mick had spent far too many years with Walker and their other best friend, Roman, to ask a question so deliberately posed. With a broad smile for Sloan, he pointed in the direction of the claim area.

"I'm sure every piece is full of well-needed items."

"Ass kisser," Grier muttered as Sloan gifted him with a broad smile.

"Nope." Feeling lighter than he had in days, he draped a casual arm around Grier's shoulders and leaned down to whisper in her ear. "I'm just very, very smart."

Also Available

Addison Fox

Wave of Memories
The Sons of the Zodiac

AN ORIGINAL NOVELLA
AVAILABLE AS A
DOWNOADABLE eSPECIAL

After a cruel twist of fate, Aquarius warrior Aiden Cage relinquished his one true love and vowed to become the most fearsome warrior in all the Pantheon. Meg, the goddess of retribution, never fully understood the reasons why she was betrayed by Aiden millennia ago—nor did she ever forgive him. Yet now he is the only one she can turn to for help. The enemy that separated them is back, and he is sworn to destroy them both…for all time.

Available wherever books are sold or at
penguin.com